THE HEARTHLORD

BETH WERBANETH

For my father,
who believed in me even when I didn't believe in myself.

Contents

High Castle
Aesterland
Fortizia
Castilla
The Frostlands

Norogard
Chernosk
N
W   E
S
Forest
Neseveen
Desert
New Port
Reese

PROLOGUE

Silas listened to the steady howl of the wind, enjoying one last moment of warmth. He could already see the light filtering in through the entrance to the snow cave he'd dug hastily the night before. This far south, he could only count on six hours of daylight before night drove him beneath the snow again—just enough time to check his traps before hiking to the next day's campsite.

When he proposed his plan to venture beyond the Icetooth Ridge to the other trappers in Serrata, they'd dismissed the idea as suicidal. The great mountain range formed a natural barrier that protected their cluster of villages from the worst of the wind and the snow. Even during summer, the great valley beyond the ridge was blanketed with frost and almost completely devoid of life. However, winter drove the rare white foxes from the Frostlands into the Serrata Valley, and a skilled trapper could make a living off three or four catches a year.

Even Governor Titus, who could be found gambling on dice at the tavern almost every night, had refused to invest in Silas's expedition. Without any financial support, it had taken Silas two years to save enough for the necessary equipment to cross into the valley beyond the mountains, including the specialized snowshoes fashioned by the royal blacksmith two hundred miles away in Fortizia.

The Icetooth Ridge was marked by steep cliffs and treacherous winds, which made it ripe for avalanches. Its boundaries had been well surveyed over the years, and there was no easy crossing. The route Silas chose required climbing well over five thousand feet of sheer ice. He'd been on the mountain for a little over thirty hours, all the while listening to the ice shifting all around him. He knew an avalanche could sweep him to his death at any moment, but the promise of the potential riches beyond kept him going.

Two weeks had passed since Silas had initially ventured beyond the ridge, and he'd already stockpiled two dozen foxes in his main camp, as well as the carcass of an elusive arctic elk. Today he planned to retrieve the traps he'd laid in this part of his territory in preparation to extract his haul. The promise of more gold than he'd ever seen dulled the bite of the cold, and he pulled his hood tight as he crawled out of his shelter. He carefully fastened his snowshoes to his boots, grabbed his spear, and set off toward the distant grove of white trees.

When he'd crested the top of the Icetooth Ridge, he had been awestruck by the endless expanse of snow that rippled before him. It was hard to imagine anything could flourish here, but the Frostlands was full of surprises. There were clusters of white trees with short pine needles and tightly interwoven roots that crested above the ice. A storm had driven him to take shelter among the trees one night, only to find himself covered with hundreds of small beetles the next morning.

Strange berries and mushrooms grew in the crevices between the white roots, some of which he recognized from his own valley. He hadn't been desperate enough to eat them—a single mistake out here could prove deadly. The insects and vegetation fed small rodents and birds, which the foxes ate in turn. However, the groves were small, so he'd had to travel between them to avoid overhunting his prey.

He'd discovered the elk carcass while moving between two groves. It was fresh—probably only a day or two old—and it was immediately clear its death had been the work of an animal. It had unnerved Silas to learn the foxes were not the apex predators in the region, which was the main reason he had decided to start making his way back with his spoils.

Silas tried to shake off his unease at the thought of the elk carcass and occupied himself with his plans for the future as he trekked. He smiled as he imagined the jealous ire he would draw from the other trappers when he hauled his sled full of white pelts into town. It would be a month or so before enough merchants passed through to sell his haul. Maybe it would be best to buy a cart and ox and take his stock north himself. He'd heard merchants could sell furs for ten times what they paid to the aristocrats in Fortizia, and that they fetched an even higher price in the distant cities of Aesterland. With such wealth, he could return to Serrata and live comfortably for the rest of his life—maybe someday even become a governor.

The wind, his constant companion in this frozen landscape, was particularly strong today, pushing him back with every determined step he took. He'd long since grown accustomed to the wind's harsh melody, often shrieking, sometimes bellowing, occasionally whispering. It was rare that he could even hear the crunch of his snowshoes, but now a foreign sound cut through the familiar howl. He tensed as the crack reverberated through his senses. He saw movement out of the corner of his eye, and he could only watch as a jagged black tendril snaked its way across the frozen ground. He followed the body of the crack until he was looking down at his feet, where he saw the dark expanse beneath the snow that was separating underneath him.

Panic filled him as the ground shifted, and he threw himself forward, but the sudden movement only worsened the tremor. His hands slid uselessly along the ice, and then he was falling. He grunted when his back slammed into a hard surface, and he stared up at the clear blue sky for several moments, afraid to do anything more than breathe.

Silas slowly sat up, praying as he carefully checked every joint. He knew an injury would be fatal, and rather than return to Serrata a legend, he would be remembered as an idiot. A flood of relief swept through him when he completed his assessment without discovering any issues. He crawled to his feet, brushing the snow away from his coat as he surveyed his new surroundings.

A thick sheet of frost had camouflaged the crevasse from above, and shards of it were now scattered all around him. The air around him felt stale and was surprisingly warm. As his eyes adjusted to the new darkness, he could make out what appeared to be a narrow corridor sloping further underground. He reached out to touch the polished stone wall to his right, amazed when his gloved hand slid across it like glass. He'd never seen such intricate stonework. He gazed into the darkness, a strange mix of excitement and dread creeping up his spine. No one could survive south of the Icetooth Ridge, yet this structure was definitely manmade.

Silas bent down and unstrapped his woven snowshoes. With one hand on the wall beside him and the other probing for obstacles, he ventured forward into the beckoning darkness. The howl of the wind outside grew ever fainter as he trudged on, until the only sound left to comfort him was the loud echo of his own footsteps against the smooth floor.

After ten minutes of blind exploration, his forward hand collided with another hard surface. His fingertips brushed against a groove, and he traced the outline of a door. He pressed gently, then, sensing some give, pushed against it with his shoulder. The door resisted for a moment, then grated open, allowing him to tumble forward into the next room. It took Silas several moments to process that the darkness of the hallway had been replaced by a pulsing light, but even as he looked at his hands, he wondered if he was dreaming. Looking around this new room, he could find no explanation for the light—there were no holes in the ceiling here, or even a torch or lantern. Instead, there was only a solitary statue set proudly in the center of the room.

Silas's hands trembled as he approached the statue. It depicted what could only be an ancient king—a bearded man who wore a crown and a full set of armor emblazoned with the sigil of an eagle. The king was nearly half a foot taller than Silas himself, and his physique suggested he had been well-practiced with the sword sheathed at his side. There was something off about the king's stern gaze. As he got closer, Silas realized he was missing both of his eyes, leaving only hollow sockets in their place.

Silas was almost close enough to touch the statue when the dim light faded, and for a moment, he was engulfed in a darkness that swallowed him whole.

He felt like he was suffocating, and he dropped to his knees. As quickly as the sensation had come, it was gone, and the room was bathed in the serene light once again. Still, he knelt before the statue for several minutes before regaining his composure.

When he finally rose to his feet once more, he noticed one of the statue's hands was open, almost as in offering. He felt a sudden urge to leave—to go outside, abandon the rest of his traps, take his furs back to Serrata, and write off this buried temple as the side effect of the concussion he must have suffered in his fall—yet he was unable to look away from the bright glint of the sapphire ring in the statue's hand.

He reached out and grasped the ring. He was no merchant, but he immediately knew the huge sapphire was worth ten times as much as the furs. He fiddled with the flap on his pocket, then paused—the ring was so small, and he didn't want to risk it slipping away on the arduous journey back across the ridge.

As he slid the ring onto his finger, time seemed to slow. It was as if he were awakening from a long sleep—now seeing everything clearly for the first time. A powerful voice flooded his mind, overwhelming his senses. He could only stare up into the hollow eyes of the ancient king, until a single idea managed to surface from his clouded consciousness. It was not a king he had found, after all, but a god—the Hearthlord.

Silas stood rooted in front of the statue for what must have been a long time. The world had forgotten the truths that had been entombed in this frozen wasteland along with the statue of the Hearthlord. Sickness, suffering, death—all of it was meaningless without his guidance. How many generations of people had been robbed of the Hearthlord's salvation?

The furs he'd risked his life to secure suddenly seemed so inconsequential in the wake of this new treasure. The people of Castilla had to learn what he now knew. There was a paradise that awaited those who proved themselves worthy, where they could bask forever in the warmth of the Hearth. He lowered his head in reverence to the statue and turned, exiting the chamber with a new purpose burning in his heart.

CASTILLA

I

You worms of the mud,
How could you fathom the light of the sun?
Would you even know
If it failed to rise?

Matteo sank onto the stump, extending his hands to the warmth of the fire. Nearby, Octavius and Evander were dressing the boar they'd caught earlier in the day. It was a juvenile male whose tusks hadn't quite grown long enough to become deadly. It would be enough to feed them for the next week or so, but short of the real prize they were after.

He hunkered forward, bathing in the heat of the healthy blaze. There were still a few weeks of summer left, but the small hunting post of Alcazar was far enough south in the Serrata Valley that there was already a layer of frost on the ground. It was the third and final foray into the wilderness that they would make for the season, and the last chance to bring back enough meat and skins for a payout to survive the winter.

Evander grunted as he shoved a spit through the butchered hock of the boar. He slung the spit onto the struts over the fire, and Matteo felt his stomach rumble when the scent of roasted pork filled the clearing. He reached inside his coat and retrieved a small flask, but Evander snatched it away from him as he raised it to his lips.

"Hey!" Matteo protested as the older man took a swig from the flask.

A mischievous smile crossed Evander's face. He had lost most of his front teeth to the bar fights that occupied him in the winter, leaving gaps in his grin. When Matteo first met him in Serrata, he'd been intimidated, to say the least. It was his first season on his own, though, and not many hunting parties had been willing to take on a greenhorn like him.

Evander tossed the flask back to Matteo and sat down on the log next to him, leaving Octavius to finish dressing their kill. Matteo took a sip of the bitter liquid, grimacing as he forced it down his throat. After a moment, a warm sensation filled his chest, and he took another drink.

He looked up at Evander, surprised to see that he was glaring into the darkness of the forest beyond the glow of the fire. "What's wrong—" Matteo began, but he jumped to his feet when he heard the rustling of leaves behind him. He looked around wildly for his spear, but it was leaning uselessly against the cabin across the clearing. He frantically turned his gaze back to the forest, expecting one of the bears that stalked the wilderness to emerge.

A dark form shuffled out of the trees, and Matteo saw a glint of metal to his side as Evander drew his knife. Matteo reached down for his own knife, cursing himself for forgetting it was there, but he stopped when he realized the eyes peering at him from the edge of the clearing were human.

A couple of seconds passed in silence as Matteo, Evander, and Octavius stared at the disheveled intruder, but then Evander called, "Silas?"

The barely recognizable trapper stumbled into the clearing, and the light of the fire fully revealed the sorry state he was in. His heavy fur coat was tattered and torn along the seams, and his face was gaunt. Matteo remembered when he'd departed Serrata months ago with a sled full of expensive supplies and the promise that he would return with untold riches. Now, there was nothing left but a wild look in his eyes.

Evander approached the trapper and helped him sit down next to the fire. Silas muttered something under his breath and tried to rise, but he was no match for Evander's firm grip. The older man offered him a waterskin, which Silas reluctantly accepted.

"What happened to you?" Evander asked gruffly as Silas took a long draught of water. "You look like you haven't slept in weeks."

"I found something beyond the ridge," Silas muttered, his voice raspy and hollow. "I—" he paused and looked frantically down at his gloved hands for a moment. He relaxed slightly, then shook his head and said, "Never mind. I'll be able to show you soon."

"Show me what?" Evander asked. He looked at the forest where Silas had come from and asked, "You really made it beyond the ridge? Was it like you thought? Where are your supplies?"

Silas ignored him and heaved himself to his feet. He stumbled past the fire towards the other side of the clearing. Evander watched him disappear into the forest, then cursed softly and dipped his torch into the fire to light it. Matteo trailed behind him as he followed Silas into the darkness.

They walked through the thick undergrowth for a few minutes. It was hard enough to navigate with the light of the torch, but somehow Silas led the way through the murky dark ahead, apparently intent on some unseen goal. Matteo reached into his pocket for the small carved token his mother had given him when he'd left for his first season of hunting. He idly rubbed his fingers across the well-worn grooves of the wooden disk. It was a crude relief of the Huntsman, one of the more popular patron spirits in the region, along with the Broodmare and the Smith. Matteo felt some of his tension melt away at the familiar weight of the token in his pocket.

He stifled a surprised grunt when he bumped into Evander's back. A loud thwack rang out just ahead, and when Matteo sidled around his companion, he saw Silas raise his hatchet once more and drive it into the bark of an overgrown thicket.

"What is he doing?" Matteo whispered.

A frown crossed Evander's scarred face, but he said nothing. They watched in silence as Silas continued to hack away at the thicket for ten minutes before Evander finally turned to return to their camp. Matteo watched the trapper for a few seconds longer, until the glow of the torch faded and left him in darkness. As he hurried after Evander, the continuous rhythm of the hatchet lingered behind him.

Octavius was just finishing up with the boar when they made it back to the clearing. He cleaned the blood off of his knife as he asked, "What the hell was wrong with him?"

"Don't know," Evander said gruffly, grabbing a jug of whiskey from the bundle of supplies near the cabin. He brought it with him to the fire and took a long drink as he sat down. "He was gone for a long time. Maybe he lost it up in the mountains."

Octavius snorted and threw a rope over a naked branch overhead. He tied the parcels of meat he'd cut and hoisted them up to protect them from any curious wildlife that happened by in the night. "That's the problem with trappers," he said, tapping the side of his head with an outstretched finger. "Too much time alone."

Evander shrugged and rotated the spit over the fire. "Did you hear the governor is going to raise the iron tax?" he asked.

Octavius barked a short laugh. "Again? That'll put half the mines out of business," he predicted. "I heard some miners talking about trying their hand at hunting. Next season will be a nightmare."

Matteo was quiet as the two older men talked politics, unable to get the image of the unkempt trapper toiling away in the darkness out of his mind. He started when Evander clapped him on the shoulder to get his attention. Evander gave him his portion of the roast, and Matteo managed a weak smile as he thanked him. His stomach rumbled as he looked down at the meat—he hadn't realized how hungry he'd been until now. He bit into it and looked up at the night sky, savoring the taste. It was only on these hunting expeditions that he got fresh meat. Normally it was salted to hell or completely dried out to prevent it from rotting on the long trek back to civilization.

Matteo remained by the fire after he was done eating, sipping his whiskey and listening to Octavius's story about the giant bear he'd encountered in the neighboring valley for what must have been the fourth time. It seemed like the bear got a little bigger with each retelling, but Matteo laughed all the same when Octavius related how he'd escaped by throwing a bee's nest at the beast. An hour or two passed before the embers of the fire dwindled and the others rose to retire to the cabin.

Matteo hesitated beside the fire for a few moments, then ventured, "That trapper is still out there."

Evander frowned as he looked at the direction Silas had gone and said, "Probably best to leave him alone, kid. He knows where the cabin is if he gets cold."

"He looks like he hasn't eaten in days," Matteo said.

Octavius began to snarl a reply, but Evander placed a disarming hand on his shoulder. "Take him a half portion. Tell him he can have the rest when he comes back with you."

"Why waste our rations on a lunatic like that?" Octavius argued.

Evander smiled. "We could let him die out there, I guess." Some of the belligerence left Octavius's face, and Evander cut off a strip of meat from the boar and handed it to Matteo. "Watch yourself out there."

Matteo nodded and accepted the ration, then lit a torch from the fire and headed into the forest. In daylight, it would have been a simple matter to follow the trail they'd made before, but it was slow going with nothing but the torchlight to search for the tracks. After fifteen minutes of blundering through the forest, Matteo was sure he'd gone the wrong way.

He had almost resolved to give up and return to the clearing when the light of his torch reflected off of something metal in the distance. He cautiously approached it, stopping to inspect the hatchet that had been haphazardly discarded on the forest floor. He picked it up and raised his torch to search for the missing trapper.

He spotted the grove that Silas had been hacking away at before. Gripping the hatchet, Matteo approached the gash Silas had created in the tightly clustered saplings. The opening to the interior of the grove was narrow, but when Matteo positioned his torch just right, he could see the trapper's back as he knelt in the darkness inside.

"Silas," he called. "I brought food for you. Come outside."

The trapper didn't move from his position inside the grove. Matteo glanced nervously behind him, not eager to spend too much time alone in the dark forest with this madman. Still, he felt bad for the trapper, so he summoned his courage and jammed his shoulder through the opening.

Someone as burly as Evander would have had trouble fitting through the small opening, but Matteo was lean, and after a little maneuvering, he pressed his way into the grove. The trees formed a living cave, their trunks and branches intertwined so tightly that Matteo couldn't see any openings to the rest of the forest. It gave the grove an odd insulating effect, and it took Matteo a couple of seconds to realize he could no longer hear the sound of crickets coming from outside.

Silas was kneeling on the ground a few feet in front of him, both of his hands resting on the forest floor. Matteo kept his distance as he circled around him, the hatchet in his hand making him feel a little safer. Silas didn't seem dangerous, but it didn't hurt to take precautions.

He paused when he felt the texture of the ground beneath his boots change abruptly. He had grown so accustomed to the soft mulch of the forest and the crisp crackle of leaves underfoot that the hard, smooth surface beneath him seemed completely out of place. He bent down to get a better look, placing his hand on the cold, polished surface of the stone beneath him. It was unnaturally smooth, with deep grooves where a large design had been etched into its surface. There was a strange tingling sensation in his fingers as he ran them across it, and he abruptly withdrew his hand.

He raised his gaze to Silas, who was staring intently down at his own hands while muttering softly under his breath.

"What is it?" Matteo breathed, backing up until he felt dirt beneath his boots once more.

Silas stopped his low chanting as he looked up. His eyes burned bright in the reflection of the torchlight, and he grinned as he said, "An altar."

"How did you know this was here?" Matteo asked.

"The Hearthlord showed me the way," Silas said before returning his attention back to the stone slab beneath him.

Matteo frowned as he surveyed the grove again. Now he took a closer look, he could see the remnants of a structure that had once been here, and suddenly he understood how the trees could have grown in their tight formation. They'd twisted around the crumbling arches of what had once been a shrine, suspending the stonework that had survived in their trunks. He raised his hand to touch one of the pockmarked blocks of the structure. It felt different than the dais beneath. Both must have been ancient, but the altar remained pristine while the sanctum that surrounded it had been eroded by years of neglect.

"I brought you food," Matteo said, wiping the dust from the old structure off on his tunic and retrieving the ration from his satchel. "Why don't you come back to Alcazar and rest for the night? All of this will still be here tomorrow."

Silas looked up at him again, his stomach growling as he eyed the pork. He hesitated for a moment, then shook his head and said, "Not now. Let me concentrate."

Matteo sighed as he turned to leave, but he paused at the passageway. The fervor gleaming in Silas's eyes looked more like determination than madness to him, and he had located this ancient structure in the middle of the night, deep in the wilderness of the valley. Matteo looked at his hand in the flickering torchlight—there was also the odd sensation he'd felt when he'd touched the altar.

His curiosity overcame him, and he returned to his spot across from Silas. The grove was warm, and it would be nice to get a break from Octavius's loud snoring for a night. Silas looked up at him irritably when he sat down, but he didn't say anything, and Matteo settled in to spend the night with the trapper.

While he tried to stay awake, he was sure he dozed off a couple of times. Every time he roused himself, Silas remained at his station, consumed by his tireless prayers. The darkness beyond the passageway steadily faded into a muted purple, and then pink as the sun rose outside.

Matteo yawned and stretched as he got back to his feet. He still had a full day of hunting ahead of him, and he knew he should return to camp before Octavius and Evander came to look for him. He could only imagine the ridicule Octavius would dump on him when he found out he'd spent all night surveying the trapper.

As he fished the pork out of his satchel to leave for Silas, he registered he could no longer hear the trapper's mumbling. He looked up just as Silas collapsed onto the slab. Matteo took a step forward to check on him, but the entire grove was suddenly consumed with a blinding red light. Matteo raised his arm over his eyes in surprise, but just as suddenly as it had manifested, it was gone.

He stood rooted to the spot as red bursts of phantom light danced before his eyes. After a few moments, his vision returned, and he knelt beside the unmoving trapper to check his pulse. He paused when he put his hand down on the stone—it was unnaturally warm beneath his touch. The tingling feeling beneath his fingers returned, stronger now, and he drew his hand away again.

Matteo sighed in relief when he discovered that Silas was still breathing. He dragged him off of the warm dais, which was surprisingly easy. Silas was a few inches taller than him, but his thick fur coat had hidden how emaciated he had become. The trapper was probably on the brink of starvation.

Matteo carefully placed Silas down at the edge of the grove and left his satchel and waterskin next to him in case he woke up, then ducked into the narrow passage again to go get help. If he hadn't seen it with his own eyes, he wouldn't have believed it, but now he knew Silas wasn't crazy. Whatever it was that he'd discovered here, it was real.

II

Welcome the stranger who comes in the night.
Set a place for him at your table.
Should he so ask,
Offer him all that you own.

A red glow filled the temple as Silas knelt in front of the stone slab in its center. He smiled—the light that pulsed through the carved runes of the altar was strong and steady today. It had been twenty-five years since he had followed the Hearthlord's voice to the overgrown thicket of vines in the Serrata Valley that had concealed the altar. Back then, it had taken an entire day of prayer for it to respond with a single pulse of divine light.

During the early years, Silas spent most of his time secretly meditating upon the ring. He didn't dare reveal its existence to the others—he knew he didn't have the means to protect it should thieves hear about it. Though the voice faded as the months wore on, it still whispered to him in his dreams.

The first divine truth he learned from the Hearthlord was their forgotten past. Centuries ago, men had lived in bliss with the Hearthlord and his angels in perfect harmony. However, they'd grown arrogant and sought to usurp the Hearthborn, which resulted in a cataclysm. The Hearthborn abandoned the mortal realm for the paradise beyond and closed the way to the corrupted. Without their guidance, men indulged their sinful nature for centuries and steadily fell further from grace.

The hunters and trappers of the Serrata Valley gradually discovered Silas's small enclave. Its location deep in the valley, well past any other established towns, quickly made it a popular hub for them to clean their kills and trade provisions. Eventually, merchants learned of the budding community, and ten years after its establishment, a path was cut through the forest to connect Alcazar to Serrata. A few merchants and hunters made the village their permanent residence, and Silas's following slowly grew as they witnessed the miracle of the altar.

To Silas's despair, the voice of the Hearthlord left him completely years ago, but after more contemplation, he realized it was because he already knew what he needed to do for the next revelation. The altar was all that separated his congregation from the paradise that lay beyond, and if they continued to pray, they would be able to open the way to the Hearth. The more followers he gained, the brighter the pulsing light became, and Silas's convictions only grew stronger in the meantime.

"Divine Hearthlord, lend me your wisdom," he beckoned quietly. "All that I have, I surrender to you. In return, show me the way. Deliver us faithful from our wickedness."

He bowed his head as he completed his prayer, then he rose to his feet and moved to the other side of the altar, where he could face the small congregation. Most of the adults were seated on wooden benches on either side of the aisle that led to the altar, where a cluster of children had been waiting patiently.

One by one, the acolytes approached the altar to pray. Many of them had been born into the congregation, although some were the children of more recent converts. The toddlers who came first were clumsy, but they were still able to kneel at the altar and pat their hands on the stone. The next group managed a short prayer. Silas smiled as the light grew warmer with each acolyte. The adults would come afterwards, but the glow of the altar always burned brightest in response to its youngest worshippers.

The temple was already bathed in a red glow by the time Auron, Matteo's young son, approached the altar. The boy knelt and quietly said the prayer, his eyes focused intently on the runes carved into the stone. He drew in a deep breath and then placed his palms on the stone.

Silas felt the hair on the back of his neck raise as he sensed a charge in the air. Auron frantically scrambled back just before the runes erupted with a blinding light. A cracking sound ripped through the shrine, and a metallic smell wafted through the air as the light abruptly faded, leaving the altar completely dark once more.

It took Silas's eyes several moments to adjust to the new dimness of the temple, but he could hear a collection of gasps ripple through his followers. Once his vision returned to him, he could make out a small silhouette swaying unsteadily in the center of the altar. He instinctively stepped forward when he saw the figure begin to collapse, lifting a surprisingly light body in his arms. When he looked down, he saw a frightened child's eyes fixed on him.

The girl was young—probably no older than four. Her head had been recently shaved, but the remaining fuzz was as white as the snow that blanketed the valley. Stranger still, her skin was a deep bronze, several shades darker than anyone Silas had ever seen. Her pale eyes lost their focus as she went limp, and Silas looked up, meeting the uncertain gazes of his congregation.

A broad smile spread over his face as he announced, "Our prayers have been answered! Rejoice—an angel has been sent to guide us!"

All at once, the mood in the room shifted from fear to jubilation. The adults left their seats and crowded around Silas, reaching forward to touch the unconscious child. Even Auron, still trembling from the revelation, approached, grasping the girl's hand in his own. Surprise crossed his small features, and Silas followed his gaze to a black mark etched into the back of the girl's hand.

Any doubt he may have had about the girl's origin vanished once he recognized the shape of the Hearthlord's eagle. Silas felt a shudder of rapture—this was the second revelation. Silas led his followers in prayer, thanking the Hearthlord for his favor.

III

Senya sat up in her bed when the bells began ringing, groggily rubbing the sleep out of her eyes. Pink rays of the early dawn scattered across her bedroom, dimly illuminating the sparse furnishings. She could see her breath in the cold morning air as she exhaled, and she shivered when she put her bare feet on the stone floor. She quickly changed out of her nightgown into a warm wool dress and pulled on her fur-lined boots.

This year's winter was the longest she could remember. It was well into spring, yet the ground outside the village was still blanketed in a foot of snow. The days were slowly growing longer, leaving more time to play outside after her scheduled activities were done. She couldn't wait for summer, when it wouldn't start getting dark until well past dinner, and she could spend the entire evening away from the stifling confines of the temple.

She washed her hands and face in her water basin, haphazardly tossed her nightgown onto her bed, and then departed, racing through the stone corridors to the great hall. Her room was situated in the isolated royal wing of the temple, which was much further away from the common areas than the acolyte dormitories. By the time she reached the hall nearly all of the boys were in their seats eating bowls of hot porridge.

Senya took her seat next to Father Silas, who had already finished and was sipping from a mug of mulled wine. His hair was more gray than black now, and deep hollows were etched beneath his eyes. The winter had been hard on him—he'd spent the first half confined to his bed with a rattling cough. Senya had only been able to watch helplessly as his condition deteriorated, painfully aware that there wasn't anything she could do to help him. Thankfully, a physician from Fortizia had come and drafted a potion to alleviate his symptoms, and he'd regained enough strength to return to his regular duties a month ago. His health was holding for the moment, but he was visibly weaker than he'd been before his illness.

Once everyone had eaten, Father Silas stood up and led them to the inner sanctum. One by one, the acolytes approached the altar and rendered their morning prayers. Although the lamps fixed to the marble columns that surrounded the altar weren't lit, the room was bathed in a soft red light. Every couple of seconds it would pulse more brightly, its steady rhythm hypnotizing Senya until it was her turn to approach.

She knelt on the warm slab and placed her hands on the stone, taking in a deep breath as the power coursed beneath her fingers. While she could feel it resonate with some of the other acolytes, she had never felt in tune with it when praying at the altar. Still, she closed her eyes and bowed. Although she had been taught the same prayer as the others, she had her own version. "Please give me your guidance. Show me what you want me to do."

As always, the altar gave no answer. After waiting for a few moments, she stood up and returned to her place among the row of acolytes while Silas knelt to pray. It was common for him to linger for ten minutes or more in silent prayer, during which time the acolytes were supposed to stand at attention.

Senya felt a nudge in her side. She looked at Auron, who'd quietly repositioned himself beside her. He leaned over and whispered to her, "My father returned from his hunt last night. My mother said she would bake cakes for all of us tonight."

A wide grin crossed Senya's face. The temple staff would sometimes make sweets in the summer when the royal court was in attendance, but they were a rare treat during the winter. Auron's father must have brought in a good haul if his family had been able to purchase butter. She opened her mouth to reply, but then she saw Petrus, a newly ordained priest, staring at the two of them.

She looked up at the marble ceiling, swaying idly back and forth on her feet as the minutes crawled along. After what seemed like forever, Father Silas stood up, and the acolytes fell into line behind him as he led them to the library. The servants had already stoked a fire in the center of the room, which they huddled around as Silas opened the wooden shutters. Sunlight flooded in along with the cold air, making Senya shiver even through her thick dress.

Three times a week, the acolytes were set to the task of copying the Hearthlord's word. The entire collection was composed of five scrolls, one for each of the Divine Embers, and each acolyte could copy one scroll a month. Senya had enjoyed this activity more when she'd been tasked with mixing ink and preparing pens to distribute to the older acolytes, who did the actual scribing.

Now that she was old enough to write, she found it tedious. Only the best reproductions were approved for release, and the rest were burned at the end of the month. In two years, not a single one of her scrolls had managed to escape the bonfire, and she didn't have very high hopes for the one she was currently working on, either.

She pulled her half-finished scroll and a wooden tablet from the shelf at the end of the room, then found a spot on one of the deerskin rugs with Auron. After a few moments, Fabian plopped down beside her. Among the sea of Castellano boys, he was an oddity with his striking red hair. His family had emigrated from

Aesterland three years ago to join the congregation. She smiled at him and scooted over to make more room for him on the rug.

One of the younger acolytes passed out their pens and small vials of prepared ink. Father Silas sat down in the wooden chair near the shelves and read from Ember of Obedience, where they'd left off the last session.

Their pens had to be re-inked every two words, so Silas only read a word every few seconds. "The way is winding," he recited gravely. "Danger looms beyond the path. To gaze too long into the fog is to stray from my side. Keep your eyes forward, and follow."

Despite the slow pace, Senya found herself working frantically to keep up at times. Every mistake had to be crossed out and re-written, by which time Silas would already be two words ahead. She'd learned early on that it was a good idea to sit next to someone who could keep up with the recital, and although Fabian was the same age as her, his accuracy was as high as the oldest acolytes. She spent most of the time looking at his scroll, quickly glancing away whenever one of the supervising priests passed by.

If an acolyte happened to get too far behind, one of the supervisors would snatch his scroll away from him and he would be marched up to Silas, who would smack him across the knees with his cane. The humiliated acolyte would then have to stand there for the rest of the session, which could last for hours. This had happened to Senya a few times, although she was spared the beating — left only to endure the resentful gaze of the acolytes. She was already the only girl among them, and the reminder of her supposed divinity on top of that made her feel even more isolated. Honestly, she would rather have the smack.

Her hand was beginning to cramp up when Silas finally announced they were done for the day. The acolytes rushed to the cubbies to store their tablets and scrolls, and then those who weren't on chore duty left to spend the rest of the day with their families.

Before he left, Auron reminded her, "Come over once you're done! You can have supper with us if you want."

Senya nodded happily and promised, "See you then."

She stood alone in the hall as the rest of the acolytes left, until the echoes of their footsteps and laughter had completely faded. Eventually, Father Silas emerged from the library, leaning heavily on his cane. As they walked through the temple, she slowly flexed the tension out of her hand.

"Is your penmanship improving?" Silas asked. She shrugged, and he smiled wryly. "Many have asked for the word of the Hearthlord in the angel's own hand. How long do you think they will need to wait?"

Senya frowned. "Why can't you give them someone else's and say it's mine?"

"The tongue that lies will smolder in its mouth," Silas said testily.

"Mine aren't ever going to be as good as the others," she replied sullenly. "I don't understand why they have to be perfect."

"Perhaps if you focused more, if you had fewer distractions..."

Senya flushed at this notion, and quickly steered the conversation to a different track. "How many people are waiting?"

"Twenty or so, I believe."

Senya felt her mouth open dumbly at the number. People came from all over Castilla to seek her divine touch, but twenty a day was high even in the summer, when it was fashionable to make the pilgrimage to Alcazar. In the winter, when the road was blanketed with a thick layer of snow, only the most dedicated braved the difficult trek. "Why so many?" she asked.

"A wagon of wounded soldiers arrived this morning. There was a skirmish at the border."

Senya felt a flare of anger pass through her. "Why waste time scribing if they were already here?"

"Your education is not a waste of time," Silas replied.

Stubbornly, Senya continued, "If there is fighting at the border, doesn't it make more sense for me to be there, rather than for them to come here? If someone was seriously hurt, they may not make it in time before—"

She stopped abruptly when Silas turned on her, the look on his face telling her to drop it. "The Hearthlord did not send you to help King Ferdinand with his wars," he said tersely.

Senya lowered her head, and they walked in silence the rest of the way. She was almost grateful when she heard the sound of moaning from the ward, and she broke away from Silas as they entered the crowded room. All twelve of the straw pallets that lined the walls were full, leaving the remaining soldiers to lie on the floor or sit with their backs against the wall. A small group of legion physicians were tending to the wounded soldiers, and some of the congregants were assisting with blankets and buckets of hot water.

The chaos of the room paused for a moment when Senya entered, although some of the semi-conscious soldiers continued to moan incoherently. She felt the eyes of the soldiers and medics upon her as she passed from bed to bed, briefly touching each soldier to inspect his condition. To her growing dismay, their injuries ranged from severe to critical. She felt her heart begin to race as she realized how much work there was to do — this was more healing than she had done in months, and their injuries were far worse than the typical pilgrim's. For a moment, she wasn't sure if she was up to the task.

She drew in a deep breath to steady herself and returned to the bed of the soldier with the most critical injuries. One of the physicians was stationed at the other side of the pallet, where he had been preparing a potion to give to the dying man. He gave Senya a skeptical look, but she ignored it as Father Silas handed her a small knife. She used it to cut away the bloody bandages wrapped around the soldier's waist, revealing a deep gash across his abdomen. She placed her hands on either side of the wound and closed her eyes.

Healing had always come to Senya as naturally as breathing, and within a few moments, she had entered the trance, extending herself into the man's damaged tissues. Bit by bit, she slowly fused the rent flesh back together. The wound was deep, but the medics had done a good job to stave off infection. After an hour of concentration, she withdrew, leaving behind nothing but a discolored scar.

When Senya opened her eyes once more, all of the physicians in the room were crowded around the bed, and their expressions had turned from doubt to amazement. Unphased, Senya wiped the sweat from her brow and stumbled away from the pallet to the next one, where a puncture wound awaited her.

By the time she finished with her fifth patient, her vision had blurred, and she couldn't catch her breath. Silas put his hand on her shoulder and said, "You're exhausted. That's enough for today."

Senya shook her head. "The others aren't as bad. I can keep going."

Silas frowned and considered for a moment, then he acquiesced and allowed her to move to the sixth soldier. This one had lost his arm in battle—a severe injury, but no longer life-threatening. A tourniquet had long since stopped the bleeding, and it would eventually become a stump on its own.

Senya's hands shook as she gently placed them on the soldier's arm. She couldn't regrow the appendage, but guiding new flesh over the wound was a simple matter. She allowed herself to fall into the trance, letting all of her other senses fade away. When she tried to explain her ability to the congregation she often likened it to floating — the sensation of the ground faded away from beneath her feet. She was untethered, as if she could drift away at any moment. At first, she was only vaguely aware of the staccato pulse throbbing in her ears, but it gradually accelerated until it became a frenzied pounding.

The next thing Senya knew, she was crumpled on the floor, and Father Silas was shaking her shoulders. The roar in her ears steadily faded as she looked up at his worried face. The physicians and soldiers were pressing around her behind him, but the congregants pushed them away to give her space.

Disoriented, she asked, "What happened?"

Silas motioned to Lycus, a burly congregant, who easily lifted her into his arms. She squirmed, protesting that she could walk on her own, but honestly, her arms and legs felt like jelly. As Lycus took her outside, Silas addressed the soldiers, assuring them she would be back the next day.

Senya felt her face flush red with embarrassment as Lycus carried her past a group of temple servants. He walked slowly to allow Silas to catch up on his cane, leaving her to try to avoid the gazes of the curious acolytes they passed along the way. When they reached her bedroom, Lycus gently placed her beneath her covers, then he bowed and left.

Senya tried to sit up, but her attempts were only met with exhausted twitches from her muscles. Father Silas drew the curtains, shutting out the cool midday sun. She looked up at him as he rested a hand on her shoulder. She set her jaw, preparing for a stern lecture about the follies of pride, but he only gave her shoulder a soft squeeze.

"Rest," he said quietly.

"I'm not tired," Senya grumbled, ignoring the heavy feeling behind her eyes. She looked up at the dark ceiling as Silas left her. After a few moments, she lost the fight against the creeping exhaustion and closed her eyes.

IV

The bells were ringing again. Senya drowsily sat up, surprised to find herself in bed. She winced when the sudden movement triggered a throbbing pain in her forehead. As her eyes adjusted to the dim morning light, she saw Lucrezia, one of the temple maids, sleeping upright in a chair that had been pulled next to her bed.

Lucrezia awoke with a start when Senya tapped her arm, a mortified look crossing her face as she realized she had been sleeping.

"Forgive me, milady," Lucrezia pleaded.

Senya waved off the apology and hopped down off of her bed and onto her feet. Her head swelled with more pain, and Lucrezia poured her a cup of water.

"Father Silas instructed that you should rest today," Lucrezia said.

"Today?" Senya asked dumbly, looking out the window at the morning sun. The last thing she could remember was healing the wounded soldiers, but that had been in the afternoon. Slowly, she registered she must have slept since then. She exclaimed loudly when she remembered her plans to see Auron the previous evening, evoking a look of disapproval from the middle-aged woman.

She ripped a clean dress out of her wardrobe and changed. Before Lucrezia could stop her, Senya bolted out of the room, clutching her forehead as she ran towards the great hall. Anxiety gripped her as she wondered what Auron would think — she had promised to meet him, and his family would have been expecting her. It wasn't often she was invited over for dinner, and she had been looking forward to his mother's cake so much. She wondered if they thought she had intentionally snubbed them, and if he was mad at her.

She slid to a stop when she reached the entryway to the great hall, scanning the room for Auron. Her heart fell when she didn't see him, but then she felt a hand on her shoulder. Startled, she whirled around, surprised to see Auron's smiling face before her.

Without asking for an explanation, he passed her a small parcel wrapped in cloth. She opened it with shaking hands, blinking tears out of her eyes when she saw a slice of the promised cake in the cloth. "Thank you," she sniffled softly.

Auron laughed and said, "You don't have to cry about it. Did Father Silas keep you here?"

Senya shook her head as she broke off a small piece of the crumbly cake. "There were a lot of soldiers from the border. I was healing them, and then—" She paused as the memory came back to her. She knew she had healed some of them, but she was sure she hadn't been able to tend to all of them. "I should go back to see them," she said resolutely.

"You will not." Father Silas's deep voice caused both children to jump in surprise. Auron took a step back from the priest, smart enough to detect the finality in his tone, but Senya clenched her fists stubbornly.

"I can help them," she argued.

"You won't help anyone until you rest, child," Father Silas said, annoyance creeping into his voice. "I instructed Lucrezia to keep you in your room."

The pain in Senya's head dulled her instinct to protest. She felt drained, and she knew the old priest was probably right. Even if she tried to heal the soldiers now, she didn't know how much she would actually be able to do. Still, the idea of spending the entire day cooped up in her room was not appealing.

Finally, she compromised, "Can I come to the ritual, at least? I'll go back to my room right after."

Clearly exasperated, Father Silas agreed, and he left them for the shrine. Once he was safely out of earshot, Auron let out a deep sigh of relief. "Anyone else would get his cane if they talked to him like that," he said quietly.

Senya frowned and broke off another piece of the cake. "He doesn't order anyone else around like me."

Auron shrugged, and they came to the silent agreement to drop the subject. Senya stashed the rest of the cake in her pocket to finish later, and they fell into the group of acolytes heading to the main part of the temple for the weekly ritual.

The front sections of the temple were already packed with people by the time the clutch of acolytes shuffled in. Fortunately, there were two benches reserved for them in the front, so it wasn't difficult to find a seat. During the summer, it was common for pilgrims to crowd the aisles when there was no place left to sit, but only half of the pews were full today. Although the strong glow of the altar was enough to illuminate the far reaches of the sanctum, the young priests still lit the lamps with fragrant oil, filling the temple with a pleasant haze.

Father Silas stood in front of the altar, adorned in the black stole emblazoned with the Hearthlord's eagle. He raised his hands, signaling for the congregation to grow quiet, and then began to speak. Although his voice was soft, the marble of the temple projected it throughout the large chamber.

He never said anything during the ritual that Senya hadn't heard a thousand times before, but the echo of his voice and the haze of the chamber made his words feel more powerful. It was as if the Hearthlord were speaking directly through him. When she'd been younger, Senya had stayed awake at night waiting for the Hearthlord to speak to her directly, as he had with Father Silas, to give her some inkling of the divine purpose she had been sent to achieve. It had now been seven years since her emergence from the altar, and still, his voice failed to reach her.

She looked down at her feet, suddenly overcome with shame. She knew there must be something she was missing—if she were really the angel, she would channel the Hearthlord and help Father Silas find the next revelation. Maybe the Hearthlord was withholding his guidance until she was worthy of it. A true angel would have been able to heal all of the wounded soldiers and write the Hearthlord's word with perfect accuracy. As it stood, she was nothing but a fraud.

A murmur rippled through the congregation, and she looked up when a familiar scent left a metallic taste in her mouth. Smoke spilled out from the altar, dyed red by the blinding light. Silas had fallen to his knees, coughing violently as the smoke surrounded him. The older acolytes rose to help him, but then an explosive crack reverberated throughout the temple, and the red light suddenly disappeared.

The flickering glow of the remaining lamps revealed a man standing in the center of the altar. Senya felt a chill run down her spine as she processed his sudden appearance. Despite his youth, his hair was the color of ash; otherwise, his features were similar to the Castellanos—he was light-skinned, with a broad face and dark eyes. His armor was strange, composed of thousands of tiny metal rings that covered his entire body. The solid iron breastplates King Ferdinand's soldiers wore weighed well over thirty pounds on their own, but he moved easily in his metal coat. A long silver braid secured his mail around his waist. He carried no shield or spear, only a long sword sheathed at his side.

The congregation watched with bated breath as the man stepped down from the altar and surveyed the gathering at the temple. Father Silas brushed off the acolytes who had helped him up and approached the man, bowing as low as he could manage.

"You must be another sent by the Hearthlord to guide us," Silas croaked reverently. "We are at your service."

The man motioned for Silas to rise, still calmly surveying the crowd. His gaze stopped abruptly when it fell upon Senya, and she felt her heart begin to beat more quickly. He stared at her for a few seconds before snapping his attention back to Silas. He asked, "Are you the chief of this—" he paused, taking in the expensive stonework of the temple, then continued, "—village?"

"I am," Silas replied.

"You have done well to open the portal on your own," the man said. "Leave the rest to me."

He returned to the altar and placed his hands on it. The acolytes beside her tensed, and as she watched the man's back, she could see the air shimmer around him. Silas took a step back, raising his arm to protect his face from the searing heat that burst out from the altar.

The altar roared back to life, brighter than Senya had ever seen it. The light no longer pulsed, but was now completely steady, and a vibrant portal of swirling colors formed at its center. A loud rumble broke out as the gateway to the Hearth opened before them, and almost as one, the congregation fell to their knees in prayer.

The man stood back up, but the portal remained suspended in midair, and a second man emerged. He had blonde hair, but his most striking feature was his piercing red eyes. He also wore strange armor, though his was composed of reticulated black plates that covered most of his body. The first man saluted the newcomer before being set at ease. They conferred quietly for a moment, too softly for Senya to hear what they were saying, but she shivered when they both looked in her direction once more.

To her surprise, more armored men continued to emerge from the portal. The first two men spoke to Silas, and by the time he instructed the congregation to return to their homes, fifteen Hearthborn had come through, with ever more appearing by the minute.

Senya nervously stood up when Silas motioned for her to join him. She felt like the unsettling red eyes of the Hearthborn were drilling through her. She was used to drawing attention in the village — she looked so different from the Castellanos that it was impossible to avoid. She knew what curiosity, fascination, and reverence looked like, but she didn't recognize the guarded expressions in the eyes of the Hearthborn. The only thing she could do was keep her own gaze firmly on the ground as she approached Silas.

Silas put his hand on her shoulder, oblivious to her tension. "The Hearthlord sent us the first angel seven years ago," he explained to the blonde man. "We knew that more would come, so we continued to pray."

"She must have told you much of Jenseits," the angel ventured.

Silas frowned. "Jenseits? Do you mean the Hearth?" The angel nodded, and Silas relaxed and shook his head. "She was little more than a babe and had nothing to tell us. She came to us with the gift of healing, for which we were more than grateful."

The man rubbed his chin thoughtfully. "Show me your face, child," he ordered, and Senya was compelled to look up at him. His expression was cryptic, but she thought she sensed a spark of recognition in his crimson eyes. "What is your name?"

"Senya," she responded mechanically.

He extended his hand, and without thinking, Senya offered him her own. He examined the mark of the black eagle on the back of her hand, then released her with a grunt of satisfaction. He called over one of the angels and said, "Send word to the Regent, and have the Leuchter regiment transfer here. We will wait for her before proceeding further."

The angel saluted and stepped back into the portal, disappearing from the temple once more. Senya stared at the gateway, barely able to stand the fear that crawled up into her stomach. The metallic taste lingering in her mouth made her sick, and her headache had returned in force.

Father Silas squeezed her shoulder and said, "You should go rest, now."

Grateful for the order, Senya quickly left the sanctum, immediately bracing herself against the cool stone wall of the corridor as a wave of nausea overtook her. She took a few seconds to regain control of her breathing before continuing to her room. A thousand unanswered questions swirled around in her mind, but for now, all she wanted to do was crawl back underneath the safety of her quilt.

V

Senya climbed up onto one of the fence posts that circled the market, looking out over the crowd at the temple. Since the arrival of the Hearthborn, Silas and the other priests had been too busy to continue school. The first couple of weeks, Senya had relished the sudden taste of freedom, but as some of the novelty wore off, she'd noticed she was being watched. Even now, she was all too aware of the blonde man surveying her from the edge of the busy market.

The regular town watchmen had also been relieved of their duties, replaced by Hearthborn soldiers in their black armor. They'd wasted no time in securing the borders of Alcazar. Although they still allowed pilgrims and merchants to enter, no one was permitted to leave. A small group of hunters and trappers preparing for their next expedition had pleaded their case to Father Silas, but he'd promised it was only temporary and asked them to have patience. Without anything to do but wait for the restriction to be lifted, most of them had taken to drinking in the market.

She looked over as Auron and Fabian clambered up onto the fence, and together they watched a small patrol of Hearthborn march across the square. There must have been hundreds of them in Alcazar now, although it was impossible to keep count. They were constantly coming and going through the portal. The inner sanctum had become a restricted area, and not even Father Silas was allowed near the altar anymore.

Fabian offered Senya a piece of dried jerky, which she gladly accepted. Although she still slept in her room in the royal wing, she did her best to avoid the temple now, which also meant skipping most meals. Without the other acolytes, she was sure she would have starved by now. She wasn't sure why she was so uncomfortable around her fellow Hearthborn. They had been nothing but cordial with her. Some would give her strange looks, but they mostly ignored her. Still, she was happier keeping her distance from them.

"Do you really think the Regent is arriving soon?" Auron asked as he chewed on his own chip of jerky.

Senya nodded. "I heard some of them talking last night. They said they had to make preparations for her."

"When are they going to take us to the Hearth?" Fabian asked.

Auron scoffed. "You only go to the Hearth when you die."

"They come and go all the time," Senya interjected. "They're not dead."

"They're angels," Auron argued. "Why haven't they taken you back there, anyway? If this is the third revelation, isn't your job here done?"

Senya frowned. "I don't know," she said. "I don't want to go back."

"Why would you rather stay here than go to paradise?" Fabian asked. "Did you ask them to take you with them?"

"No," Senya replied, already tired of this line of questioning. "They haven't told me anything, and I don't know anything."

Sensing her exasperation, Auron and Fabian let the topic drop. The three chewed the tough jerky in silence for several minutes, until the fence shook slightly as a man leaned back against it. The children looked up to see the ashen-haired man who had opened the portal beside them.

Without his chainmail, he was much less intimidating. His brown eyes lit up as he smiled disarmingly at the three of them. "I don't think I ever properly introduced myself," he said. "My name is Alphonse Nichts." He set his gaze on Auron and said, "You are the one who opened the portal seven years ago, aren't you?"

Auron turned red as he shoved his hands in his pockets. "I don't really remember that," he stammered.

Nichts grinned and casually raised his hand. He snapped his fingers, causing a tiny flame to spark into life over his thumb. Auron and Fabian stared at the fire in amazement, but Senya's eyes were drawn to the mark of the Hearthlord's eagle on the back of his hand. She hadn't noticed it before, but it matched her own brand. After a few moments, the flame disappeared, and Auron jumped off the fence and circled around in front of the man, pleading for him to repeat the trick.

He laughed and said, "I can teach you how to do it yourself if you want. It probably won't be very difficult for you."

Senya watched silently as he demonstrated the trick again, and Auron began furiously snapping. She glanced at Fabian, who was watching raptly from the fence. Nichts gave Auron a few pointers, and to Senya's surprise, the next time he snapped, a thin trail of smoke rose from his fingers. A wide grin crossed his face as he looked up at the Hearthborn.

Senya finished off her morsel of jerky before climbing down from her perch and excusing herself. She didn't need to be told she wouldn't be able to learn it herself — it was the same discordant power that pulsed from the altar. She couldn't teach Auron how to heal, and he wouldn't be able to teach her his stupid trick.

Without realizing it had been her destination, she found herself at the temple ward. She relaxed as she walked inside. The group of wounded Castellano soldiers from the front lines had long since recovered and vacated the beds, but new arrivals continued to trickle in. The weather had improved considerably in the last couple of weeks, exposing large patches of ground from beneath the snow. It wouldn't be long before the summer rush began in force.

Sophia, the head nurse on duty, looked up in surprise when she entered — she wasn't scheduled to come until later. Still, she directed Senya to a pallet occupied by a young boy. His mother rose from his side and took Senya's hands. A series of incoherent pleas tumbled out of her mouth, and Senya smiled and assured her that her son would be fine.

Sophia gently disengaged the mother from Senya, and she turned to the boy. His cheeks were stained with tears, and he whimpered softly when she gingerly touched his arm. He had broken it badly — it would be a difficult injury to heal. When it was busy, Silas usually turned away these cases because they could take hours to address, but the boy was the only patient today.

Senya knelt down beside him and closed her eyes, quickly losing herself in the rhythm of reconstructing the boy's arm. It was easy to forget everything else while she was healing. The hours slipped away unnoticed, and by the time she regained her senses, the sun hung low in the sky and the boy was sleeping peacefully.

Senya almost lost her balance when the boy's mother threw her arms around her, barraging her with blessings. Again, Sophia gently pulled the woman away, allowing Senya a moment to catch her breath. When she looked up, she noticed a small group of Hearthborn observing her from across the pallet. She felt her heart clench in her chest when she met the crimson gaze of the woman in the center.

The woman was fairly young, probably in her late twenties, and beautiful. Her silky blonde hair was pulled up into a tight bun, and her skin was pale and smooth except for a dark scar that cut across her right eyebrow. She wore the black plate of the other Hearthborn, but hers was inlaid with the Hearthlord's eagle in ivory. Like Nichts, she wore a silver braided cord around her waist. There was no doubt in Senya's mind - this was the Regent of the Hearthborn.

Before she knew what she was doing, Senya found herself on her knees, her head bowed low as she trembled in the Regent's presence.

Unphased by Senya's reaction, the woman remarked, "Your power has grown."

Senya slowly looked up, shocked out of her fear by confusion. There was something familiar about the woman, but no matter how hard Senya tried, she couldn't remember her. She stammered, "Have we met before?"

A thin smile crept up to the Regent's lips. "They told me you didn't remember." She gestured to the black mark on Senya's hand and continued, "You were once in my service, before you came here." She paused for a moment, reconsidered, and corrected herself. "Perhaps you never left it."

Senya stared at her dumbly. The Regent motioned for her to rise, which Senya obliged, although her legs felt weak beneath her. Now the initial shock of encountering the Regent had passed, she recognized the man to her right — it was Major Koehler, who had arrived from the portal directly after Nichts. He'd led the Hearthborn while they waited for the Regent. A blue-eyed woman with short, mossy hair stood to the Regent's left. Senya's eyes traveled down to her hand, where she could see a black mark she guessed matched her own.

Finally, Senya broke the silence and admitted, "I couldn't remember why you sent me here."

"You helped these people reactivate the altar," the Regent replied. "Now, you will help us release my ancestor, the Imperator." At Senya's bewildered look, she clarified, "The priest calls him the Hearthlord."

This only served to confuse Senya further. "Release him from where?"

She noticed Koehler's lips twist into a snarl, but the Regent continued to smile. "That's enough questions for now," she said. "Don't stray too far. We will depart once I have made the necessary preparations."

With that, she left with her entourage, and Senya sat down on the nearest pallet, a sudden wave of exhaustion passing over her. Sophia approached her, a concerned expression on her face, so Senya forced a smile and assured the nurse she was fine. Wanting to be alone, she left the ward, ignoring the Hearthborn who trailed her on the way to her room.

VI

Lower your head.
Fix your eyes below.
You, who was born of dust,
Ask not how the eagle soars.

Senya felt a strange mixture of excitement and anxiety bubble up through her chest as she donned the pack heavy with supplies for the Regent's expedition. The town square was packed with members of the congregation, all of whom had come to pray as thirty Hearthborn loaded the last provisions onto the saddlebags of the dozen oxen that had been donated to the endeavor. Silas was giving a speech about the momentous occasion, promising that when they returned, it would be with the Hearthlord.

A pair of fleshy arms wrapped around Senya, and she smiled as Auron's mother kissed the top of her head. She had barely been able to close her pack with all the dried fish and bread Auntie Mariana had stuffed into it. Auron's little sisters somehow slipped underneath their mother's arms, and Senya soon found herself completely immobilized by hugs.

Once they disengaged, Auron's father prodded him forward, and he hugged her, as well. She stood still for a moment in his warm embrace, wishing he was coming as well.

"You'll have to tell me what it's like on the other side of the ridge," Auron said, awkwardly stepping back.

"I'll tell you everything," she promised. "They said we shouldn't be gone for more than a month—I'll be back before you know it."

Auron smiled and snapped his fingers, summoning a steady wisp of flame. The little trick had turned out to be a sort of initiation — all of the acolytes who'd mastered it had been inducted into a new school the Hearthborn had started. Senya had watched both Auron and Fabian spend countless hours practicing. While Auron had quickly perfected the trick, Fabian had rubbed his fingers raw without anything to show for it. She glanced at the edge of the crowd, where the red-headed boy was watching them with a muted expression. When he noticed her attention, Fabian quickly dissolved back into the throng of congregants.

Senya frowned as she turned back to Auron. She had never seen him happier than when he'd announced he had been chosen as a holy knight of the Hearthlord. As much as she wanted to share his enthusiasm, somehow she knew the afternoons the three of them had spent romping through the outskirts of Alcazar were coming to an end.

Sensing her ambivalence, Auron let the flame die and boasted, "I'll learn something new to show you by the time you come back."

Senya glanced over her shoulder when she heard the caravan begin to move, and she quickly turned back to Auron and gave him another short hug. Then, she trotted off to join the group of soldiers moving along the southern road out of town, resisting the urge to look back. Within fifteen minutes, they had passed the last cluster of houses that belonged to Alcazar, and it was already the furthest Senya had ever been from the temple.

She walked beside Father Silas, who was keeping up with the steady march of the angels fairly easily. Senya had been skeptical about his inclusion in the expedition, but the promise of freeing the Hearthlord had breathed new life into him. He was barely using his cane, and his eyes were bright with purpose.

Diana Feracht, the Hearthborn Regent, marched at the front of the party, accompanied as always by her blue-eyed bodyguard. Most of the rest of their party consisted of the blonde Hearthborn, aside from a small cadre of orange-haired men and the short, yellow-eyed man who had taken to walking directly behind Senya. They all shared the same mark as her, and they all donned chainmail instead of the heavy plate armor the blonde Hearthborn wore.

The southern road quickly became little more than a trail, but it was used often enough by the hunters and trappers of Alcazar that it wasn't hard to follow. The angels talked and joked as they marched, and Senya noticed them marveling at the scenery more than once. She too was enthralled; the deeper they went into the forest, the larger the trees became, until they towered over them like giants. The woods were alive with the sounds of birds, and it wasn't long until Senya noticed the first deer watching them warily through the brush.

Their speed was checked by the slow pace of the oxen, but even so, she felt exhausted by the time they made camp. It was by far the longest she had ever walked in one day, probably many times over. She glanced at Father Silas, who grimaced as he sat down next to the fire. He rubbed his knees through his thick vestment. Without thinking, she placed her hand over his, easily reducing the swelling that was causing him pain.

He smiled in appreciation, but Senya couldn't help but question the logic of bringing him on this expedition once more. The first time he'd reached the Hearthlord, he had climbed the Icetooth Ridge. He had been a young man then, but now his joints were gnarled with age. She didn't know if she would be able to scale the cliffs, let alone how Father Silas could manage it.

Senya looked over in surprise when Lady Diana joined them at their fire. Her bodyguard served her a bowl of thin soup, then offered Silas and Senya their rations. Another Hearthborn, Lieutenant Eichmann, sat down as well, and the five of them began to eat in silence.

The Hearthborn soup wasn't like anything Senya had tasted before. The angels had brought over a dozen sacks of a strange yellow grain through the portal, which they'd rendered into this watery slop. They'd loaded the oxen with little else in the way of rations. Senya was used to eating venison, fish, bread, and fruits and berries in the temple— compared to that, this was bland.

"Is it not to your liking?" Diana asked.

Senya looked down at the soup, her cheeks burning red in embarrassment. "It's not that," she said. "I just didn't remember it."

Diana laughed. "You don't have to lie. It may not be good, but it will keep for months." She looked over her shoulder at the darkness of the woods and mused, "Perhaps we will hunt for game once we reach the ridge."

"It's too rocky for deer further south, but there are mountain goats," Silas said. "If we come across any hunting parties, I can pay them for some of their quarry."

"Excellent," Diana said. "Meat is hard to come by in Jenseits. Most of my men hadn't tasted it before coming here."

The other Hearthborn both looked at her uncertainly, but Senya was intrigued. "What is it like there?" she asked.

Diana thought for a moment, then answered, "It's similar enough to this country, though without the trees."

Senya looked at the light flickering off the massive trunks around them, unable to imagine the Serrata Valley without its thick forest. "Why aren't there any trees?"

Diana shrugged. "There were trees, centuries ago. Once we revive my ancestor, they will grow again."

Silas bowed his head reverently. He took off one of his gloves, and Senya saw the sapphire of his ring flash in the harsh firelight. She was surprised; she had only seen him wear it a few times on the anniversaries of the first and second revelations. As far as she knew, she was the only other person who was even aware of its existence.

Silas took the ring off of his finger and offered it to Diana, apologizing, "I wanted to wait until we were away from Alcazar to present this to you, my lady. This is the holy relic the Hearthlord bestowed upon me, but you are more deserving of it than I."

Diana leaned over, inspecting the brilliant gem in Silas's hand. Finally, after a few seconds of thought, she gently closed his fingers back around the ring. "He gave it to you," she said. "You can return it to him yourself."

By the time Senya crawled into the tent she shared with Father Silas, she felt more at ease than she had since the Hearthborn had arrived. She didn't know why she had felt so tense when she had first encountered Lady Diana. The Regent had entertained more of her questions throughout dinner, never becoming impatient with her. She looked at the black eagle on the back of her hand, and though she was still buzzing with excitement, she forced herself to close her eyes.

The expedition trekked through the forest for another two days, their progress slowing steadily as the snow deepened. By the time they hit the rocky foothills that skirted the imposing ridge ahead, the trail had become a maze of animal tracks. The Hearthborn established a more permanent camp near the exposed base of the cliffs.

This close, Senya had to crane her head all the way back to see the top of the gargantuan ridge. The sheet of rock looked imposing from Alcazar, but up close, it seemed impossibly tall. The cliffs were pitched at ninety-degree angles in most places. Massive icicles hung treacherously like fangs across the rock face, and she couldn't help but imagine what would happen if one were to fall above a climber. She looked back at Father Silas, unable to believe he had once scaled this colossus.

As the angels unpacked the supplies from the oxen, Senya was surprised to find that they hadn't brought much rope with them, nor did they have any of the more specialized tools Father Silas had used to complete his summit. That evening, she broached the subject with Lady Diana, asking how they intended to scale the ridge.

"We don't need to climb it," Diana replied, smiling in amusement at the absurdity of the idea. "The mountain will let us through."

Senya found out what she meant the next day when Diana and the three orange-haired men approached the face of the nearest cliff. She consulted with them for a few minutes, then stepped back and allowed the largest of them to place his hands on the stone. Even standing among the cluster of angels a hundred feet away, Senya could feel his power ripple through the air. It was similar to the sensation she'd felt when Nichts had opened the portal, but rather than sending chills up her spine, it hit her low in the stomach.

She looked up in alarm when she heard a violent crackling sound, sure for a moment that an avalanche was about to bury them. Instead, she only saw the unmoving face of the mountain, and when she looked back down, there was a concave section in the rock the man had touched, blanketed by a fine layer of dust.

The first man stepped aside, and the next replaced him, repeating the same process. This time, Senya did not look away when the mountain rumbled. The rock turned to dust beneath his fingers, and by the time he relinquished his position, the nascent tunnel was another foot deep.

As the men settled into their labor, Diana returned to the soldiers and issued a set of crisp orders. They immediately scattered to their tasks, leaving Senya and Father Silas alone to watch the excavation. Senya was amazed at their stamina — she could feel how much effort they put into each push, and they only had a couple of minutes to rest in between. She knew if she were to exert herself at the same level, she would collapse after thirty minutes, but an hour passed without them showing any signs of fatigue.

She frowned when she heard a violent cough to her side, and she turned to Father Silas in alarm. He brushed her aside as he retched into his handkerchief. Although he assured her it was nothing, she could only think of the rattling pneumonia that had incapacitated him at the beginning of winter. The arrival of the Hearthborn made it seem like that had been ages ago, but she had to remind herself it had only been a couple of months since he'd been confined to his bed.

Silas rose with a heavy sigh and said, "I think I will lie down in camp." He looked down at Senya fondly and said, "The power of the Hearthborn never ceases to amaze me."

"Do you want me to come with you?" Senya asked.

He shook his head and said, "No, stay here if you like. Maybe you can be useful to them."

As she turned to watch Silas return, she noticed Rolf Kaufmann, the short, yellow-eyed man who had been shadowing her since they left Alcazar, standing a few feet behind her. The corner of his mouth twitched when she met his gaze, but then she quickly looked away, trying to ignore the pinpricks crawling across her back.

By mid-morning, the excavators disappeared into the darkness of the tunnel. The soldiers brought a steady stream of newly cut timber, which they used to construct supports inside the shaft. Lieutenant Eichmann returned to the base of the cliff to oversee the construction operations. When he saw Senya was still there, a look of exasperation crossed his weathered face, and he admonished, "You're in the way."

Senya felt her cheeks flush as she asked, "What should I do, sir?"

Eichmann seemed surprised at her response. He rubbed the back of his neck as he thought, before he finally replied, "I suppose the cook could use some help."

Senya nodded and trotted back towards the camp, painfully aware Kaufmann was following her. She knew his order had probably been to watch her, but there was something about him that made her uncomfortable. She quickly located the party's cook, a middle-aged Hearthborn called Aberdeen.

He sat on a log, idly stirring the same thin soup they'd eaten for the last three nights. He frowned when she reported that Eichmann had directed her to him, cursing softly under his breath. When he saw Kaufmann following directly be-hind her, he sighed and tossed a heavy sack of potatoes towards her.

Senya looked down at the sack uncertainly, and Aberdeen pushed the handle of a small knife into her hand. "Peel those," he ordered. She sat down and took the first potato out of the sack, but before she could start, he warned, "Any skin you leave on, I'll have Kaufmann peel off you."

Senya looked down and slowly shaved away at the potato with the knife. Although she was sure the threat had been the cook's idea of a joke, she still checked each potato meticulously before placing it carefully in the wooden bowl Aberdeen dropped next to her.

She winced when she felt the blade nick her finger, but the wound had disappeared by the time she wiped the blood off onto her dress. She hadn't ever peeled vegetables before — there was a rotation of congregants who took care of all the cooking in the temple. The constant disapproving glances from Aberdeen and the phantom gaze of Kaufmann made her feel self-conscious at first, but after a while, she fell into a sort of rhythm.

It took her all day to work her way through the entire sack, and by the time the Hearthborn returned to camp to eat, her hands were cramped and shaking. Still, she helped Aberdeen serve the hungry soldiers. When they had all retired to their campfires to eat, Aberdeen dismissed her, and she took two bowls to search for Father Silas.

The sound of a rattling cough drew her to their tent, where she found him sleeping. She placed the bowl beside him before returning outside. She cautiously made her way to the closest fire and sat down, soaking in its warmth as she ate her dinner. The soldiers ignored her and continued to talk. When she was done, she immediately returned to her tent and crawled beneath her blanket, drifting to sleep as she listened to Silas's harsh breathing.

VII

Senya looked up from the pot she was supposed to be tending when she heard the clash of steel, watching as Lady Diana parried the blade that came hurtling toward her. Senya had learned the perfect spot to position herself when the soldiers trained, so she could watch while still pretending to focus on whatever task Aberdeen gave her. With a fluid motion, Diana caught her attacker's arm and twisted it behind him, forcing him to drop his sword. The Regent smirked in satisfaction and released him, motioning for the next opponent to approach her.

The first time Senya had seen the Regent spar, she wondered if the other soldiers were going easy on her. Diana defeated them all so easily, without ever losing a point against them. The longer Senya watched, though, the more she became convinced otherwise. After the matches, Diana's opponents were covered with sweat, and they weren't any faster when they faced each other. The Regent's every movement looked both effortless and precise — it was as if the bout had already been choreographed.

Senya could only watch transfixed as Diana felled two more challengers in quick succession. The Regent sheathed her sword, the expression on her face betraying her boredom. Natalia Vogel, her bodyguard, rushed to her side with a towel, which Diana accepted with a smile. They left Eichmann to run the remainder of the training, and Senya returned her attention to the stew, which had begun to boil over.

A couple of quick stirs caused the bubbles to dissipate, and she glanced at Aberdeen to see if he'd noticed. She breathed a sigh of relief when she saw he was still engrossed with butchering the goat one of the Hearthborn had killed the previous day. The chunks of meat he'd managed to extract so far were small and misshapen, but her stomach still rumbled at the sight of them.

The angels finished their training after another hour and crowded around the stew pot, where Senya served them lunch. Once the blonde Hearthborn had been fed, she filled a spare pot with the soup and called out to Aberdeen, "I am going to bring the Rothschilds their lunch, sir."

Aberdeen waved her away, and she carried the heavy pot towards the cliff face, carefully navigating the uneven terrain. The first time she'd had this task, she'd tripped on her way back with the empty pot, badly skinning her knees and elbows. It had only taken a few moments to heal, but she wasn't eager to relive the experience.

As always, Kaufmann trailed a few steps behind her, casting his shadow wherever she went. He was quiet — in all the time he'd watched her, he'd never said a word to her. Still, she couldn't shake the needling sense of unease whenever she looked back at him.

Kaufmann and the Rothschild brothers didn't train with the blonde Hearthborn, and they didn't sit at the same campfires. Their tents were isolated on the opposite side of the camp from the others. While all the other angels reported to Lieutenant Eichmann, Kaufmann and the Rothschilds answered directly to Lady Diana.

She shivered as she entered the tunnel. Torches had been set into the ground every ten yards, allowing her to see, but the passageway was so smooth and straight it was hardly necessary. The temperature dropped sharply as she progressed into the depths of the mountain, and she clung closer to the pot in her hands for warmth.

She walked for fifteen minutes before she was able to hear the echoing sounds of the Rothschilds in the distance, and it was another couple of minutes before she could see them. Every day added another minute to her commute, and she wondered how long it would be before they broke through to the other side. They paused when they saw her, and the oldest, Harald, relieved her of the pot.

Senya waited, shivering, as the three of them ate. She tried not to think about the unfathomable tons of rock above her head, but she jumped every time she heard the wooden supports creak from the strain. The air was filled with a thin layer of smoke from the torches that lit the way. She didn't know how the Rothschilds could stand to be here all day.

Another treacherous rumble from deep within the mountain made Senya quiver in terror, which elicited a chuckle from Augustus, the middle brother. "Did you bring us any water, girl?" he asked.

Senya quickly shrugged the waterskin off her shoulder and handed it to Augustus. He took a heavy draught before passing it on to Joseph, the youngest. Augustus looked past her at Kaufmann, who was leaning back against the smooth wall of the tunnel.

"You got an easy assignment this time, didn't you?" he asked, a taunting smile crossing his face.

The edge of Kaufmann's lip twitched, but he didn't respond. Augustus snickered despite Harald's look of disapproval. The brothers finished their meal, stretched, and stood up, returning to their excavation. Senya snatched up the empty pot and waterskin and took off towards the entrance of the tunnel, jogging to try to restore circulation to her frozen appendages.

Every sound in the tunnel was amplified by the smooth rock surrounding her. She could see Kaufmann's shadow flit in front of her every time she passed a torch, and she imagined that he was no longer tailing her, but now chasing her. Her heart raced as she quickened her pace, but no matter how fast she ran, his steps loomed ever closer. Suddenly, she realized she was out of breath, and she staggered to a stop as she gasped for air.

A few moments passed before she could breathe again, and she didn't dare look behind her as she forced her legs to move once more. To her immense relief, the sound of Kaufmann's boots steadily grew more distant. Still, she wasn't able to shake her imagined terror until she was back in the sunlight once again. She quickly returned to Aberdeen's fire, where he chided her for taking so long.

Exhausted from her journey into the tunnel, she sat down on the log beside the fire and poured herself a bowl of stew. She paused as she raised the first spoonful to her mouth, looking up at Aberdeen and asking, "Did Father Silas come to eat?"

"Haven't seen him," Aberdeen grunted.

Senya lowered her spoon and fixed a second bowl for the priest. She took a bowl in each hand and made her way to her tent, where she heard the muffled sounds of the priest's coughing. She crouched to enter and placed both bowls on the ground next to Silas's pallet before turning to inspect him.

His forehead was hot and damp with sweat, which she wiped away with the sleeve of her robe. His face was pale, and his breaths came in short gasps. He reached out for her, and she quickly helped him into a sitting position. His body shook from a series of violent coughs, and when he took his hand away from his mouth, Senya could see the blood in his palm.

His condition had deteriorated slowly over the last two weeks, but this was a sharp decline from how he'd been in the morning. Senya rolled up her pallet so Father Silas could sit against it, her mind racing. She had never seen him this bad before. She helped him take a drink from the waterskin, then promised, "I'll go get help."

She scrambled outside and made a beeline for Lady Diana's tent on the other side of the camp. Natalia was stationed at the entrance — a sure sign the Regent was inside. The bodyguard frowned as Senya approached, holding her hand up to stop her.

Natalia looked over her shoulder at Kaufmann with thinly veiled distaste, then turned her gaze to Senya. "What do you want?" she asked.

"I need to talk to Lady Diana," Senya pleaded. "Father Silas is sick."

"Wait here." She disappeared into the tent for a few moments, then returned to hold the flap open for Senya to enter herself.

Senya rushed inside and knelt before the Regent, who had been inspecting a large map sprawled out across the floor. Diana looked at Senya expectantly, and Senya quickly explained, "Father Silas has gotten much worse. Please, you have to take him back to Alcazar."

"Can you not heal him?" Diana inquired.

Senya looked down at the floor in shame and admitted, "I can't."

"I see," Diana said. "We will breach the mountain in a few days. Unfortunately, the priest is the only one who has seen the Imperator's tomb — he must stay here to serve as our guide."

Diana returned her attention to the map, and Natalia tapped on Senya's shoulder, signaling it was time for her to leave. Senya slowly got to her feet, and, summoning her courage, she blurted out, "There is still medicine back in Alcazar. I could go back and—"

"Enough," Diana said, her cold tone cutting through Senya like a knife. Senya trembled when the Regent stood up and approached her. Diana's gaze held her rooted in place, and she could not look away as the Regent commanded, "You will stay here."

Senya felt herself nodding helplessly, and then she was released from Diana's spell. Diana frowned as she considered, then she looked up at Kaufmann, who had remained near the entrance. "Go back to Alcazar and retrieve this medicine," she ordered. "Hurry. We mustn't keep the Imperator waiting."

Senya felt Kaufmann's gaze fall upon her once more. "What about her?"

"She won't run," Diana said confidently. Her tone was final as she commanded, "Go."

Kaufmann dipped his head and left the tent without another word. Natalia grasped both of Senya's shoulders and steered her outside. Senya stood numbly in the cold sunlight for a moment, allowing her anxiety to dissipate. She knew she should be relieved that Father Silas would soon have the medicine he needed—so why was she so uneasy?

VIII

A blast of cold air nearly knocked Senya off of her feet as the tunnel flooded with light. Harald Rothschild lowered his hands and stood to the side as Diana ventured into the endless white snowfield beyond the Icetooth Ridge. Senya felt a sharp prod against her back, and she stumbled out onto the snowfield, shivering violently even beneath the heavy fur coat she'd been given.

She moved aside as an angel led one of their oxen onto the snowfield. It was outfitted with a makeshift sled, where Father Silas was sleeping. Kaufmann had returned with the potion the previous day, which had helped to suppress his cough, but the illness had left him so weak he could barely walk. The Hearthborn had packed furs around him to keep him warm, and Diana had promised the Hearthlord would restore his strength once they released him.

Two Hearthborn led the snorting ox further down the snowfield, and Senya followed them as another two left the relative warmth of the tunnel. She was surprised to find that neither Natalia nor Kaufmann was accompanying them on this part of the expedition, but she couldn't say she missed the constant overbearing presence of her chaperone.

Before her, the arctic valley sprawled out as far as Senya could see. Even the sky was a pale gray; she could barely tell where the valley ended and the horizon began. While the ox pulled most of their supplies, Senya and each of the Hearthborn were outfitted with backpacks, as well. The snow was a hard crust beneath her feet, making it easy to walk, but the wind sometimes howled so fiercely that she almost lost her balance under her heavy load. It wasn't long until her hands grew numb even through her mittens, but all she could do was squeeze them beneath her armpits.

Diana led them into the tundra for a few hours, and the crust slowly softened into snowdrifts. Senya's own feet sank a few inches with each step, but the ox was up to its breast in the snow. Senya waited atop a gentle hill, watching the angels coax the heaving beast forward, and she suddenly wondered why the Hearthborn hadn't thought to bring snowshoes with them.

She glanced at Diana but thought better of saying anything when she saw the look of frustration in the Regent's eyes. After twenty minutes, the ox laboriously crested the hill, and they continued into the next valley. The ox's gait flagged as the day wore on, and by the time Diana stopped them for the night, the animal was shivering uncontrollably. The heavy fur coats Senya and the Hearthborn wore were enough to stave off the frigid temperatures, but it was clear the ox was freezing to death.

They made camp in a small alcove that offered some protection from the wind. While the Hearthborn built a fire, Senya approached the ox where it had collapsed in the snow. She knelt beside it and placed her hand on its thick neck, waiting for it to relax before probing it for signs of injury. Two winters ago, she'd reversed the damage frostbite had inflicted on a trapper who had survived a blizzard, but she wasn't sure if there was anything she could do for an animal suffering from hypothermia.

After a few minutes, she frowned and withdrew her hand. Just as she had been powerless to help Father Silas, she knew there was nothing she could do for the ox. She looked back at the Hearthborn as they struggled to light the frozen logs they'd brought along with them. For all of their divinity, it was obvious that they were grossly unprepared to deal with the conditions south of the Icetooth Ridge.

The ox closed its eyes, and she reluctantly left it to join the others at the fire. The wind howled noisily overhead as they ate. The usually talkative angels were silent, and Diana only stared into the fire in quiet contemplation. After Senya had eaten, she coaxed Father Silas to have a few bites of his porridge. As the fire died, two of the angels moved Father Silas into one of the tents. Diana still had her own tent, but everyone else shared the other two tents, and Senya found herself crammed between two Hearthborn. Although uncomfortable, it was warm, and after a long day of walking, sleep found her easily.

When she crawled out of the tent the next morning, she found Diana standing over the unmoving body of the ox. Senya felt her heart sink when she realized it must have died in the night. Diana conferred quietly with the others, and then they unpacked the sled. While the angels sorted through the supplies, Diana returned to the tent where Father Silas had been sleeping.

After a few minutes, the Regent crawled out along with Father Silas, who leaned heavily on his cane as he drew himself to his feet. The angels turned to her as she announced, "We will reach the Imperator within the day. Pack only the essentials — we will return here by nightfall."

The Hearthborn quickly executed her order. Within fifteen minutes, they were on the move again, everyone but Father Silas donning light packs. Two of the angels supported Silas's weak form between them, and although he tried to walk, his feet barely touched the ground.

Senya's breathing grew heavier as they climbed a large ridge, which took the better part of two hours. When she finally scrambled up to its crest, she was amazed at the sight of the valley below. She'd always imagined the Frostlands as an endless expanse of barren ice, but sporadic patches of white trees littered the landscape beyond the ridge. Further to the south, the phantom peaks of more mountains rose into the horizon — these perhaps reaching even higher than those of the colossal Icetooth Ridge.

When the others reached the top of the ridge, Silas pointed to one of the small groves in the distance and said, "Just to the west of there is where I found the Hearthlord."

Excitement rippled through their small party as they made their way down into the valley. The snow was deep here — Senya found herself sinking to her shins with each step, and she lost her footing and fell into the powder more than once. Still, the promise of meeting the Hearthlord kept her going at a brisk pace. Diana stopped her a couple of times to wait for the angels carrying Father Silas to catch up, but she could sense the Regent was also anxious to reach the tomb.

The snow was more tightly packed at the bottom of the valley, allowing them to progress more quickly. A bitter wind swept perpendicular to their route, but it wasn't quite as strong as it had been the previous day. After another three hours of hiking, they reached the bare plain to the west of the forest, and Diana accompanied Silas as he staggered forward on his cane.

Senya heard an odd skittering sound, and she looked at the ground, where tiny pellets of ice danced sporadically at her feet. She dully became aware that the horizon was shaking, and before she could grasp what was happening, the ground beneath Diana and Silas opened with a deafening crack.

The angels immediately surged towards the newly formed crevasse. Senya didn't realize she hadn't been breathing until she heard the Regent's voice bubble up from the crevasse, assuring them that she was fine. Senya cautiously approached the edge of the crack, peering down into the semi-darkness below. The opening plunged twenty feet down, where a dazed Silas was lying in a mound of snow. Senya felt her heart flutter with relief when he rolled into a sitting position, seemingly uninjured from the fall.

Diana looked up and ordered, "Fix a rope. Kolsch and Schneider, stay up there. Everyone else, with me."

One of the angels pounded a stake into the ground a safe distance from the hole, then produced a length of rope and fastened one end around the stake. He tested its purchase, then, satisfied, threw the other end into the crevasse. Senya watched as the first angel descended, rappelling deftly against the wall of ice that formed one side of the crevasse.

She took the rope Schneider handed her and looked down into the cavern, biting her lip nervously. If she lost her grip and fell from here, it was a long way to the bottom, and only the middle of the cavern was protected by a fresh layer of snow.

Diana glanced back at her, and, sensing her fear, commanded, "Close your eyes and climb down."

Senya did as she was told, screwing both of her eyes shut and clenching the rope tightly. She crawled out over the edge and slowly descended, lowering herself hand over hand until she felt the cold ground beneath her feet. She quickly let go of the rope and scurried out of the way so the remaining angel could rappel down.

One of the angels helped Father Silas to his feet, and Diana retrieved a torch from her pack. She lit it, revealing a long corridor that plunged deeper into the ice. Without looking back, she proceeded down the hallway, leaving Senya, Silas, and the angels to trail behind her.

Oddly, the stale air grew warmer the further they progressed. Senya removed her hood and loosened her coat when she began to perspire. The steep decline of the hallway leveled off after a few minutes, and Diana paused when she reached a massive stone door. Diana handed her torch to the angel behind her and pushed against the door, which grated loudly as it gave way. A pale light flooded into the hallway from the chamber beyond, and Senya followed the others into the sanctum.

As soon as she entered, she felt as if she were being enveloped in the Hearthlord's divine presence. The air was heavy with it, and even breathing took a concentrated effort. Her attention was immediately drawn to the statue on a pedestal in the center of the room. A muted light pulsed rhythmically throughout the room, much like the altar had before the Hearthborn arrived.

She heard a soft thud behind her, and she turned in alarm when she saw Father Silas had fallen to his knees. He grasped at his chest as he struggled to breathe, and she rushed to his side, putting her hand on his back to steady him. His gaze was fixed on the statue, and tears flowed freely down his cheeks.

Senya frowned as she turned her own attention to the statue. It didn't quite conform to her image of the Hearthlord. The tall man it depicted was adorned with the regalia of a noble; a crown rested on his brow and he wore a long cloak around his shoulders. One of his hands was at the hilt of the sword at his side, and the other was open as if offering something. Most unnerving, though, were the empty sockets where his eyes should have been. Somehow, Father Silas had never mentioned that in his sermons.

Diana removed her gloves as she approached the statue. She drew a dagger from her belt and, in a swift motion, dragged the blade across her palm. A splash echoed throughout the small chamber as blood erupted from the deep cut, and Senya felt her own power spark in response.

The Regent grasped the statue's outstretched hand with her own. From Senya's vantage point, it almost looked like her blood was being absorbed by the statue. Before she could question the strange phenomenon, Diana turned back to her and motioned for her to approach. Senya's feet moved on their own, and she soon found herself looking up at the fearsome visage of the Hearthlord.

From behind her, Diana gently placed a hand on her shoulder. "Are you ready?" she asked.

Senya looked down at the black mark on her hand, reminding herself this was the reason she had been sent to Castilla in the first place. The cut on Diana's hand looked painful, but she knew it was something she would be able to heal in seconds. She drew in a deep breath to steady herself and nodded.

Diana smiled disarmingly and instructed, "Close your eyes. This will only hurt for a moment."

Senya looked back at the statue one last time, then closed her eyes obligingly. Anticipation gnawed at her nerves as she waited for Diana to cut her palm. For a solitary moment, she felt something cold against the side of her neck, and then her body grew very warm as hot blood spilled down her throat.

The pulsing light abruptly disappeared, and Senya felt a powerful hand close around her neck. Her feet left the floor as she was lifted into the air. When she looked down, she could see the statue below her, but in the flickering torchlight, the stone looked more like flesh. She opened her mouth to protest, but the only sound she could make was a weak gurgle. Blood filled her mouth, and when she realized she could no longer breathe, her thoughts ground to a halt.

Senya barely felt anything when the statue released her, allowing her to crumple onto the ground. She raised a trembling hand to the deep gash along the side of her neck. When she glanced up, she saw the statue had left his pedestal and now stood before Diana. The other Hearthborn both dropped to their knees, bowing before the imposing figure, but Diana remained on her feet.

A deep, unfamiliar voice filled the chamber as the Hearthlord asked, "Who are you?"

Although Diana was visibly unnerved, her voice remained steady as she replied, "I am Diana Feracht, Grandfather. I am the seventeenth Regent who has served in your absence."

"Have you come to challenge me?"

Diana seemed taken aback by this question. "No, Grandfather," she replied. "I came here to free you, so you can restore Jenseits."

The Hearthlord laughed dryly. "In that case, show me your loyalty, Granddaughter."

He placed his hand on Diana's face, and her panicked scream suddenly filled the room. The shrill sound pierced through the murky swamp that remained of Senya's fading consciousness, and she tried to summon her power to heal herself. The warmth that normally came so readily to her fingers was nowhere to be found, though. Her vision blurred as she rested her head in the pool of blood rapidly forming around her.

Silas felt as if his heart had stopped when Lady Diana drew the knife across Senya's throat. Though his body felt as if it were made of lead, he dragged himself across the room to her unmoving form, ignoring the Regent's screams of pain as she clutched the right side of her face. Panic surged through him as he moved Senya's cold hand to inspect her wound. He threw his own gnarled hands over the gash, desperately trying to stem the blood gushing out over her neck.

He looked up when he felt the Hearthlord's divine presence looming over him. Ever since Lady Diana told him of her intention to revive the Hearthlord, he had been waiting for this moment, when he would finally kneel before his god in the flesh. Now, though, all he could do was tremble as he gazed into the Hearthlord's single red eye.

The Hearthlord looked down at his hands, and Silas followed his gaze to the sapphire ring around his finger, now slick with Senya's blood.

"You brought them here," the Hearthlord said, glancing over his shoulder at Diana and the angels, who were assisting her as she struggled to regain her composure. She had removed her hand from her face, revealing a dark bruise around the hollow socket that remained of her right eye. Silas turned his attention back to the Hearthlord as he continued, "You have my gratitude."

Silas bowed his head, too ashamed to meet his gaze. He'd never understood why the Hearthlord had picked him to deliver his teachings to the people of Castilla. He had been blessed with an idyllic life in Alcazar for thirty years. The Hearthlord had not only given Alcazar an angel, but he had also given him a daughter. Despite that, he had transgressed against each of the five pillars of the Hearthlord's teachings. Faith, honesty, hospitality, obedience, and patience — he had made a mockery of each, and now this was the punishment he had wrought.

"I am but a worm before you," he said hoarsely. "I know I am unworthy to beg anything of you, but please, save her."

The Hearthlord's lip twitched as he said, "You could ask for anything. Is this what you choose?"

Silas nodded, and the Hearthlord knelt on the other side of Senya. Silas moved his hands away, and the Hearthlord brushed his fingers across the gash on her neck. The skin stitched back together, leaving a translucent web where the gash had been. A moment later, Senya coughed weakly. Silas lifted her head as she ejected a foam of blood from her lungs, and she drew in a rattling breath. His eyes burned with tears as he drew her head into his chest — though unconscious, she was still alive.

The Hearthlord stood up once more and extended his hand expectantly. "The ring," he prompted, and Silas frantically pulled the relic off of his finger. He wiped off as much blood as he could onto his fur coat before handing it over.

The Hearthlord deposited the ring into a small pouch hanging from his belt. He glanced down at Senya, his gaze lingering for a moment on the black eagle on the back of her limp hand, and a grim smile crossed his face. Without another word, he was gone, with the other Hearthborn trailing a respectful distance behind him.

Silas stared at the empty door, the cold reality of the situation striking him all at once. He opened his mouth to beg them to stay, or at least to take Senya with them, but no sound came out. A cold sweat broke out across his body as he looked down at the girl in his arms.

When they had left Alcazar in search of the Hearthlord, he had known there was a real possibility he would not return. The last few winters had wreaked havoc on his aging body, and he knew from experience the trauma the Frostlands had in store for him. However, the promise of meeting the Hearthlord had made the risk of death seem a small price to pay. Now, though, the embers of a fire he'd thought long dead burned in his stomach once more. If for only a bit longer, he had to live. He would not allow Senya to die here.

IX

Cast not aside suffering.
Embrace it as an old friend.
Seek neither comfort nor satisfaction.
Suffering is eternal.

Smoke filled Senya's lungs, and, for a few relaxing moments, she imagined she was back at the temple, performing her morning ritual before the altar. She began to utter the prayers that had been ingrained into her over the years, but every syllable caused a dull ache in her throat. She opened her eyes, allowing the illusion to fade away as she stared at a small campfire.

She raised a quivering hand to her neck, where she felt a rough piece of cloth. She winced; even the gentle touch caused the wound beneath the bandage to throb. The memory of Lady Diana opening her throat in front of the statue trickled back to her, and she wondered how she was still alive. She gritted her teeth as she tried to pull herself into a sitting position, but a firm pressure on her shoulder halted her progress. She looked up at Father Silas, who shook his head and instructed, "Save your strength."

The fire cast deep shadows onto the hollows of his skeletal face, and Senya wondered how long she'd slept. His heavy fur jacket now served as her blanket, allowing her to see how much his robes sagged off his bony shoulders.

She opened her mouth to question him, but her throat protested any attempt to speak. Her stomach rumbled audibly, and Father Silas retrieved an iron pot and a stick from the ground. There was a thick brown paste plastered to the bottom of the pot, which he stirred for a few seconds before forming it into a small ball. He carefully propped Senya's shoulders up on his knee and put the suspect glob into her mouth, supporting her as she swallowed the substance. It had the faint taste of meat, although it had the texture of wet bread. Father Silas fed her one more glob, then let her drink from a waterskin that had been left behind, and finally allowed her to lie flat again.

"There is enough food for a few more days," Father Silas said quietly as he heaved a remnant of a white branch into the fire. "There is a cache of supplies in a cave not far from here. If we're lucky, some of the traps may still work."

Senya shivered as she thought about venturing back into the frozen wilderness, and she nestled beneath the warmth of Silas's fur coat. She noticed the backpack she'd carried to the tomb lying a few feet away from the fire. The angels and the rest of their supplies were nowhere to be found.

She looked away gloomily as she thought about the Hearthborn. It seemed like a surreal nightmare now, how the statue of the Hearthlord had come to life, but the pedestal at the center of the chamber was still empty. She shuddered when she felt the phantom blade of Diana's knife pressed against her throat once more. Her hand twitched reflexively back to her neck, but Father Silas gently grabbed her wrist.

"It will be slow to heal," he explained. "The Hearthlord closed it, but the binding is thin. Leave it alone."

Senya struggled for a moment, trying to summon her power to reinforce the thin layer of skin, but the warm sensation that usually welled up in her fingers didn't come. She looked at her useless hand, tears of helplessness forming in her eyes as she surrendered to her growing despair. The Hearthlord had immediately seen right through her— she wasn't the angel Father Silas and the rest of Alcazar had taken her for. He had taken away her ability to heal, leaving her a worthless husk.

Father Silas held her hand as he wiped the tears away from her eyes. "It will be alright," he promised. "Do you remember the forest just to the east of here?" When Senya nodded, he continued, "Even if you can't find the traps, you can still forage berries and roots there. This is a good shelter — it's warm and protected from the wind. If you ever find yourself unable to return here before nightfall or during a storm, you need to dig a snow cave. Keeping yourself warm and dry is the most important thing out here."

Senya listened as he detailed the survival minutia he'd learned from his time in the tundra more than thirty years ago. He told her about the different species of berries she could expect to find, how to locate fox nests, how to set traps, and what type of wood to gather for fires. He described the nearby landmarks and explained how to triangulate one's position in the seemingly endless white abyss using the significant features of the landscape.

His confidence was surprisingly infectious, and by the time he finished talking, Senya was beginning to believe they could survive here, at least until they regained the strength to make the journey back to the mountains. She put anything beyond that out of her mind for now.

Five days passed before Senya was able to venture outside of the safety of the tomb. The moment she pulled herself over the lip of the crevasse, the wind smashed into her like a hammer. Once she had steadied herself, she turned around and helped Father Silas crawl out onto the ice.

They had both lost weight since the Hearthborn had abandoned them, but he swayed like a dead leaf in the fierce gale. She didn't know how he'd managed the short journey to the nearby forest by himself until now. Just climbing out of the crevasse had exhausted her, and it was another mile or so to the grove. They braced against each other as they fought through the wind, slowly carving their way across the gentle slope of the valley to the eastern ridge.

She glanced at the Icetooth Ridge, which stretched endlessly in the distance to the north. It was easy to make out what the priest had referred to as Eagle Peak, a great protrusion with a high hooked ledge that vaguely looked like the silhouette of a beak. Its right wing was raised, forming the tip of a neighboring peak nearly twice the height of its head, but the left wing rested at its side. It was almost directly north, near where the Rothschilds had carved the tunnel.

While she had rested, Father Silas ingrained the descriptions of his landmarks into her. Eagle Peak was the most important because it could be used to reliably determine north, but there was also the giant fir tree that rose above the rest of the forest, as well as the cluster of hills to the southwest.

She frowned as she glanced over her shoulder at the hills. One of them hid the entrance to the cave Father Silas had used as a shelter during his last expedition, where he'd left a cache of supplies. Even if none of his traps had survived, he had been almost certain his spare pair of snowshoes would still be there, which would make traversing the drifts much easier. It was much further away than the grove, though, and he hadn't had the luxury to explore. As it was, the roots and berries he'd foraged in the forest were barely enough to sustain them.

She was glad she could finally help him. The tenuous scab on her neck still ached as she moved, but the pain was no longer unbearable. She'd spent most of her time over the last five days sleeping, as there wasn't much in the ancient tomb to occupy her when she had been awake. When Silas wasn't teaching her about survival techniques, she'd only been able to stare listlessly up at the curved ceiling, trying to figure out what she could have done differently. She much preferred to be out here, where she had something to do.

It took the better part of an hour for them to reach the top of the eastern snowbank. Beyond, the grove of trees stretched out for miles. They carefully made their way down the gentle slope on the other side. The wind subsided halfway down, and by the time Senya reached the bottom, the feeling returned to her fingers and toes as her body regained its warmth.

The trees at the edge of the grove all appeared to be the same species. Their bare branches curled out like skeletal fingers, forming a thick canopy of gnarled ivory. Their roots intertwined into a lattice over the snow, which supported the sparse undergrowth. Senya stopped at the edge of the forest and peered through the uniform stalks into the semi-darkness beyond. The wind rippled through the canopy, causing a constant clicking noise to reverberate throughout the grove, but beneath that, she thought she could detect the cautious movements of wildlife.

Silas dropped the pack he'd been carrying to the ground and swept handfuls of brittle sticks into it. Senya spotted a fallen branch a little further in the forest. She dragged it out onto the ice and stomped on it, breaking it into two smaller pieces she could stuff into the bag.

Once they had enough firewood, Silas led her further into the forest, where he'd laid the rudimentary noose traps he'd made from stripping bark. One of them had triggered, but its noose was empty. Senya knelt beside him as he showed her how to reset the trap. He gestured to the dark hollow beneath a nearby tree and explained, "Hares like to nest in these types of burrows. These traps have a low success rate, but the more we lay, the better the odds we'll get something. We have to check them every couple of days, though, or else something may steal our quarry."

"Like foxes?" Senya rasped. She could still barely manage a whisper without causing her throat to swell with pain.

Father Silas nodded as he continued the delicate work of resetting the trigger. "Foxes, maybe owls." He carefully repositioned the twig that served as the trigger, then withdrew to admire his handiwork. "You can set the next one."

Once they finished checking the traps, Silas showed Senya one of the bushes with the berries they'd subsisted off for the last couple of days. He'd already picked it mostly clean, but they robbed it of the rest of its fruit.

Silas gestured to the crest of the snowbank, where the sun was already sagging into the horizon. "We have to go," he said softly.

Senya frowned as she looked at the measly collection of berries they'd gathered. She leaned close to his ear and whispered, "You go ahead. I can look for a little longer."

Silas followed her gaze to their provisions, and his shoulders slumped. "You can stay for half an hour, but then you need to return."

Senya took the pack from Father Silas and trotted further into the forest. Within a few minutes, she found a fresh bush heavy with berries, and she filled the pack until it was overflowing with them. The white bark of the trees turned purple as twilight fell, and she picked her way through the maze of trunks until she was back out on the ice.

It was dark when she reached the top of the ridge again, and she realized she'd lost track of time in the forest. When she finally reached the crevasse, her entire body was shaking violently from the bitter cold. Her arms and feet were completely numb. Unable to grasp the ledge to lower herself down, she was forced to jump, landing heavily on her feet and praying she hadn't twisted an ankle as she tumbled into the snow. She clawed her way out of the powder into the stone corridor beyond and hurried down until the air was warm again.

Father Silas met her at the door to the chamber. She looked down in preparation for a lecture, but instead, he helped her take off the heavy backpack. She sat down next to the fire, pulling her mittens off with her teeth and holding her hands near the flame. In the dim light, she could see the tips of some of her fingers were gray with frostbite, but the color returned after a few minutes. She waited until the feeling returned to her fingers before carefully removing her boots. She grimaced when she found nearly all her toenails had turned black.

As she warmed herself, Father Silas heated the berries in a pot over the fire. They were too hard to eat in their raw form, but after cooking for an hour, they melted into a soft jam. It wasn't long until the chamber was full of the sweet scent of the simmering berries, and Senya heard her stomach growl.

She looked at Father Silas in alarm when he coughed, but he waved his hand and said, "It's just the smoke."

She nodded uneasily. Compared to the brittle old man who had needed to be carried out of the camp beyond the Icetooth Ridge, he'd seemed like a different person over the past couple of days. He alone had kept them alive since the Hearthborn had abandoned them.

She had been trying to avoid the topic of the Hearthborn, but as the thought of them resurfaced in her mind, she could no longer help herself. In her hoarse whisper, she asked, "Why did the Hearthlord leave us?"

Father Silas's brow furrowed at the question. "A trial to strengthen our faith," he suggested, although he didn't sound as sure as he usually did when it came to the will of the Hearthlord.

"I don't understand," Senya said.

"It is not for us to question the Hearthlord's designs," he said grimly. Senya dropped her gaze to the ground, but then she felt Father Silas's reassuring hand on her shoulder. "Do not dwell on it, child. Don't forget - the Hearthlord spared your life. He meant for you to survive this trial and return to his service."

Senya nodded, comforted by the thought. The only identity she had ever known was as a servant of the Hearthlord. As long as she could cling to that, there was still a life to look forward to beyond the Icetooth Ridge.

X

Senya chewed on her lip as she stopped at the edge of a cliff, now positive she was no longer traveling along the same route the Hearthborn had taken to the tomb. She'd set out that morning with the brilliant plan to locate the ox that had died in the neighboring valley, but it was seeming more foolish by the minute. She looked up at the sun, trying to calculate how much time she had before nightfall. If she left now, she could still check the traps, and, if she was lucky, return with something to show for the day.

As she was mulling this over, she heard a low growl. She looked down over the side of the cliff, freezing when she saw the bared fangs of the massive wolf below. Its fur was white, and it was the size of an ox — three times bigger than the wolves that roamed the forests of the Serrata Valley.

After the initial wave of terror, she realized there was no way it could reach her from the bottom of the cliff. The wolf lowered the object it had been carrying in its mouth to the ground. Senya squinted at the dark shape, slowly making out the form of a leg covered with dense black fur.

Senya watched as three pups emerged from beneath the cliff, where the wolf must have made a den. The mother kept her yellow gaze on Senya while the pups tore through the frozen flesh of the leg. Senya backed away from the ledge and climbed up the ridge once again. All of the animals she had seen thus far had the same white fur as the wolves, so the leg the wolf mother had scavenged could have only come from the ox.

She was lucky she had stumbled on the wolf from afar. If she had been able to find the ox first, she could have become the meal the pups were feasting on. It was a stark reminder that no matter how good she got at trapping and foraging, she was far from the top of the food chain in this land.

The hike back to the southern valley consumed the majority of her remaining daylight. She detoured through the forest on her way back, checking the traps. A few of them had tripped, but there was no quarry waiting for her. She reset them and spent a few minutes digging for tubers to bring back to the tomb.

She made it back to the crevasse just as the sun set. She tossed the bag full of the beets she'd foraged into the pit, then carefully climbed down herself. She knew the route fairly well now, although the icy handholds still made her nervous as she descended. Once her feet were safely on the ground, she knelt beside her bag and shoveled as much snow as she could into it. Once the bag was full, she slung it over her shoulder and proceeded down the tunnel, trotting along the smooth passageway despite the darkness. She slowed down after a few minutes and wandered forward with her hand outstretched until she felt the heavy stone door beneath her fingers.

Senya exhaled a breath of relief when she entered the warmth of the tomb. Father Silas was sleeping, so she busied herself with rekindling the smoldering embers of their campfire. Once it was burning with a healthy glow again, she dumped the snow she'd gathered into the cooking pot the Hearthborn had left behind. She placed it on a makeshift grate over the fire and waited for it to melt.

She filled both her and Father Silas's waterskins, leaving the rest of the slushy water to boil over the campfire. Like the berries, the beets had to be cooked before they were edible. They made a heartier meal, but it would take a long time to boil enough water to cook them over the small fire. She took off her blood-stained coat and sat down. As she waited, she imagined the ox leg roasting over the fire, and her mouth began to water.

Although she hadn't lost as much weight as Father Silas, Senya could distinctly feel her ribs as she wrapped her arms around herself. She knew they wouldn't be able to live off berries and roots forever, let alone gain the strength to make the arduous journey back to the tunnel. The noose traps were too unreliable to provide a steady source of meat.

Her thoughts turned to the cache of supplies Father Silas had left on his last expedition. If his traps were anything like the iron jaws the fur trappers of Alcazar used, they would be much more effective. She'd resisted the urge to hunt for them so far — there was no guarantee they had survived over the years, and Father Silas's description of the location of the cache was based on landmarks that no longer existed. One of the hills to the southwest had a cave where he'd sheltered, but the deep snowdrifts meant the terrain was constantly changing, and there were dozens of hills.

She'd thought scavenging the ox was a better bet, but now she knew its carcass rested in wolf territory, finding the cache would give them the next best chance of survival. She blinked when she heard the pot bubble, and she dropped in a few of the beets, being careful not to splash any of the water onto the fire.

Senya impatiently fished out one of the beets with a stick after fifteen minutes. It was still tough beneath her teeth, but her hunger roared to life after the first bite. She scarfed it down, hardly minding when it burned the roof of her mouth. She ate two more before forcing herself to stop, leaving the rest for Father Silas.

She cooked his portion for another thirty minutes, periodically poking the beets with her stick to judge their softness. The pneumonia had left Father Silas too weak to chew much, so she mashed the beets in a small wooden bowl with a rock. Once the pulp was ready, she gently woke him up.

"Is it time for the morning prayers?" the priest asked as Senya helped him into a sitting position.

Senya shook her head and fed him a small portion of the pulp, which he swallowed with some difficulty. The clouded look of disorientation slowly left his eyes as he managed a few more bites, but then he said, "You eat the rest."

"You hardly ate anything this morning."

Father Silas stubbornly refused to open his mouth, and Senya gave up after a few seconds of resistance. To be honest, she was still ravenous. As she ate the rest of the pulp, Father Silas looked wistfully at the fire.

While she scraped the last bits of the beet pulp from the bowl, Senya considered telling him about the wolf she'd seen, but she quickly decided against it. It would make him worry, which would only be a drain on what little strength he had left. Instead, she said, "I'm going to look for your supplies tomorrow."

"I left them in a natural cave in the foothills to the southwest," he said dreamily, repeating the information for what must have been the twentieth time. "There are three hills clustered together that are a bit taller than those surrounding them. The terrain was different than I remembered, though. You'll have to be careful."

Senya nodded patiently. She lifted his head and coaxed him to take a sip of water, but he sputtered, which deteriorated into a fit of coughing. Senya helped him sit up so he could clear his lungs. He laboriously spat up a mass of phlegm and blood, and he was shivering by the time Senya laid him down again.

She could only watch helplessly as he gasped for breath. A few days after Father Silas's health began to decline, when she had returned to the tomb with feet so frostbitten she could barely hobble on them, she'd felt the familiar currents of her ability to heal stir in her fingers. In the wake of their desperate situation, a sense of euphoria overcame her as she repaired the damage. The Hearthlord had set them on this trial, but he was still watching over them, giving them the tools to succeed.

While she could heal the odd scrape and the frostbite that recurred day after day, there was nothing she could do to fight the sickness ravaging Father Silas's body. Her hands shook with a mixture of anger and grief. Of the five pillars, faith had always been the one she had most struggled to grasp. Now more than ever, she failed to understand the Hearthlord's will. Father Silas had devoted thirty years to his service. What had the priest ever done to deserve such punishment? Why had the Hearthlord restored her power only to have her watch him suffer so?

Senya dipped a rag in the lukewarm bowl of cooking water and draped it across Father Silas's burning forehead. His breathing settled into a steady rattle as he drifted back to sleep, and she returned to the fire to clean the cookware. Once the chore was done, she laid down and surrendered to her exhaustion.

The fire had been reduced to embers by the time she stirred again. She drowsily rekindled it, noting she needed to gather more firewood as she drew from the scant pile. Her stomach growled as she pulled on her coat and her pack. She clenched her jaw and ignored her hunger; there was nothing left in the tomb to eat, anyway.

She checked on Father Silas, but he was still in a deep sleep. Not wanting to disturb him, she slipped past the stone door into the dark hallway and made her way up towards the surface. She was relieved when she saw the pink light of dawn flooding into the crevasse, and she climbed up onto the ice. She hunkered her shoulders and pressed against the wind towards the hills to the southwest.

The base of the hills was further from the crevasse than the forest, but it was flat and the torrential wind cleared the hard crust of any snowdrifts, making it fairly easy to traverse. She was glad she had gotten up so early; it would give her plenty of time to explore the hills and hopefully find the cave. It was still mid-morning when she made it to the snowbank that skirted the edge of the hills. Her feet sank into the snow as she climbed the powder to the top of the first mound. Using her hands to claw for purchase, she managed to reach the top, though she was sweating beneath her heavy coat. Father Silas's warnings replayed themselves in her head — she had to be careful; excessive perspiration could freeze beneath her clothing.

From the top of the hill, dozens of smaller hills spanned out before her, rippling across the frozen landscape until they grew into a small mountain range that sliced the southwest horizon. She checked the position of the great fir tree over her shoulder, then studied the peaks of the distant Icetooth Ridge, orienting herself against Father Silas's landmarks. She searched the sea of uniform white mounds until she found a cluster of three larger peaks another mile away, which looked similar enough to what Father Silas had described.

Senya stumbled down the hill to traverse the maze of valleys in the general direction of the cluster. The snowdrifts here were deep, making her progress painfully slow, and she had to climb the nearest mound from time to time to reorient herself. It wasn't long before exhaustion crept up her numb limbs, but she ignored it and continued on. By the time she could see the cluster from the valley, her optimism was faltering. She was now several hours away from the relative safety of the tomb. If she didn't find the cave, it would be a long, cold walk back with nothing to show for it.

She climbed the nearest hill in the cluster to get a vantage point on the ridge that connected the three peaks. When Father Silas found the cave, the opening had been obvious. Senya's heart fell as she gazed across the drifts blanketing the ridge, unable to see anything that indicated a cave. She carefully made her way onto the broad ridge, hoping that if she walked along the top of it, she would spot a depression in the snow on either side.

She made it halfway to the center point of the ridge when she heard a low rumble, and cracks appeared in the surface of the snow around her. Panic gripped her when she noticed the maw of a crevasse open a few feet to her left. As the snow beneath her feet rushed away, she threw herself forward, desperately grasping for the newly formed ledge. For a moment, it tolerated her weight as she struggled to pull herself up, but then it collapsed, as well, and she was swept downwards with an avalanche of snow.

A blur of white enveloped Senya as she thrashed against the current of snow, but then everything abruptly turned to black. It took a moment for her to realize she was no longer in motion. She could hear her own frenzied gasps for air, and although she felt the weight of the snow pressing in on her from all sides, she could still move her arms and legs.

After the initial shock receded, Senya took a deep, calming breath, and then she began to dig. Her progress was slow, but after a few minutes of steady crawling, the resistance of snow beneath her hands disappeared. She pulled herself out of the tunnel she'd made, gasping for breath.

Although she was free from the avalanche, everything was still dark. She carefully pulled the rest of her body out of the mound and crawled down a gentle slope until she felt the rough texture of rock beneath her hands.

She sat down on the uneven surface and was still for a few minutes, allowing her breathing to return to normal. It was significantly warmer here than it had been outside, and as she listened to the steady patter of dripping, she realized the temperature had crept above freezing. She brushed the snow out of her hair before it could melt. The sound of a river echoed through the cavern, and she could detect a trace of sulfur in the air.

She shrugged the pack off of her back and retrieved a torch and a scrap of flint. After a few tries, she lit the torch from a spark, and a warm glow illuminated the wall of snow behind her. She unsteadily rose to her feet and turned the light forward, revealing the hollow cavern she'd fallen into.

Giant crystal stalactites stretched down from the roof of the cavern, some of them nearly touching the rocky floor below. Every surface in the cave glistened with moisture, and a large pool had formed near the center. Senya approached the glassy surface of the pool, careful not to lose her footing on the damp floor. In the middle of the pool, two columns gracefully curved ten feet into the air, where they ended in sharp points. As she got closer, she realized the structure was not crystal, but rather the ribs of some enormous animal. Other bones were scattered around the cavern, including a skull with a pair of tusks as long as any of the ribs. Senya could only imagine the size of the animal that had left these remains behind.

She knelt beside the pool and removed one of her mittens, dipping her cupped hand into the cool surface to take a drink. After she took her fill, she wandered around the edges of the room, locating four passageways that exited the chamber.

She returned to the mountain of snow that had collapsed with her, but the light of her torch didn't reach far enough to show where she'd fallen from.

Unable to return the way she came, she knew she had to press deeper into the cave system and hope one of the passageways led to an exit. She listened intently at each passageway, finally choosing to take the one where the sound of the river was loudest.

The passage led steadily downwards, but the sound of the river continued to grow louder, so Senya marched onward. The temperature rose as she progressed until her body was damp with perspiration. She took off her heavy coat and continued on.

She emerged into another cavern, this one filled with a constant spray of mist and the roaring echo of the river. It was impossible to shield the weak flame of her torch from the onslaught of water, but the light remained even after the torch went dark. She looked up at the glowing slime that coated the stalactites in this chamber. The light emanating from the slime threw the chamber into a dim blue relief. It was easily four times as big as the first chamber, and it was dotted with more pools, although most of these were boiling idly.

Senya stowed her wet torch in her pack and approached one of the steaming pools, holding her arm over her nose as the smell of sulfur grew stronger. Despite the stench, she enjoyed the intense heat of the steam for a few minutes before making her way towards the river that cut a path through the center of the chamber. It was ten feet across and probably just as deep, and the current was so strong the water was white with turmoil.

The tail of the river disappeared beneath a low rock edge, but the cavern remained a little wider towards its mouth, forming a narrow riverbank. She took her mittens off and kept a hand on the craggy rock, aware one false step could send her plummeting into the vicious current. Fortunately, the slime illuminated the way forward here as well.

She followed the river upstream until she reached a sprawling chamber, where another low rock ceiling obscured its source. She stopped abruptly when she turned away from the river, staring at the mountain of white fur scarcely twenty feet from her. The creature was so big she couldn't take all of it in at once—she saw a set of claws, each razor-sharp nail longer than her arm, an exposed fang bigger than her head, but also a closed eyelid, and finally, she attuned to the rhythmic rise and fall of the beast's breathing. Somewhere amidst her instinctual terror, she recognized that the behemoth was sleeping.

Senya held her breath and pressed her back against the smooth wall of the slumbering beast's den. Despite her urge to get as far away from the animal as quickly as possible, she forced herself to slowly skirt the edge of the chamber, slinking away from the receding glow of the blue slime and back into the darkness of another passage. She didn't breathe again until she was well away from the monster, and her heart rate didn't return to normal for a long time after its snoring faded into the distance.

She didn't bother trying to light her wet torch again, rather keeping her hand on the smooth wall and following alongside it. After a few minutes, she felt an icy breeze sweep past her, and then she heard the familiar whistle of the arctic wind outside. She dried herself off as best as she could and shrugged her coat back on. She turned a sharp corner, smiling when a narrow ray of light blinded her.

Senya climbed up a rocky ledge to the high passage where she could see daylight. It was narrow enough that she had to take her pack off and squeeze herself through before she could reach back and bring the rest of her meager supplies. She sat in the snow and basked in the light for a few minutes, allowing the relief to flutter in her heart. A wall of snow had piled up at the entrance of this cave, as well, but there was a small pocket near the top that hadn't yet been obscured.

She stood up, preparing to leave the snow cave, but then an odd texture caught her eye. She made her way to the protrusion and scraped at it until she unearthed a tarp that had lain almost completely buried. Senya's hands trembled as she unfolded the tarp, revealing a neat bundle of pristine arctic fox furs and a variety of iron trapping implements.

Senya sorted through the traps, removing those rusted beyond repair, and piled the remaining three on top of the furs. She grinned when she unsheathed the hunting knife and found the blade was still sharp and clean. She tucked the knife into her coat, then turned her attention to the set of snowshoes Father Silas had promised, relieved to find they, too, were in good condition. The shaft of his hunting spear had rotted away, but the head was still serviceable, and it would be easy to repair in the forest.

Thanking the Hearthlord, Senya piled the pelts and traps into her pack and fastened the snowshoes to the soles of her boots. She scaled the steep slope of snow at the entrance of the cave and crawled outside, then reoriented herself against her primary landmarks. She had emerged near the base of the southernmost point of the triple mounds, and she made a mental note in case she needed to use the shelter again. Despite her misadventure, the sun was still a safe distance above the horizon, so she headed back towards the tomb with the supplies.

She was amazed at how quickly she was able to move with the snowshoes. Without her feet sinking into the powder with each step, she felt as if she was gliding across the landscape, and she cleared the distance it had taken her several hours to traverse in the morning in a little less than an hour. The sun was still high when she reached the crevasse, so she decided to return to the forest to lay her newly gained traps.

Although ineffective, the noose traps had taught her which areas saw the most activity. She set the metal traps where she'd had to reset the primitive traps the most, then foraged for another half hour, gathering enough berries for a meager dinner. As she headed back to the crevasse, she was sure this would be the last night she and Father Silas would be without a proper meal.

Father Silas was sitting next to the fire when she slipped past the heavy stone door. His expression brightened when she held up the snowshoes victoriously, and he spent the next few minutes helping her unpack the remaining supplies from her heavy bag. While she cooked the berries she'd foraged, she told him everything — about the mysterious bones, the boiling pools and blue slime, and even the enormous hibernating beast she'd encountered. His eyes were alight with wonder

— he'd had no idea such an extensive cave system was connected to his small refuge.

For the first time in days, Father Silas ate his full portion, although he had to pause regularly to allow his rattling cough to pass. The rag he used as a handkerchief was so stained with blood that it was hard to tell how much he hacked up with each new retch.

Senya watched him as she scraped up the sludge of berries from the pot, the reminder of his illness putting a damper on her mood. The supplies would soften the hard edge they'd been tracing to survive, but Father Silas needed medicine. It would take at least two days to reach the tunnel, but probably longer considering his condition. She couldn't see any way around spending a few nights out on the ice. She frowned as she finished her meal and reached for her waterskin, trying to calculate how much food they'd need for the trip. She figured bringing enough to get past the tunnel would be sufficient — once they reached the other side, it would be easy enough to scavenge in the forest, especially if spring had melted the remainder of the snow.

She rubbed Father Silas's back as another fit overtook him. Once it passed, she helped him lie down on the heap of moss that served as his bed. She retrieved one of the soft fox furs from the bag and placed it beneath his head, and he smiled wearily.

"I'm proud of you," he said huskily. "When you return to the Hearthlord, he will be, too."

Senya was taken a bit off guard by the unexpected praise. She felt his cheek, which was hot beneath her touch, and quickly poured some of her water over a spare rag and laid it on his forehead. Still, she couldn't help but smile as a warm feeling spread through her chest.

A wave of exhaustion crashed into her as she waited for him to drift to sleep. Once his breathing had evened out, she crawled over to the fire and scraped the last of the jam out of the pot and into a bowl to serve as their breakfast for the next morning. She filled the cooking pot with the few handfuls of snow she'd brought in with her. Normally, she would watch it melt before turning in for the night, but her muscles throbbed from the day's escapades and her eyes were burning from the smoke that filled the poorly ventilated room. She left the pot on the dwindling fire, crawled to her makeshift pallet, then curled up to sleep.

The room felt unnaturally still when she awoke again. A deep-seated ache pulsed through her legs when she rolled into a sitting position. She placed her hands on her thighs and quickly healed the damage. Before, a little bit of discomfort wouldn't have been worth the exertion, but with the promise of a steady source of nutrition, she could afford to splurge a bit.

She stretched as she made her way to the embers of the fire. She was eager to go out and check the traps, so she scarfed down half of the leftover jam from the previous night. She spent a few minutes reviving the fire, illuminating the chamber with its cheerful light once more, then took the remaining jam in the bowl and set it next to Father Silas. She touched his shoulder to wake him.

He did not stir, so Senya gently shook him, surprised at how light his body felt beneath her touch. She had never known him to be a heavy sleeper, but he remained still after her increasingly forceful attempts to rouse him.

A heavy sense of dread crept up Senya's spine, and she finally pulled on his shoulder hard enough to roll him flat on his back, causing his fur coat to fall off of his skeletal body. His glazed eyes stared blankly at the ceiling overhead, and Senya felt cold as she placed a finger beneath his emaciated jawline. Tears streamed down her cheeks as she waited for a pulse, but the seconds ticked away and still she felt nothing.

Without thinking, she placed her hands on his sunken chest and closed her eyes, extending her power. She felt a vacuum beneath her fingers, and after a few seconds, she was as drained as she had ever been in her life. Her vision spun wildly as she drew away, sure that if she tried to heal him any longer, she would follow him into the void.

Dazed, she automatically began to recite a prayer, but the words felt vulgar now — an empty appeal to an apathetic god. True anger flared up in Senya for the first time as she clutched the priest's cold hand. Was this part of the Hearthlord's trial? Father Silas had served the Hearthlord for most of his life, and was this his reward — to die cold and starving hundreds of miles from his home? If this was part of the Hearthlord's plan, what kind of god was he?

The anger burned out as quickly as it had come, leaving a hollow pit in Senya's stomach. She looked at her own hands as a feeling of utter powerlessness settled upon her. After everything Father Silas had done for her, she had failed him when he had most needed her.

Unable to do anything else, Senya buried her face in the priest's vestment and cried.

XI

The ground on the windswept plain was too hard for Senya to perform a proper burial, so the following morning she excavated her supplies out of the central chamber of the tomb. She washed Father Silas's face and removed his heavy fur coat before wrapping him in the tarp she'd found with his old supplies. She stood over him silently for several minutes, wanting to apologize but unable to find the right words. In the end, she laid the bowl of jam on his chest as a meager offering and left, sealing the heavy stone door of the tomb to leave the priest to his rest.

She built a shoddy camp halfway up the stone corridor. It wasn't as warm as the central chamber, but it still retained some heat from the earth, and it was protected from the wind. She climbed the crevasse and made the journey to the forest to check her traps. None of them had caught anything yet, so she spent the rest of the day stripping bark to make twine. Once she had enough, she cleaned up a long stick and affixed the spear tip to it. She returned to her camp with more firewood and blackberries, and she melted snow in the iron pot to refill the waterskin before drifting to sleep.

The days blended together in Father Silas's absence. The time when she was out on the ice wasn't so bad — it was easy to lose herself in the tedium of checking traps, improving her tools, foraging, and gathering wood and water. When the sun set, she tried to keep herself busy with cooking and processing her quarry, but the grief she could ignore during the day always seemed much stronger in the dark.

Sleep never came easily, and the exhaustion followed her into the next day. Still, desperate to get away from the tomb just down the hallway, she always set out as soon as the sun rose in the morning. Her efforts eventually paid off—she caught her first arctic fox three days after Father Silas's death. She relocated some of her traps deeper into the white forest, and, after that, there was never a night she didn't have meat roasting over her fire.

Over the course of the next couple of weeks, she regained all of the weight she'd lost since the Hearthborn left. She made a bed of the furs from her prey, and, nestled under Father Silas's coat, she was as warm as she'd ever been in her bed in Alcazar. As spring turned into summer, she accumulated a stockpile of excess food, and she set her gaze north once more.

She sorted through her supplies, carefully thinking about what she could afford to leave behind. The iron pot was good for camping, but it would be easy to replace once she crossed the ridge. Her collection of furs was probably priceless, but each weighed a few pounds and provided little survival value. Her knife, spear, and snowshoes were essential, but she decided to leave all of her traps behind.

After another week, she'd saved enough food to make the journey. She filled her waterskin, then, with a last farewell to Father Silas, left the crevasse. The sky overhead was a pale shade of gray and flurries of snow swept up around her as she left the valley. She cast her gaze to the horizon, where she could see darker clouds gathering in the distance. It was difficult to predict how soon the storm would be upon her, but now she was on her way, she couldn't stand the thought of turning back and returning to the tomb. Her legs continued to automatically carry her forward, and after a few more minutes, she convinced herself she would make it to the ridge well before the clouds reached her.

She walked all day, stopping only to eat. Though she'd packed carefully, her bag still weighed over thirty pounds. By the end of the day, her muscles were aching from the unfamiliar load. As the sun set, she dug a snow cave and crawled inside with her pack. She wrapped herself in Father Silas's coat and ate the last of the food she had rationed for the day, then laid down.

Despite her exhaustion, sleep eluded her for hours. Now her escape from the Frostlands was so close, she could no longer stave off the needling concerns about what would happen when she returned to Alcazar. What had Auron and Fabian and the other acolytes thought when she hadn't returned with Lady Diana and the Hearthlord? What would they think when she returned without Father Silas?

She must have eventually dozed off; the next thing she knew, daylight was peeking through the web of hoarfrost that had formed at the entrance of her cave. She rolled up Father Silas's coat and fastened it to her pack, then scurried out of her snow cave into the light. She released a small sigh of relief when she saw the storm was still a safe distance away.

Without wasting any time, she set off towards the mountains. The rolling snow-banks gradually steepened as she approached the ridge. The flurries of the previous day had escalated into a mild storm, and by the time she reached the sheer cliffs, her visibility was reduced to a few yards from the torrent of snow.

She turned west and followed the frozen boulders along the base of the cliff. She found herself shivering with nervous energy. The tunnel entrance couldn't be more than a few miles away, and then she would be on her way back home. The storm was quickly becoming a full blizzard — easily the worst she had seen since she had been stranded. The fierce wind created a distinctive whistling noise as it rushed across the cliffs, and the mountain rumbled as the snowpack higher up shifted dangerously. While she was afraid of avalanches, she didn't want to stray too far from the cliff for fear she would miss the entrance of the tunnel.

Senya's heart jumped in her chest when she saw the perfect indentation of a circle against the cliffside, and she hurried into the tunnel. Inside, the shrill whistle of the wind became a jarring shriek. She didn't recognize the piercing sound from the journey south, but she supposed the wind could be blowing at a different angle than it had been before.

She stopped a few feet in and sat down, unstrapping her snowshoes and retrieving a torch from her pack. She lit the torch and stood up, turning the light into the tunnel. She blinked stupidly as she stared at the smooth rock wall a few yards further down the path. She approached the obstruction, telling herself she was imagining it, but when she reached out to touch it, the solid rock remained beneath her fingers.

Senya pushed on the wall, gently at first, then with increasing force. When it didn't budge, she rammed her shoulder into it, grunting in pain when she bounced off inconsequentially. Panic flooded her thoughts as she felt around the corners of the tunnel, searching for any creases or potential signs of weakness. There was a perfect seal between the smooth edges of the tunnel and the wall. She imagined the Hearthborn watching the white hell they had escaped disappear as the Rothschild brothers reformed the rock.

Senya howled with desperate rage as she thrust her spear into the rock, but it only served to chip the metal tip. The shriek of the wind turned her anger into despair, and she slowly understood her attempts were futile. Even if the wall of rock was only a few inches thick, she didn't have the tools to break it. For all she knew, the tunnel could be sealed all the way through.

Although the tunnel provided some shelter against the wind, Senya couldn't stand the noise any longer, so she ventured back out into the blizzard. She sat in the snow to strap her snowshoes back on, but she remained there for a long time after they were secured to her feet, staring blankly into the white abyss before her. Her trial wasn't over after all.

It occurred to her that she had been naïve to overlook the possibility the tunnel would be unusable. She had been too optimistic, too impatient, and now she was far from the relative safety of the tomb. With a great effort, she stood back up, shaking off the thick layer of snow that had accumulated on her shoulders and hood. If she remained exposed to the blizzard, she would freeze before she figured out a way to cross the mountains, so she made her way south to the eastern edge of the nearest foothill.

The slope of the hill was spared the brunt of the wind, allowing her to dig out a new snow cave. She opened her pack and took stock of her remaining supplies — she only had enough food and water for another day if she rationed sparingly. She wouldn't be able to make any meaningful progress back to the tomb until the blizzard passed, so all she could do for now was wait and try to conserve her energy.

She wrapped herself up in Father Silas's coat and closed her eyes, listening to the storm as it raged on. She slept for a few hours at a time, but each time she awoke she was greeted with the howl of the blizzard. Her shelter darkened as night fell, and after sleeping all day, she stared blankly up at the ice above her, trying not to think about her growing hunger.

She blinked when a fine dust of snow fell from the ceiling into her face. After a few seconds, another wave hit her, and she raised her arm to cover her eyes when it became a rhythmic pattern. She could hear a low rumble accompany the disturbances, which grew more pronounced when the earth shook beneath her. She sat up when a large section of the ceiling caved in on her, and her hair stood on end when a monstrous bellow reverberated across the cliffs.

Senya clutched her pack and tunneled out of her collapsing snow cave into the blizzard. Three gargantuan silhouettes, each one towering at over thirty feet, were making their way through the torrential gale, slowly pressing east. The shaking ground beneath her gradually calmed as they moved further away. She dug a new shelter, but the phantom rumble warded away any notion of sleep.

The storm raged on throughout the next day, finally breaking around midnight. Senya trudged south as a calm wind animated the fresh powder around her, ignoring the hollow pit in her stomach. Her pack was completely empty now. Despite two days of rest, she felt utterly exhausted. Her supply of water was also running low, but without the means to make a fire, she couldn't melt snow until she reached the frozen oasis of the tomb. The only thing she could do now was walk.

Everything became a blur of white as she trudged onwards. The sensation left her hands and feet first, and then the numbness crawled up her limbs until she no longer felt that cold anymore. She reached up to loosen her coat, but her fingers were too clumsy to unclasp the buttons. After a few seconds of futile effort, she allowed her hands to drop and proceeded onward.

At some point, she must have collapsed, because the next thing she knew, she was lying in the snow. She dully tried to pull herself to her feet, but her arms and legs felt so weak. The powder beneath her was soft, although it burned her cheek when she rested her head against it. Suddenly very tired, Senya closed her eyes.

"Get up," a distant voice said. Senya frowned, a little annoyed at whoever was trying to disturb her sleep. The voice returned, louder and more insistent this time, and said, "Your trial is not over."

Senya slowly opened her eyes and looked up. Through the fuzzy haze that remained of her vision, she could see the Hearthlord standing a few feet in front of her.

"I let Father Silas die," she whispered desolately. "This is what I deserve."

"You would have him die for nothing," the Hearthlord replied. "You must return to me."

"The tunnel is sealed—" Senya began, but before she could finish, the Hearthlord was gone. She frantically looked around for him, but she was alone once more.

She drew in a deep breath, and then with a cry of effort, she stumbled back to her feet. The first step she took sent bolts of pain down her leg, as did the next one, and the one after that. Her entire body burned as she continued onward, and the white hell around her became an inferno as she pressed further south.

It was dark again when she tumbled down the snowbank into the familiar crevasse. She sat by the remains of her campfire and pulled off her mittens, ignoring the blackened, dead flesh on her fingers and scrounging what little kindling she had left behind beneath the half-burned logs. Somehow she managed to start a fire, and an hour later she drank for the first time in well over a day.

The next thing she knew, it was morning. She held her aching head as she sat up, and slowly drank more water. She vaguely remembered her fingers had been frostbitten the night before, but when she inspected them, they were healthy, and her feet showed no signs of permanent damage. Her stomach rumbled audibly, so she retrieved her traps from the hole she'd stashed them in and dumped them into her pack.

The memory of her encounter with the Hearthlord was now hazy and dreamlike, but still, it filled her with warmth as she climbed out of the crevasse and struck out toward the forest. She'd never heard his voice in all the years she'd prayed in Alcazar, yet in her moment of need, he'd been there to encourage her to keep going. The Hearthborn had sealed the tunnel, but who was she to think she could understand the Hearthlord's will? Any doubts she'd had before were gone now, replaced by a singular mission. No matter how long it took, she would cross the mountains and return to him.

XII

The arena fell quiet when Diana hit the sand. She raised her hand to her throbbing temple, surprised at the slick texture of blood beneath her fingers. She glanced up at her sparring partner, whose face mirrored the shock of the other soldiers who'd been watching. He lowered his practice sword and took an uncertain step back when she climbed to her feet. He looked like he was about to apologize when she bashed his nose in with the blunt edge of her sword.

She couldn't even remember the last time she'd taken a blow during training, but she hadn't seen it coming at all. She thought she'd learned to cope with the dark void left by the loss of her right eye, but the steady stream of blood trickling down the side of her face proved otherwise. Still, it was better to find out here than on the battlefield.

She turned her gaze to the sergeant. He had been staring at her with his mouth slightly agape, but he regained his composure when she gave him a pointed look. "Back to training!" he roared to the other soldiers, who scrambled to resume their drills.

"Have him taken to the medic," she ordered, gesturing towards her unconscious partner.

"Yes, Your Grace," he replied, signaling to two cadets to carry the soldier off the training field. He hesitated for a moment, then asked, "Shall I have a soldier escort you to the medic as well?"

"I'm fine," Diana said dismissively.

"It looked like a heavy blow, ma'am, and normally we keep an eye on soldiers with head wounds—"

"I said I'm fine," Diana said, annoyance hardening her tone.

The sergeant immediately shifted his eyes to the ground, and she tempered her irritation. She retrieved a handkerchief from her belt and wiped the excess blood from her face, then held pressure against the cut. As she waited for the wound to clot, she felt the skin on the back of her neck crawl, and she looked past the sergeant to the balcony that connected the arena to the palace. Her lips twitched into a scowl when she saw the Imperator looking down on her. She didn't know how long he'd been watching, but she was sure he had witnessed her humiliation. The Imperator lifted his hand when she met his gaze, beckoning her, and then he turned and disappeared back into the palace.

"Give that soldier double rations tonight," she said, glancing at the medic's tent. "And tell him to keep his guard up next time."

The sergeant saluted, and Diana left him, crossing the arena to the archway that led into the palace. King Ferdinand's court had once enjoyed blood sport here, but since the beginning of the occupation it had only been used as a training field for the soldiers stationed in the palace. At first, the prize fighters who'd performed for the court migrated to the streets of Fortizia, scrapping in dingy underground rings, but it hadn't taken long to convert most of them to mercenaries. They'd joined Ferdinand's dismantled legions in the camps outside of the city, along with a good number of the strong Castellano workers from the smaller cities.

It had already been a year since Diana first marched on Fortizia with the four regiments who had then made it through to Alcazar. She'd been prepared for a long siege, but King Ferdinand had welcomed them into the city and entertained them in his palace. It had been his honor to meet the gods of Alcazar, and he'd proudly introduced them to his niece, who had been healed at some point by the angel.

So far, everything had been all too easy, but she supposed that was to be expected with the Imperator paving the way. With Fortizia pacified, she'd returned to Jenseits to oversee the initial reconstruction while the Imperator remained in Castilla. She had only been gone a few months, but when she returned, the atmosphere in Fortizia had shifted. She rarely saw Castellanos around the palace anymore, aside from Ferdinand himself. All of the serving staff had been replaced with Jenseiters. The Imperator had reorganized her regiments and moved her special forces, the Reinbann, to a camp outside the city. He was building his own army now, and she wasn't familiar with most of the new commanders.

As she approached the great hall, Diana lowered her handkerchief and probed her temple, confirming the flow of blood had ceased. She mopped up the remnants as best as she could and neatly folded the dirty cloth. Normally, she would have retired to her quarters to clean up after training, but the Imperator was not a patient man. Once she made herself as presentable as she could, she stepped past the threshold.

The great hall was charming in a primitive way. Most of the shacks that littered Fortizia were constructed of wood, but the palace was almost all roughly hewn stone. Torches lined the crooked pillars, casting the way to the silver throne in flickering light. King Ferdinand was sitting on his throne, staring blankly at his empty court. The confident Castellano bull who had welcomed Diana and the Imperator into his palace was gone now, replaced by this hollow approximation. He'd lost weight, and the glazed expression on his face didn't change as she passed him. She couldn't help but flick her gaze to the familiar sapphire ring on his finger, and a small shudder ran down her spine.

She entered the offices behind the great hall, where the Imperator was waiting for her. The chamber had been converted into a war room of sorts, with a map of the Motherland sprawled out across the large granite table. He looked up at her when she entered, confronting her with the eye he had stolen from her.

It was always hard for her to tell what the Imperator was thinking, but she got the distinct impression of disappointment whenever she was around him. He studied her for a few moments before finally turning his attention back to the map.

"The Castellano king is fully committed to me now," he said. "The time has come to reclaim Aesterland." He gestured to the barrier mountains that separated Castilla from the sprawling nation to its north. Two passes connected the countries—one to the west, only a day's ride from Fortizia, and another far to the east.

"We will march from two fronts," he continued. He traced a route from the western pass to Highcastle, the capital of Aesterland. "I will pacify the country and take the brunt of their forces." He tapped on the eastern pass and said, "I will give you command of the east. You must take back Rauheneck. I don't expect you will meet heavy resistance."

Diana nodded. "How would you like to divide the troops? There are ten regiments in Castilla now."

"I will take three regiments with me. Two will remain in Castilla to maintain order. You can have the rest."

Diana frowned — if he truly expected to meet the bulk of Aesterland's resistance, it didn't make sense to take so few troops. She refrained from pressing the issue. Her ancestor had lived ten lifetimes, and her decade of experience as a commander was nothing to him. "There are also three hundred Reinbann," she ventured. "I can organize a unit to embed with you, if you would like."

The Imperator's lip curled slightly at the mention of her special forces. "I have no use for them," he said shortly. He scanned the empty room behind her and asked, "Where is your Nord?"

"Natalia is attending to her father," Diana replied evenly. It took some effort to keep her expression neutral. She'd brought Ivan Vogel back with her when she returned from Jenseits per the Imperator's request. Since his audience with the Imperator, though, Ivan had fallen gravely ill. The doctors were baffled by his symptoms — his neck was mottled, and his veins were swollen and black — but Diana knew what had happened. The Imperator had taken something from him.

"Use the Reinbann as you will, but keep the Houses in reserve," the Imperator said, disrupting her thoughts. "It would be a shame to squander another bloodline."

Diana nodded, deciding not to engage on the issue, and he flicked his wrist to dismiss her. She gratefully left his office, waiting until she was outside to draw in a calming breath. She felt something wet on her temple, and when she raised her hand, she found her wound had re-opened.

AESTERLAND

XIII

Siegfried shifted uncomfortably in the summer heat, stepping into the shadows alongside the dirt road. He could already feel the pools of sweat forming beneath his thick leather cuirass. It was a little cooler in the shade, though, so he straightened up slightly and stood at attention as he watched the distant trade cart creep closer.

Wiltshire was a small town that bordered the central and eastern provinces of Aesterland, remarkable only as a crossroads. Like most villages of any note, it was situated along the eastern highroad, which trailed the border of the Black Forest from the mountains of Castilla all the way to Norogard. One of the few roads cut through the dense swamps of the eastern provinces originated here, thus the trickle of merchants who passed through.

Compared to Siegfried's family estate in the heart of the Black Forest, even tiny Wiltshire seemed like a bustling city. He had been shocked by the number of people when he arrived to report for his assignment six months ago. His father kept a skeleton crew of servants to tend to the crumbling ruins of his ancestral home, but aside from them and the odd traveler, there had been few other people for Siegfried to interact with in the depths of the swamp. He could only imagine what the capital must be like.

He had been somewhat disappointed when he learned he'd be stationed here. He would have preferred to go to the border with Castilla or Norogard, where there were still skirmishes from time to time. Aesterland had a long history of conflict with its neighbors, although it hadn't gained or lost any territory in years. He frowned as he raised his hand to stop the approaching wagon. He knew he had to be patient; it would be a few years before his skill was acknowledged and he was swept up through the ranks and to the front lines.

"Young Master Siegfried!" a familiar voice called, and his frown softened when he recognized the rotund figure climbing down from the cart. Thomas Gainsley was one of the few merchants who ventured into the Black Forest and passed by the family estate. "Your brother told me you were stationed here!"

"You're coming from Castilla?" Siegfried asked, taking the manifest from the portly merchant. He scanned over the list of items, confirming his suspicion when he saw it was mostly furs and iron bars. He walked alongside the cart, checking for undeclared goods, and asked, "How was Berthold?"

Gainsley accepted the manifest Siegfried handed back to him and said, "He was in fine health. He gave me a letter to give to your father. I don't suppose you have mail you'd like me to pass along?"

Siegfried shook his head, and Gainsley laughed. "You may be seeing Berthold again soon enough, though. When I left the border, there were three times as many soldiers as there were in the winter, and I saw more heading south on the road."

"Why?" Siegfried asked.

Gainsley shrugged. "Something strange is going on in Castilla. Something to do with one of the cults in the mountains. They are a superstitious lot there—one of my local suppliers swears a cultist healed him of his gout. Anyway, the last I heard they were going to close the border, so I'm just lucky I made it out in time."

The merchant climbed back up onto his cart and tapped the ox leading it with a stick. As he passed, he promised, "I'll give your family your regards." Siegfried watched the cart as it clambered towards town, then stepped back into the shade and set his eyes on the southern road again. His shift dragged on for another four hours, with only a few farmers hauling carts full of vegetables coming up the road. By the time the old village bell rang to signal the shift change, the news Gainsley had brought was long gone from his mind.

He sauntered up the narrow dirt road to the wooden outpost, where some of the other soldiers were already eating dinner. Siegfried grabbed a bowl and knelt in front of the cookfire, where a large pot of stew was bubbling away. He ladled a portion into his bowl and sat down on one of the logs in the shade of the building. He took off his helmet and wiped the sweat out of his thick black hair.

The other recruits were red-headed, as were the villagers and the servants who worked at his family estate. Siegfried's mother had also been Aesterkind, although he and all of his siblings had inherited his father's black hair and crimson eyes. His memories of her were hazy now; mustard fever had claimed her when he was young. His father had been left alone to raise him, his two brothers, and his older sister.

When he'd first come to Wiltshire, the way people stared at him had bothered him, but after a while, he'd grown accustomed to it. The Feracht house was one of the most ancient noble lineages of Aesterland, although its fortunes had been steadily declining over the last century. Were it not for the elite Feracht Corps, the name would have been all but forgotten.

Berthold, his father's second son and ten years Siegfried's senior, had quickly risen through the ranks after he enlisted and assumed control of the historic unit. He'd become the fifteenth generation of Feracht to command the ancient outfit. Siegfried had no doubt that he, too, would eventually join his brother in the elite squad and add his name to his family's proud tradition.

He picked at his stew, mindlessly swallowing each bland mouthful. The mess sergeant's stews were usually composed of just two or three ingredients, and he didn't believe in wasting precious salt or spices on rookies. Siegfried washed the taste out of his mouth with a gulp of water, then dropped his bowl into a crate next to the door. He put his helmet back on and circled the outpost to the training yard, waiting as the other recruits trickled in for their evening drills.

The line of soldiers stood at attention when Sergeant Whitaker appeared from inside the outpost. The officer was short and brawny with a permanent scowl etched across his lips. The rumor was that he'd once been an elite soldier on track for rapid promotion, but those hopes were dashed when a knee injury recalled him from the front lines.

Whitaker prowled along their formation, inspecting each boy and periodically chiding one of them for an untidy uniform or lax posture. Siegfried stared ahead when the sergeant stopped in front of him. The sergeant examined him for a few moments, but Siegfried already knew his uniform was immaculate, his posture unassailable. The sergeant passed on, and Siegfried relaxed slightly.

Once Whitaker was satisfied, he split the recruits up into three groups and sent them to different parts of the training yard. As usual, Siegfried went with Crawford and Bennett to the archery range. Castilla had its heavy armored divisions and Norogard had hordes of spearmen, but neither could compare to Aesterland's archers. Derek Crawford, tall and slender, picked up the longbow and began to shoot with practiced ease.

There were three logs set downrange, one at fifty yards, one at a hundred yards, and one at three hundred yards. Siegfried watched Crawford shoot ten arrows at each target, unsurprised that his groupings were as tight as usual. Once the arrows in the quiver were exhausted, the three soldiers trotted down range to retrieve the arrows, and then Bennett had his turn.

Sergeant Whitaker limped up next to Tim Bennett and watched him intently as he shot, the grimace on his face deepening with each stray arrow. Although Bennett was well over six feet tall and probably fifty pounds heavier than the stout sergeant, he shrunk in the older man's shadow, and his shooting only continued to degrade when his hands started shaking. Finally, after the last arrow landed a few yards left of the far target, Whitaker chided, "Pathetic."

Bennett looked down at his feet, and the sergeant departed as they went to retrieve his arrows. It took Siegfried a few minutes to locate the scattered arrows around the far target, but eventually, he found all ten and returned to the station. He picked up the bow himself and steadied his breathing, then methodically pulled back the string.

His groupings on the near target were almost as good as Crawford's, but they became less focused on the hundred-yard log, and he missed entirely once on the far target. He couldn't help but breathe a sigh of frustration as he replaced the bow in its stand and joined the others to retrieve his arrows.

While Siegfried waited for the other two to shoot, he watched the other groups. Another trio, the three newest recruits who had only joined a few weeks prior, were receiving instruction with spears and shields. The standard formation of Aesterland's army was two lines of spearmen in front protecting two lines of archers behind. As long as the spear wall did not fall, the archers could pick off the enemy.

The final group of six was sparring. In case the formation was breached, each member of the army carried a sword at his side. Fighting in those circumstances was the worst-case scenario, but it was also the specialty of the Feracht Corps. Siegfried trained in swordplay with his father and brothers since he was old enough to hold a stick. Although he was one of the younger members of the unit, no one could beat him during sparring.

Siegfried's group continued to practice at the range for another hour and a half until darkness fell. Sergeant Whitaker called for the soldiers to assemble, and then he had them run around the perimeter of the training yard for another half hour before dismissing them. The soldiers left for the barracks, where the servants had prepared a hot bucket of water for each of them. Siegfried took off his leather cuirass and washed the dirt and sweat from it, then wiped himself down. He changed into a fresh tunic and hung his armor up on a hook to let it dry overnight.

Siegfried followed the others outside and sat around the cookfire with them, listening disinterestedly as they chatted. Crawford sat next to Siegfried and produced a deck of cards. Crawford was a notorious cheat, but Siegfried played with him anyway, gambling away a few pebbles he found on the ground. He yielded his spot when one of the newer recruits appeared with a handful of coins and watched silently as Crawford took the boy's money.

It always surprised Siegfried how loose the soldiers were with their gold. They were paid with a small bag of coins once a month, and half of them spent all of it in Wiltshire's tavern the first night. Siegfried always stashed the entirety of his earnings in a locked trunk beneath his bunk. It had taken Berthold four years to save enough for custom iron armor emblazoned with the Feracht eagle, and that was with some assistance from their father. Siegfried knew there was nothing left for his inheritance, and even if there was, he would not ask for help.

The fire smoldered, and the exhausted soldiers rose and migrated back to the barracks. Siegfried lay in his bunk and stared up at the dark ceiling for a while, listening to the steady chirp of the crickets outside. Sleep never found him easily, and he often lay in bed for hours waiting for it to claim him. This night was no different, and it seemed as if he had just closed his eyes when the old bell clattered outside.

Siegfried rubbed his eyes as he sat up in the pale light of dawn. He pulled on his boots and heavy leather vest, then fastened his bracers. He straightened the wool blanket on his bunk and stood at attention at the end of it, waiting for Sergeant Whitaker to appear in the doorway for inspection. This morning routine was one of the first things Sergeant Whitaker drilled into recruits when they reported for duty at Wiltshire — if a soldier's bunk was even slightly untidy, he would be ordered to practice making and remaking it while everyone else ate breakfast. Few repeated the mistake after a morning of drills on an empty stomach.

Whitaker limped into the barracks and walked down the center aisle, scouring each bunk for any imperfection. Siegfried continued to stare forward when Whitaker walked behind him and knelt beside his bunk, suppressing the snarl that rose to his lips after thirty seconds passed. He knew his bunk was fine, but the more time that passed, the more his certainty wavered.

After another two minutes, Whitaker reappeared in front of Siegfried, and he drew so close Siegfried could smell his rank breath. Finally, Whitaker growled, "Remake it."

Siegfried continued to stare at the sergeant for a few more seconds, but then he raised his hand into a salute of acknowledgment, and the sergeant passed on. The other soldiers quickly returned to attention as Whitaker inspected the rest of them, and then they all filed out of the barracks to eat breakfast while the sergeant remained behind.

Once the other soldiers were gone, Siegfried turned around, closely inspecting each detail of his bunk for the imperfection Whitaker had found. As far as he could tell, it looked exactly the same as any other day, and the blanket was pulled tight of creases, unlike the bunk directly next to his. Siegfried tore the wool blanket off and hastily remade the bed, tucking the sides beneath the mattress and smoothing the wrinkles out with his hand.

When Siegfried returned to attention, Whitaker made his way to the other side of the bed and glanced at it, then insisted, "Again."

Siegfried took the sheet off and remade the bunk, but Whitaker didn't even look before ordering him to do it again. Siegfried set his jaw and continued to remake the bed, over and over until he lost count. He was sure his growing irritation was evident on his face, so he kept his head down. The bell outside rang again, signaling morning training, but Whitaker shook his head when Siegfried looked up and said, "One more time."

Siegfried continued to remake the bed for another hour, until Sergeant Whitaker finally said, "That's enough for now, Feracht. You're late for morning drills."

Siegfried rose to his feet and saluted, then left the barracks. Normally, he would have jogged five miles along the dirt road with the other soldiers, but they'd already returned, so he joined them in the training yard behind the barracks.

He immediately noticed a group of four officers clustered together in the shade. The first, the elderly Lieutenant Barrow, was the commander of the outpost, although he only emerged from the comfort of his office when other officers passed through Wiltshire. Siegfried was surprised when he saw one of the others wore the regalia of a major. He had never heard of such a high-ranking officer visiting the small outpost to observe training.

All four of the officers were intently focused on a makeshift ring that had been constructed in the yard, where two of the younger recruits were boxing. Siegfried slipped into the line of soldiers standing on the far side of the ring next to Crawford. As he watched the recruits clumsily bash into each other, he whispered, "What's going on?"

"It's an exam," Crawford muttered. "They already had us shoot down the range and do line drills."

Siegfried frowned and asked, "An exam for what?"

Crawford shrugged. "I heard they need more people on the southern border."

The irritation that had been growing in Siegfried's stomach all morning simmered into a dull broth of anger. He raised his gaze from the panting recruits to Sergeant Whitaker, who had joined the officers in the shade. The sergeant had surely known the officers would be here and had delayed him in the barracks to deny him the opportunity to leave Wiltshire. Siegfried didn't know why he had been singled out, but his fury only grew as he waited for the recruits to finish their match.

When one of the recruits finally collapsed from exhaustion, Lieutenant Barrow stepped forward and dismissed both of them back into the line. He clasped his hands behind his back as he scanned the row of soldiers, then he said, "Let's have Bennett and Feracht next."

Siegfried stepped forward and removed his helmet and leather cuirass. He laid them neatly on the ground and stepped into the ring, turning to face Bennett. The older boy's usually jovial expression had twisted into a scowl, and Siegfried took it the previous portions of his examination had not gone well.

Both raised their fists, and Lieutenant Barrow said, "You may begin."

As soon as the words left the lieutenant's mouth, Siegfried darted forward, quickly landing two blows to Bennett's side. He ducked beneath a slow haymaker and peppered Bennett's ribs with a series of jabs, but hitting him was like punching a brick wall. Unfazed, Bennett struck back, and Siegfried narrowly avoided another powerful blow.

Siegfried knew he should just step back - if he kept his distance Bennett would tire himself out with his explosive punches, and he could chip away at him at his leisure. Still, there was something about fighting at close range, in constant danger of a decisive blow, that made Siegfried's blood burn. He could tell Bennett was getting frustrated by how easily he dodged the telegraphed punches, and Siegfried's anger dissipated with each hit he landed.

It wasn't long until Bennett was panting for breath, and Siegfried was sure the damage was building up. He watched the older boy through his fists, waiting patiently for a tell he could counter to end the match. Bennett drew in a deep breath, steadying himself for his final assault. The expression on his face turned from frustration to desperation. Siegfried gasped for air when Bennett unexpectedly slammed his entire body into him, tackling him to the ground.

Siegfried instinctively crossed his arms in front of his face when Bennett pinned him, but Bennett slammed his fists into Siegfried's sides. Lieutenant Barrow's bark for Bennett to disengage was distant over the sound of his own ribs cracking. Bennett landed a few more blows for good measure before finally rolling off Siegfried, leaving him gasping for air in the dirt.

After a few seconds, Siegfried placed a hand on the ground and unsteadily rose to his feet, wincing when tendrils of pain shot through his torso. Bennett was leaving the ring, but he stopped when he saw Siegfried raise his fists once more. Lieutenant Barrow looked at Siegfried doubtfully but did not say anything to stop the match.

Siegfried watched Bennett approach through the blurred lens that had settled over his vision. Every breath he drew was agony, and his legs felt weak. He knew he wouldn't be able to move now even if he wanted to, so he planted his feet and waited for Bennett to come to him. Siegfried felt the blood throbbing in his hands as Bennett reared back to deliver the final blow.

Siegfried felt Bennett's fist graze across his cheek as he swayed to the side, and Bennett's face cracked against his fist as Siegfried countered the blow. The throbbing sensation coalesced for a moment in Siegfried's fist, then it dispersed all at once, and Siegfried was left standing over Bennett's unconscious form.

He straightened up as Sergeant Whitaker ordered two of the recruits to take Bennett to the barracks, surprised to find that most of the pain in his ribs was gone. He gently probed his sides, checking the damage, but he could find none of the cracks he had felt before. He returned to attention when the visiting officers approached him.

"What is your name, soldier?" the major inquired.

"Siegfried Feracht, Sir."

The major rubbed his chin and mused, "You're related to Berthold Feracht?"

"I am his younger brother, Sir."

The major motioned to one of the captains, who made a note in the diary he was carrying. "That will be all," he said, turning his heel and returning to his position in the shade.

Siegfried rejoined the line of soldiers, and Lieutenant Barrow called for the next two recruits to spar. The next match was another drawn-out fight without any definite winner, and then Crawford and the recruit he had cheated the previous night fought. Crawford was six inches taller than the boy and made quick work of him with his long reach. After the match was over, Barrow dismissed the soldiers for their regular duties, and Siegfried hurried to the front of the barracks, where the servants had just finished preparing lunch.

Siegfried sat on one of the logs and began wolfing down his stew. Crawford joined him after a few minutes and asked, "Did you go see Bennett?" When Siegfried shook his head, Crawford frowned and said, "You broke six of his ribs."

Before Siegfried could respond, Lieutenant Barrow appeared in front of them. Siegfried quickly swallowed the stew in his mouth and stood up with Crawford. Lieutenant Barrow smiled and said, "You two have been selected for service at the southern border. You will leave with Major Gardener tomorrow morning."

Crawford and Siegfried saluted, and Lieutenant Barrow left them. Crawford grabbed a bowl of stew, and they both sat down and ate in silence.

XIV

Siegfried scanned the disjointed horizon as he marched along the patrol line, searching the ridge for any sign of movement. When he first arrived at the border, the forest covering the southern mountains had been completely green, but now, two months later, it was painted in bright shades of red, yellow, and orange. The trees in the sprawling Black Forest remained dense and green all year, so Siegfried couldn't help but marvel at the wave of color that had erupted across the hills.

Of the fifty recruits Major Gardener had selected from the outposts dotting the long road to the border, half had been assigned to serve as spearmen in the Fifth Infantry Division at the eastern pass. Siegfried was glad he'd been sorted into infantry, although he had been mildly disappointed when he'd found out Berthold and the Feracht Corps were embedded with the First Infantry at the western pass, three days' march away. Crawford and the other recruits had rested at the eastern border camp for a night before continuing onward to join the Second Ranged Division, which would support the First Infantry.

Life at the border was surprisingly quiet. The Fifth Infantry had closed the trade road to Castilla, but word had spread far enough that few merchants wasted their time approaching from the north. No one had even attempted to approach from the south since Siegfried reached the front.

Wooden watchtowers poked out of the treetops near the top of the mountains, just a few miles over the border. Callahan, a veteran on the same patrol shift as Siegfried, had explained that they were usually manned by Castellano guardsmen, but half of them had disappeared one day, and then the number had again been cut in half the next. After three days, the towers stood empty, and no one had seen anyone climb them since.

There were plenty of rumors about what had happened in Castilla. Most of the soldiers agreed there had been an uprising, but there were conflicting reports as to whether it had been triggered by a coup in the legions or some sort of plague. Without any merchants passing through from the south, there was no reliable news source, so the soldiers spun wild tales about the fall of Fortizia to the cultists who lived deep in the mountains.

The force stationed at the border had swelled to four times its original size, and Siegfried had overheard some of the veterans discussing the possibility that the mass movement of troops wasn't just a defensive maneuver. The price of iron, coal, and furs had already skyrocketed in the great cities without the steady influx from Castilla. If King Ferdinand had truly been overthrown, there was no better time for Aesterland to strike and claim the spoils of the revolution.

Siegfried patted his pocket, reflexively checking that the note he had received three days back was still there. Soldiers normally paid merchants to carry their mail, but with the border closed, the price of sending correspondence had risen far above what Siegfried could afford. Siegfried had been surprised when a captain shook him awake in the middle of the night and presented him with a sealed envelope. Before he could ask the soldier who he was or how he had found him among the tens of thousands of soldiers clustered in the sprawling camp, the captain disappeared without a word.

Siegfried had torn the mysterious envelope open and pulled out a small scrap of paper, upon which was inscribed a single sentence.

The enemy bears our sigil.

He had read it again, then turned the envelope inside out, unable to believe anyone would have paid such a high price to relay such a short message. To his dismay, there was nothing else, and the captain who had delivered the message was long gone.

After a few days of mulling the enigma of the note over, Siegfried was fairly certain the handwriting was Berthold's. Still, though, he could make little sense of the words. Castilla's coat of arms was a bull flanked by a sword and a hammer, while the royal sigil of Aesterland was Oriane's golden rose. He wondered if the Castellano legions had somehow infiltrated the Aesterland camps, but even if that was the case, there was no reason for Berthold to inform him with such secrecy. He also considered the message was some sort of code, but no matter how many times he read it, its meaning was beyond him.

He paused when he saw something shimmering in the distance beyond the mountains. Callahan looked back at him, then followed his gaze to the sky. He frowned as the wisp of smoke steadily grew darker against the gray sky and said, "Go report this to the Sergeant."

Siegfried nodded and turned, running back along the patrol line towards the camp. As he went, he noticed several other trails of smoke begin to rise from beyond the mountains. He heard the distant sound of a bell ringing in the main camp — the signal for all units to report to their combat assignments. Siegfried felt his heart begin to beat more rapidly as he veered off from his direct path towards the main camp, heading instead for the right flank line.

The line was almost fully formed by the time Siegfried reached it, with only a few holes from patrols who had been further out when the bell had rung. The road leading through the pass was still empty, but the sky behind the mountains had grown dark with countless tendrils of smoke. The soldiers planted their shields and spears where they stood at a nervous attention, waiting for further orders.

The center line, which defended the majority of the archers in the Fourth Ranged Division, spread perpendicular to the road, one hundred yards from the edge of the narrow pass. The archers would be able to hail arrows on top of any army that attempted to squeeze through. Most of the Castellano soldiers would be equipped with iron breastplates and helmets, but the sheer volume of arrows would find their fur-clad arms and legs, and the majority of them would bleed out before even reaching the first spear line.

The two flanks extended from the center line at a shallow angle, and their only job was to guard against surprise attacks from the forest. The mountains were steep enough that it would be difficult for an army to pass with any kind of coordination, and the Sixth Ranged Division was split between the two flanks to pick off any stragglers who attempted to cross.

It was unlikely either flank would see any action, and Siegfried was a reserve behind the front line. He knew the best hope he had for any real combat was to be called in to reinforce the center line, but he didn't see how that would be necessary with Aesterland's position on the pass. The Castellanos would be insane to attack them when they had such a dominant defensive position.

Siegfried and the other soldiers in the line watched the smoke for another few hours until the dark plumes blended into the night sky. The night was overcast, obscuring the moon and stars and rendering the field leading up to the mountain pass completely dark. A group of porters lit torches along the lines, creating small halos of light every thirty feet. An hour into the evening, the flank commander, General Bridges, ordered them to assume combat watch. Siegfried, who was in the second watch rotation, picked up his shield and spear and shuffled back to camp with half of the line. There, they would rest for four hours before returning to the line to relieve the other half.

It would have been difficult any other night for Siegfried to utilize the four hours he had been granted to sleep, but it was impossible with the nervous buzz of excitement in the air. Instead of returning to his tent, he joined a mix of veterans and recruits around the campfire and listened as the veterans regaled the small cluster with stories of previous skirmishes with Castilla.

Callahan sat silently on his log and sipped from his flask, scowling as each veteran ended his tale of heroism. Finally, he interjected, "There isn't going to be any battle. No one is going through the pass now. We'll be here for another year until the generals miss their wives and decide to go back home."

His words struck a chord of truth with the other veterans, and the group grew quiet. After a few minutes, the soldiers drifted away from the fire back to their tents to recoup a few hours of sleep before reporting to their positions at the line, but Siegfried remained until only he and Callahan were left.

If the generals were serious about invading Castilla, they should have done it before Castilla moved their troops to the other side of the pass. Siegfried knew Callahan was right, that there could only be a stalemate until the two nations agreed to de-escalate and move troops away from the border.

In a way, Siegfried was disappointed. Berthold's military career had only really taken off after he served in a minor border skirmish with Norogard seven years ago because he'd been able to prove himself in battle. Siegfried had hoped a full-scale invasion of Castilla would allow him to climb the hierarchy and join Berthold in the Feracht Corps, but there was no glory to be had in a stalemate.

Siegfried pulled the note out of his pocket and dropped it into the fire, watching the edges curl before turning black. The old soldier didn't ask him about it, and they enjoyed each other's company in silence until the camp bells rang again, signaling the change of the guard. Siegfried stood up and left for his post as Callahan headed for the center line.

Siegfried joined the wave of recruits who were returning to the right flank, stumbling along by torchlight to the rear line of shields. He planted his shield and spear in the ground and stood at attention as the first watch retired to their tents. Lt. General Miller, who had held command overnight, put the soldiers at ease, and Siegfried relaxed as he set his eyes on the dark outline of the mountain.

The line was quiet as the soldiers weathered the small hours of the morning. By the time the first tendrils of pink bled across the eastern skyline, most of the soldiers were dozing on their feet. Siegfried's eyelids felt heavy, but he shook himself awake and turned his gaze back to the edge of the forest.

He frowned when he saw movement along the edge of the trees, squinting to make sense of the conglomeration of dark shapes in the dim light. As his mind processed the army clustered in the forest, Siegfried considered he must have fallen asleep during his watch and this was a dream. There was no way any sizable force had come through the pass undetected during the night, yet the soldiers waiting under the cover of the trees easily numbered in the thousands.

Siegfried jolted when he heard the bell ringing again, and he looked down the line, his anxiety steadily growing when he realized all of the soldiers were fixated on the same mirage. He scanned the treeline, horrified to find that the forest was thick with soldiers as far west as he could see. As he picked up his shield and spear, he wondered if the western pass had already fallen. He was vaguely aware that Lt. General Miller was shouting orders as he strode up and down the line, and someone pushed Siegfried from the reserve line to the front to fill in a gap.

He mechanically raised his shield and rested his spear on top of it, forming a wall with the soldiers at either side of him. Even at this distance, he could tell there was something strange about the phantom army. They did not wear the distinct solid iron cuirass of the Castellano royal legions, rather they were all clad in shells of black plates. One of them, a slender figure whose armor was trimmed with gold, stepped out of the cover of the trees, followed closely behind by two soldiers bearing banners.

Siegfried swallowed uncomfortably as he gazed at the black banners, both of which bore the sigil of a white eagle. He looked nervously around him, but none of the other soldiers reacted to the obscure sigil. He supposed he shouldn't be surprised — the Feracht House had not been a great noble power for centuries, and even he had only ever seen the once proud eagle in the ruins of his family estate.

Before he had time to process what this meant, the enemy commander raised a hand, and the rest of the soldiers left the cover of the forest and marched on the line. Siegfried felt a surge of adrenaline pump through his veins as he watched them approach. A hail of arrows rained down on them, but the projectiles bounced harmlessly off of their heavy armor, and the massive force continued to encroach on Siegfried's line.

Siegfried fidgeted impatiently as they neared striking distance, ignoring the unintelligible orders that were shouted over the cacophony of bowstrings behind him. Some of the arrows found their mark at the shallower angle; although the enemy was well-protected, there were still small gaps in their armor at their neck, eyes, and groin. As long as the spearmen were able to hold the line, they had a chance against this phantom force.

Just as Siegfried braced himself to meet the attackers, he felt a strange sensation reverberate through his body, and a low-pitched grinding sound rumbled beneath him. He felt the ground quake, and he looked down as the grass and dirt erupted beneath him. Startled, he darted left, getting as far away as he could while a solid wall of dirt rose from the ground.

The soldier who had been to his right disappeared as the wall rose up eight feet, completely separating him from the western section of the line. He glanced to his left, where a similar barricade had appeared thirty feet away. Including the soldiers in the rear line, only twenty spearmen remained in Siegfried's newly isolated section.

Siegfried gasped in surprise when he felt an impact from the front, and he turned his attention to the black-armored soldier who was pressing against him, quickly swaying to the side to avoid the spear that came at his neck. He instinctively struck back, wincing at the blood that sprayed across his face when his own spear found its mark. The enemy raised a hand to his torn throat in surprise, and for a moment, Siegfried held his red gaze. After a few seconds, the enemy disappeared into the mass of black armor, and Siegfried turned to his next opponent.

For a few minutes, the stream of arrows from the archers continued as Lt. General Miller roared a battle tirade, but after Siegfried dispatched a few foes, he noticed the supporting fire had thinned and the general's gruff voice was gone. He pushed back another enemy and glanced over his shoulder, then his blood ran cold when he saw the black-armored soldiers swarming the archers. Somewhere, one of the sections of their broken line had fallen.

A low chorus of wailing drifted from beyond the earthen walls, and, unable to see anything but the sea of black armor, Siegfried could only imagine the devastation. He looked to his left at the rest of his section, horrified to see that half of the rear soldiers had moved up to replace their fallen comrades in the front line. Just as Siegfried finished off another enemy, he felt a hand on his shoulder, and he reached for his sword in panic as he turned to face his attacker.

He managed to stop himself from cutting through the Aesterkind soldier who shouldered past him to take his place in the front, and he drew in a calming breath as he fell back into the rear line. After a few minutes, his head was clear again. The enemy had surprised them with their tricks, somehow sneaking up on their flank in the middle of the night and preparing the walls to divide them, but they were only the auxiliary line. It was only a matter of time before the center line pivoted and came to their aid, and the barriers offered some protection until then.

The enemy dispersed to the fallen sections of the line, more intent on breaking the archers than finishing the remaining spearmen. Without anyone to give them orders, Siegfried and the ten remaining spearmen held their position. Siegfried was surprised to see how many soldiers were still crowded beneath the trees, where their commander remained.

The commander gave an order, and a small retinue of fifteen soldiers emerged from beneath the trees. They wore lighter armor than the other soldiers — rather than heavy plate, they were clad in coats of black chainmail. They separated as they approached, each of them heading to a different segment of the line. Siegfried watched as a single man approached his section, wondering if he was an emissary sent to negotiate their surrender. The remaining soldiers in front raised their shields, and Siegfried readied his spear.

The man paused as he neared them, resting the heavy maul he carried on the ground. He was truly a giant, towering a foot over the rest of them, and his muscles bulged from beneath his chainmail. Besides his unusually light orange beard, Siegfried would have guessed he was Aesterkind. The giant surveyed their small squadron for a few moments, then he knelt down onto one knee and placed a hand on the ground.

Siegfried shuddered as a chill ran down his spine, and he blinked in disbelief when he saw a fine cloud of dust rise from the ground around the giant. The cloud steadily grew thicker, obscuring the man from view, and then larger clumps of grass and dirt floated into the air. A low murmur passed through the front line, and Siegfried realized the strange phenomenon was not just his imagination. Small globs of clay from deeper in the earth joined the dirt and grass, and then it all collapsed into the cloud, forming the shape of a golem that took the place of the man.

The monster retrieved the heavy maul, and Siegfried felt a wave of horror pass through him as the abomination approached. His face had become an inhuman mask of earth, with abyssal black holes where his eyes and mouth had been. Every instinct told Siegfried to run, but the soldiers forming the shield wall remained where they were. Siegfried forced his hands to stop shaking and held his spear at the ready, trying to clear his head as he searched the mass of earth for vulnerabilities.

The golem raised the maul into the air as he entered striking distance, and Siegfried and the other soldiers all plunged their spears into him at the same time. The tip of his spear sank a few inches to the clay surface before it struck metal. Before he could pull it out, the monster swung, and the shaft of Siegfried's spear was wretched out of his hands as the golem turned his body. There was a deafening crack when the head of the maul collided with the shield of the soldier directly in front of Siegfried, and they were both thrown back from the sheer force of the blow.

Siegfried and the soldier landed in a heap a few feet back, and the golem continued his assault, tearing into their line mercilessly as the soldiers attempted to pierce it. Siegfried shoved the unmoving soldier off of him and scrambled to his feet. He drew the sword at his belt and watched closely as the golem smashed through another soldier's shield and crushed him against the wall.

The golem's movements were slow, but his earthen armor shifted seamlessly along with his body, forming a perfect defense none of the spearmen could penetrate. Every blow he landed with the maul was devastating — he splintered their shields and cracked their bones as if they were twigs. It wasn't long until the monster dispatched the rest of the spearmen, and then he turned back to Siegfried.

Siegfried didn't bother to retrieve his shield, rather raising his sword and circling around the golem. He stepped over the bodies of his brothers-in-arms, carefully keeping his distance as the monster advanced towards him. Siegfried paused when he felt the rough texture of the dirt wall behind his back, and he waited patiently for the golem to raise his maul once more.

Just as the giant swung the heavy weapon, Siegfried darted forward, avoiding the deadly maul and drawing his sword across the golem's side. He felt his blade sink a few inches into the earthen armor before stopping. He withdrew it before the giant could recover and backed up, noting the clump of dirt that fell away from the golem's ribs. Although his attack hadn't exposed any flesh, it did give Siegfried some hope.

The giant raised the maul again, and Siegfried darted. He controlled his distance, staying just outside of the golem's striking range, and waited for the attack. Once the giant committed to a swing, it was a simple matter to sidestep or roll out of the way, and then Siegfried could continue to hit the target of crumbling earth on the giant's side. By the third time he executed this maneuver, he could see the glint of chainmail beneath the earthen armor.

As Siegfried danced away, he heard a rhythmic cavernous sound come from the golem, and after a few seconds, he realized the man beneath the armor was panting for breath. He had not yet lifted his maul again, and, emboldened by his success, Siegfried surged towards the vulnerability he had created.

Just as Siegfried entered striking range, darkness burst across his field of view as something slammed into his side. He vaguely felt his back smash into one of the barricades. His vision slid back into focus as he watched the golem approach him, now unencumbered by the heavy maul. He attempted to raise his sword but was left staring at his empty hand. The weapon was lying on the ground a few feet away from him, and as he reached for it, the golem slammed his fist into Siegfried's stomach.

Siegfried gasped for air as he crumpled to the ground, but each inhalation was agony against his shattered ribs. He tried to get back to his feet, but his strength was gone, and he could only watch the golem through blurred vision as the monster raised his foot. A white blanket of pain settled over Siegfried's mind when the golem stomped on his left leg. His vision returned for a moment, just long enough for him to see the pale piece of bone protruding through his shin before everything faded mercifully to black.

XV

Auron raised his sleeve to his nose, blocking out the nauseating stench that had settled over the battlefield. It was another moonless night, but there were so many bonfires he could see the full extent of the carnage in a hellish red light.

When Lady Diana herself had appeared at the Reinbann training camp in the northern mountains, Auron had been unable to contain his excitement. It had been two long years since he and the other acolytes left Alcazar, and he was eager for a chance to prove himself in service to the Hearthlord.

He had been a little surprised when the Reinbann rounded up all of the recruits to march north, even the children that had trickled into the camp over the last couple of months. Now, Julia and Valeria, his little sisters, trailed behind him, marveling at the aftermath of the battle. He frowned, but they didn't seem scared by the moans of the dying Aesterkind soldiers around them. They were both probably too young to truly understand what was happening.

At first, he'd been disappointed when the recruits were ordered to stay behind in the tunnel while the Hearthborn engaged the Aesterkind forces. The fighting had dragged on into the evening, and it had only been an hour ago when the Reinbann officers split the recruits up into groups of five to comb through the battlefield. He, his sisters, another acolyte named Felix, and two boys from Fortizia had all been assigned to the squad led by Lieutenant Nichts, who'd supervised most of the Reinbann training thus far. As Auron led his sisters around an unmoving body, he was secretly glad he'd been held in reserve. He didn't know what he had been expecting, but it wasn't this.

Lieutenant Nichts led the way ahead, his black chainmail glowing with the reflection of the bonfires all around them. An involuntary shimmer of fear passed through Auron's stomach as his mentor glanced back at him. It was hard to reconcile his jovial teacher with this professional soldier who moved through the battlefield as if he were born on it. Nichts was one of the few officers who wore a braided silver cord around his waist — a symbol that he was an elite warrior.

"Just a little further," Nichts said, smiling from behind his helmet. Auron felt some of his anxiety drain away, and he forced himself to lower the arm blocking the stench. He didn't want to look weak in front of his mentor.

After a few more minutes of walking, they arrived at their destination. The Reinbann had raised a neat line of walls to break the enemy's lines, and Nichts led the recruits into one of the newly formed segments, where a cluster of wounded Aesterkind were languishing on the ground. A Hearthborn triage surgeon was already there, marked by his bloody leather apron, and he and Nichts greeted each other cordially.

"These two are salvageable," the surgeon said, gesturing to two soldiers among the group.

Nichts nodded and approached the first soldier, who was lying unconscious on the ground. He had been stabbed through his thigh and his pants leg was sopping wet with blood, but his breathing was still strong. "Gather around and watch," Nichts instructed the recruits.

Auron stepped into the circle that the recruits formed around the wounded man. Nichts removed his gauntlets and said, "Remember what we practiced. Hot enough to sear, but not enough to burn."

With that, he traced two fingers over the wound in the man's leg, cauterizing a neat line where the cut had been. Auron carefully studied his technique. In the training camp, they had mostly practiced on the corpses of animals the soldiers caught in the surrounding forests. It was rare to be able to apply anything they learned on a live specimen.

Auron frowned as he inspected the red burn. What Nichts had done was certainly a miracle in its own way, but it was still a poor imitation of what he'd seen Senya do countless times. It struck him as odd that there didn't seem to be any true healers like her in the Reinbann. In the first few months of his Reinbann training, he had eagerly awaited Senya's return from her expedition with Lady Diana. A year had passed without any news of her, until one day, Lady Diana returned to inspect the recruits.

Trembling with anticipation, Auron approached the regal woman and asked directly if Senya would be coming to join their training camp. Lady Diana had smiled and told him, "Your friend resurrected the Hearthlord. She returned to the Hearth as a reward."

Auron rose to his feet and followed Nichts and the group of recruits to the next soldier, who was bleeding from his chest. He supposed it shouldn't have come as a surprise that Senya would be the first of the acolytes to ascend to the Hearth, but he missed her. Since that day, he had redoubled his training efforts. If he could become a holy knight of the Hearthlord, he knew he, too, would someday ascend.

"Help me get his armor off," Nichts ordered, drawing him back to reality. Auron bent down next to Felix, and together they pulled the leather cuirass up over the semi-conscious man's arms. His helmet came off in the process, revealing a smooth face underneath. This soldier was probably only a few years older than Auron himself.

Nichts retrieved a leather strap from his pocket and offered it to the young man to bite down on. He obliged, stifling the scream that came when Nichts seared his wound. Tears of pain streaked down his cheeks as Nichts helped him to sit up. "You'll be okay," Nichts said reassuringly, patting the young man on the back. He glanced up at the triage surgeon and gave him an almost imperceptible nod, and the surgeon marked something down in the notebook he carried.

Before they could move on to the next segment, a breathless Hearthborn messenger jogged up to the scene. Auron had seen a dozen of these runners racing around the remains of the battlefield, relaying orders from central command to the various units that were processing the aftermath. The young Hearthborn paused for a moment to catch his breath, then said, "Lieutenant Nichts, I'm to take you to assess a special asset. If you will please follow me."

Nichts nodded, and he and the recruits followed the messenger out of the shelf and across the battlefield. They walked at a brisk pace for fifteen minutes before reaching their destination - a pair of stone barricades where yet another cluster of Aesterkind soldiers had been decimated by the assault. After a few moments of inspection, Auron realized there was something profoundly different about this part of the line. Many of the men lying on the ground had limbs positioned at odd angles, and one poor soldier's chest had caved in as if he had been crushed. Auron knew devastation like this had to be the work of one of the Reinbann.

A Hearthborn officer stood with his hands crossed behind his back at the edge of the shelf. Nichts and the messenger saluted, and the officer waved his hand to put them at ease. The officer raised a finger to point at one of the soldiers who was still alive — a young man sitting against one of the barricades, eyeing them suspiciously. One of his legs was mangled, and even from his distance, Auron could see the ghostly white shard of bone protruding from his shin. He wore the leather armor of the Aesterkind, but his hair was black, and his eyes glowed red in the light of the bonfires.

XVI

The macabre light of the bonfires danced in the reflection of the blade Siegfried had dropped earlier, taunting him just out of reach. When he had first regained consciousness, he'd tried to stand, but the pain in his leg was so severe it had made him dizzy. All he'd been able to do was wait, simmering in the miasma left by his fallen brethren. The battlefield beyond the barricades was littered with bodies now, and he could tell from the matte reflection of their leather armor that they were overwhelmingly Aesterkind. After the enemy had broken their flank, they must have met the main line in battle, and he could only surmise Aesterland had been handily defeated.

He turned his gaze to the group that had appeared at the edge of the barricades. The officer who'd been watching him for the last hour was still there, but now he was talking quietly with another man clad in the same black chainmail as the monstrous golem who had annihilated Siegfried's unit. The two men were accompanied by a troop of Castellano children, all of whom were staring at him uncomfortably.

The soldier in chainmail concluded his conversation with the officer, then he approached. Siegfried watched him warily as he knelt next to him and motioned to the children, all of whom silently gathered in a circle around him. The soldier grimaced as he inspected Siegfried's leg. He produced a small knife from his belt and sawed through Siegfried's pant leg at the knee.

Siegfried lunged forward for the knife, but the soldier reflexively caught his wrist. The soldier frowned and said, "I'm trying to help you."

Fury bubbled up in Siegfried's stomach at the absurdity of it all, and he continued to struggle violently, ignoring the spasms of pain that jolted from his shin. Finally, the soldier directed one of the older boys to hold him still. Siegfried thrashed in rage as a pair of strong arms wrapped beneath his shoulders and behind his neck, but in his weakened state, he was unable to escape.

The soldier sighed and continued his work. He removed the remaining section of fabric, fully exposing Siegfried's bruised shin and the wound where his fractured bone had pierced his skin. Siegfried felt his stomach turn when he faced the full extent of the injury, but none of the children seemed distraught by the gruesome sight. The soldier spoke softly to the children, motioning around the injury with his hands, and then he offered Siegfried a strap of leather.

Siegfried stared at him blankly for a few moments before the soldier explained, "You can bite down on it during the operation."

Siegfried turned his head away, and the soldier shrugged and replaced the strap in his pocket. He placed his hands on Siegfried's shin to either side of the wound. "I have to set the bone before I stop the bleeding," the soldier explained to the children. He shifted his weight forward, and Siegfried's vision exploded into unstable patterns of light when the soldier pressed the dislocated bone back into his body.

He felt a scream bubble up in his throat, but he swallowed it back down. Instead, he clenched his jaw and stared forward, waiting patiently for his vision to return. Blood was seeping freely from the newly agitated wound, but the soldier wiped it away with a piece of cloth and placed a hand on the jagged cut. The soldier held pressure on the cut as he explained, "Now I can close the wound." The children all leaned in a bit closer, and Siegfried felt the tension on his shoulders release as the older boy shuffled to get a better look at what the soldier was doing.

Siegfried shuddered when the hairs rose on the back of his neck. He was suddenly enveloped with the same feeling he had experienced when he'd watched the giant transform into the golem, but before he could examine the strange sensation, a new spectrum of pain exploded in his leg. He could not suppress his scream of anguish this time, and tears welled in his eyes as flames erupted from beneath the soldier's fingers.

After a few seconds, the soldier removed his hand, revealing a strip of cauterized flesh in place of the wound. Siegfried leaned weakly back against the barricade as the children crowded around his shin to inspect the treatment. The soldier moved aside so one of the girls could carefully wrap his leg with bandages and splint it.

The officer gave an order, and Siegfried grunted when two of the boys pulled him to his feet. The officer led them back into the darkness of the battlefield, leaving Siegfried to limp weakly as they dragged him along. He glanced over his shoulder at the soldier and the rest of the children, who had moved on to treat the other wounded.

Their progress through the battlefield was slow, as they had to make their way around the corpses of soldiers who hadn't yet been fed to the fires. Now his vision wasn't obstructed by the walls, Siegfried could see the true extent of the massacre. The burn pits littered the horizon, casting the eerie flickering light upon miles of corpses. There had been thirty thousand soldiers stationed at the eastern pass, and from the looks of it, more than half of them had met their end here. Eventually, Siegfried lowered his head, resting his gaze firmly on the ground beneath him.

They passed the nearest burn pit and turned along a path, where the grass had been matted down by heavy foot traffic. They walked for half a mile until they reached a cluster of tents guarded by fully-equipped soldiers. One of the soldiers stopped them, and he and the officer spoke quietly for a few minutes. Finally, the soldier stepped aside, and they were allowed to enter the camp.

The officer pulled aside the flap of a large tent, and the boys escorted Siegfried inside. The tent was filled with rows of sleeping pads, about half of which were occupied by wounded Aesterkind troops. Siegfried felt a flutter of relief pass over him when the two boys set him down on a pallet.

While Siegfried rested his leg on the soft pad, he watched the officer approach one of the soldiers guarding the entrance of the tent. Siegfried noticed the man gesture back towards him, and the guard nodded and touched the pommel of the sword at his belt.

One of the boys gave Siegfried a blanket. He followed Siegfried's gaze to the soldier, then said, "Don't worry. They're going to take you to see Lady Diana with the other recruits."

"Lady Diana?" Siegfried asked, looking back at the boy.

"She will decide if you are worthy to serve the Hearthlord," the boy said with a smile.

Before he could ask any more questions, the officer returned and gestured to the two boys. They rose to their feet and followed closely behind him as he left the medical tent. Siegfried glanced at the soldier, who was still monitoring him intently. He lay back against the sleeping pad and closed his eyes, surprised at how exhausted he suddenly felt.

Siegfried dozed through the rest of the night. The next time he woke, the empty mattresses from the previous night were filled with wounded Aesterkind. Some of the prisoners were sobbing, others were chatting nervously, but most were silent — either sleeping or contemplating their fate.

He propped himself up on his elbows to see past the wounded around him. Two soldiers now stood guard at the tent's entrance, and several more patrolled up and down the aisles of pallets. A few medics were tending to the prisoners. They wore clean white aprons, and Siegfried noticed one of them was accompanied by another Castellano child.

The morning passed fairly uneventfully. One of the medics stopped by Siegfried's pallet early in the afternoon. He inspected Siegfried's leg, and, satisfied with the field treatment, helped him sit up. Siegfried had spent the entire morning watching the medics go through the same procedure with every prisoner, so he took off his leather cuirass and bracers and surrendered them without being asked. The medic dropped the bloodied armor into the aisle at the foot of Siegfried's bed.

Siegfried sat still as the medic examined him, wincing when the doctor probed his broken ribs. Compared to some of the other prisoners, his injuries were minor. Although he was crippled and sore, his life was clearly in no danger. The medic finished his examination quickly and jotted something down in his notebook, then moved on to Siegfried's neighbor.

A group of Castellano children served the prisoners their lunch, which consisted of a slice of bread and half a dried sausage. Siegfried recognized the girl who gave him his ration as one of the children who'd gathered around him on the field. She didn't look him in the eye when she handed him his portion, and she hurried on without a word.

Siegfried ate his ration and rested his head on the pallet once more, staring blankly up at the canvas ceiling of the tent until two soldiers appeared above him. "Get up," one of them ordered in a clipped accent. Siegfried frowned, not wanting to put weight on his leg again. The soldier repeated his command impatiently, but when Siegfried didn't respond, he grasped his arm and jerked him to his feet.

Pain shot up Siegfried's splinted leg as he was pulled into the aisle, but he had no choice but to limp along as the soldiers escorted him out of the tent. After spending the day in the dim light of the tent, the harsh sunlight outside was blinding. Siegfried automatically dropped his gaze to the ground, allowing his eyes to adjust. The soldiers dragged him across the camp, where they finally allowed him to stop beside another prisoner.

Siegfried glanced up at the line of five prisoners, all Aesterkind soldiers his age or younger. Their hands were bound in front of them with iron manacles, and they were chained together in their line. One of the soldiers clamped a pair of manacles around Siegfried's wrists, linking him to their chain.

Beyond the first boy, two other soldiers were tethering oxen to a cart. Siegfried was surprised to see the soldier who had set his leg standing beside the cart. The two Castellano boys who'd carried him were loading supplies into the back of the cart, along with another boy who sported the red hair of an Aesterkind. Siegfried scowled, wondering how the boy could so quickly turn on his own people.

A soldier emerged from one of the smaller tents and approached them. His black plate armor was inlaid with gold details, and the way he held himself made it apparent he was an officer. He carried his helmet beneath his arm, so Siegfried could see his long blonde hair and striking red eyes.

The officer stopped in front of the line of prisoners and inspected them, but his gaze paused for a brief moment when it rested on Siegfried. Before Siegfried could interpret the smirk that rose to the officer's lips, he turned and addressed the soldiers who were preparing the oxen.

One of the soldiers finished adjusting a harness and hurried towards the first prisoner in the line, picking up the end of the chain and yanking him forward. Siegfried stumbled along with the others towards the cart. One by one, the soldiers loaded their prisoners into the back, where they squeezed onto two benches set into either side of the cart.

By the time Siegfried struggled up onto the bench, his leg was burning from the strain of the ordeal. The soldier fastened a rope across the open back of the cart while the officer climbed up into the driver's bench. The remaining soldier who had been attending to the oxen finished adjusting the rigging and joined him in front, and, with a flick of his whip, he spurred the animal into motion. The wooden axles creaked for a moment, then shifted, and the cart rumbled forward.

A few soldiers and the boys fell in behind the cart, easily keeping pace as it jostled along the grassy path. The cart bounced unpredictably on the makeshift road, causing Siegfried to wince with pain every time the floorboards shifted beneath his injured leg. He gingerly rested his calf on a supply crate and watched the prison camp gradually recede into the distance. As the cart continued, the air grew hazy with the smoke from the burn pits. The Castellano workers were still clearing corpses, but they had made considerable progress overnight. Although the sections of the field nearest to the path were completely clear, the stench of death was still heavy in the air.

After a few miles, the path met the high road, and the cart turned left. The ride became much smoother as they headed north, but Siegfried's relief was tempered by the heavy traffic that accompanied them. Soldiers were marching north as far as he could see, both ahead and behind. The previously quiet pass had become a busy thoroughfare, spitting out invaders by the thousands. Their cart moved a bit more slowly than the soldiers' marching pace, so Siegfried was left to watch as the army advanced further into Aesterland.

As he looked north, the implications of Aesterland's utter defeat at the eastern pass dawned on him. A third of the army had been shifted to the southern border, including many of Aesterland's elite soldiers. With the front broken, there was nothing to stop the enemy's advance into the interior of the country.

XVII

Senya plunged her hatchet into the sheet of ice, clinging desperately to it as the tempest grew around her. What had begun as a small flurry had grown into a full blizzard, and when she looked behind her, all she could see was the two-thousand-foot drop to the white abyss below. Loose shards of ice cut her cheek as she braced against the gale.

She'd thought she knew the cold, but the mountain pushed everything to extremes. Even through two layers of coats and the extra furs she'd packed around her body, she was freezing. She could barely feel the handle of her hatchet beneath her numb fingers, but she knew if she lost her grip, she'd be swept away. She gritted her teeth and pulled herself forward. She struck at the ice with the dagger in her left hand, patiently chipping away at the thick sheet until she was able to establish another anchor.

Bit by bit, she crawled along in the storm until the ground beneath her turned into hard snowpack. She scrambled onto the crust and lay there for a moment, exhausted. She gazed up into the blizzard, wanting to close her eyes — to rest. With a great effort, she climbed to her feet and pressed onward.

The terrain beneath her steepened as she staggered blindly into the storm. The wind pummeled her, determined to bar her from the upper reaches of the Icetooth Ridge. Any semblance of the course she'd charted was long gone now.

A year and a half of preparation—all erased by a rogue storm. She knew that she should be worried—that if she didn't find shelter soon, she would freeze to death—but instead, she was only numb. It didn't matter, anyway. The snow on the mountain was too hard to dig into, and her visibility was limited to a couple of feet in front of her. The only thing she could do was pray the Hearthlord would see her through this newest trial.

Since that day he'd appeared to her on the ice, she'd often felt his presence, although it was always a whisper in the wind or a shimmer in the fog. In the depths of winter, when the sun did not rise for an entire month, she'd been sure he was with her, sitting just outside the light of her campfire. She thanked him for every hare or fox that wandered into her traps, and for the larger carcasses the wolves left behind.

Though he had been merciful, he hadn't left her completely untested. An unusually warm day towards the end of autumn had spoiled her entire stockpile of meat, leaving her with almost nothing to see her through winter. In her desperation, she'd ventured deep into wolf territory, and when the winds had changed, one of them had caught her scent.

All she could remember from the encounter was a flash of claws and teeth. She knew she wouldn't have survived if the Hearthlord hadn't taken pity on her and guided her flailing knife into its eye. It had retreated, leaving her with deep lacerations on her arm and chest. Somehow, she made it back to the safety of the tomb and closed her wounds before passing out, but the white scars remained to remind her of her hubris.

The storm around her settled by small degrees until it became a thinning fog. A few minutes later, the sun emerged, revealing the rocky spine of the ridge. Senya smiled, thanking the Hearthlord for his favor, and wearily continued her ascent. Thirty minutes later, she realized there was nothing else in front of her, and she looked out at the vast green valleys and mountains that filled the horizon beyond the ridge. After being enveloped in a world of white for so long, the introduction of the vibrant color was almost a shock.

From this height, she could see all four valleys of Castilla, all the way to the northern range that separated the kingdom from Aesterland. Once she overcame the initial burst of color, she noticed the gray swath of land that spread over the central part of the Serrata Valley. She squinted, but aside from the odd discoloration, she couldn't interpret any details.

A surge of emotions swelled up in her, but she quickly tamped it down, reminding herself she was still only halfway. She peered at the northern face below her, taking her time to study it as she tried to intuit the safest path down. It was much steeper than the southern side had been, with sheer cliffs composing most of its five-thousand-foot plummet to the distant ground.

She opened her pack and retrieved the rope she'd spent countless nights weaving from the viscera of her quarry. She tied the center of it around her waist, then secured the ends to two hooks she'd made from the bones of an elk. She'd practiced rappelling during her months of preparation, but only for short distances. Her gaze fell upon a thin traverse that cut across the face for a few thousand feet. Taking the traverse wouldn't be as fast as rappelling, but it would be safer.

She carefully walked along the top of the ridge to the high point of the traverse, then she strapped on her snowshoes and lowered herself down onto the undisturbed powder. With her spear in one hand and one of the hooks in the other, she inched forward, listening to the snow beneath her as she walked. From above, it was difficult to tell how stable the traverse truly was, so whenever it creaked, she plunged the hook into the nearest crack along the wall and waited to see if her footing would collapse beneath her. After a few false alarms, she gained some confidence, and by the time night fell, she had descended three thousand feet to a rocky plateau.

It was considerably warmer on the north side of the ridge. She could taste the moisture in the warm breezes that sailed by her on this side, and she quickly became too hot beneath her double layer of coats. She took off Father Silas's coat, but she held it close for a while afterward before carefully folding it and tucking it into her backpack. She smiled - the Hearthlord wasn't the only one who had been watching over her.

She had enough kindling left to build a small fire, but after she'd melted enough snow to refill her waterskin, she kicked it out. She sprawled out beneath the stars as she chewed on the last of her jerky.

Senya began her final descent shortly after dawn the next day. Her muscles were sore from three hard days on the mountain, but it did little to dampen her mood. She could see trails of smoke rising up in the distance. Alcazar would be another three days away, but smoke meant trapper camps. Her heart fluttered at the prospect of human interaction after her long solitude. If she was lucky, the trapper would be someone who had wintered in Alcazar and could tell her what had happened since she'd left.

The traverse she'd followed the day before wound back towards the east, but it steadily became thinner as it went. She followed it down another five hundred feet, where it spilled out into a shallow snowfield, which sprawled out as far as she could see. She was able to move much more quickly here, and she descended another thousand feet in an hour. She followed the curve of the slope downward, entering a sunny bowl where the body of the mountain merged with its neighbor. The grade was steeper here, but it was still manageable. She continued down another hour, stopping abruptly when she found the ledge that led into the cliffs below.

She peered over the edge at the rocky ground that lay another two hundred feet below. Instead of the cliff face she'd expected, there was only open air beneath her. Just as she realized the danger, she heard an unsettling crack rumble through the snow as the cornice shifted beneath her.

Senya took a step backward, then the snow slipped out beneath her weight like sand. Thunder rang in her ears as she fell along with the false ledge, and she blindly clawed at the snow in front of her. As soon as she felt purchase with her hook, she was dragged down violently with the cascade of snow, and the rope cinched tight around her waist.

The avalanche continued to rain down around her for another thirty seconds, but she remained still for a long time after the last wisps of ice drifted past her.

She dangled senselessly, swaying gently in the wind. Dazed, she clung to her rope until she could see again.

After her disorientation faded, she followed the length of the rope twenty feet up to the outcrop she'd managed to find with her hook. Her other hook was dangling below her, and her spear was gone. There was a sharp pain in her ribs as she reeled in her second hook, but she gritted her teeth and ignored it for the moment. Once she had retrieved the hook, she swung it into the cliff face in front of her until she caught the edge of a rock with it. She pulled herself in until she was able to cling to the square rocks before her.

She looked down, letting out a rattling breath when she saw she was only fifty feet away from the ground. Had she fallen for a few more seconds, she would have been smashed against the boulders below. She jammed her second hook into a crag and tugged on the rope to make sure it would stay put.

Slowly, she climbed the twenty feet up to retrieve her first hook. With the extra length of rope, she descended back to her anchor and untied the knot that secured the rope around her waist. She grasped the rope with both hands and rappelled down to the bottom.

Senya knelt as soon as her feet touched the ground below, blinking away unbidden tears. She was possessed by the strange sensation that she was dreaming — that she would wake up and find she was still at her camp in the crevasse, or worse, that she was still lying in the tomb, gasping for breath as blood filled her lungs. Her only solace was the excruciating pain in her ribs, and after a few minutes, she placed her hand on her side and healed the cracked bone.

She removed her coat and packed it away, then wiped the grime from her face. With one last look at the impassable ridge, she made her way into the forest.

XVIII

Senya had never imagined she would miss the howling gale that forever blanketed the snowdrifts, but without it, the dense forest seemed much too quiet. The wet leaves squished softly beneath her feet as she followed a narrow animal trail. She'd grown so accustomed to the gentle, refined smells of her white forest, but the foliage here reeked in the humid breeze. Life teemed everywhere she looked, and she had to stop herself from inspecting every berry and mushroom she encountered to make any meaningful progress.

In all her years living in Alcazar, she never realized how many different songs rattled through the trees. She counted at least seven bird species in the first hour of her trek, and she didn't even try to keep track of the number of insects lazily buzzing past her trail. As pungent as the forest was, it couldn't mask the dank scent of animal droppings. She reckoned she could track down the boar that had left its calling card behind within the hour if she was so inclined.

The only thing that kept her from exploring the wonders of this luscious forest was her growing unrest. As soon as she had set foot on this side of the Icetooth Ridge, all of her neglected feelings of loneliness burst to life again, and she longed for the familiar faces she had left behind. Auron, Fabian, the acolytes, the nurses, the servants, the trappers, even the pilgrims — she wondered what they would say when she returned. A shadow of fear passed over her when she thought of how she would explain what had happened to Father Silas, but she stifled it for the moment. She could cross that bridge when she came to it.

It wasn't long before the animal trail widened into an overgrown path. The branches on nearby trees had been broken irregularly, probably with a hatchet in years past. Judging from the dense underbrush, it seemed like this particular hunting trail hadn't been used all summer. Still, Senya followed it, and after another hour she spotted a small trapper's lodge nestled in a neglected clearing.

She couldn't help but smile as she approached the wooden structure. She passed the stale remains of a cookfire and walked up the rickety steps. Like the trail, the lodge had also fallen into disrepair, but she didn't let that bother her. There were bound to be useful supplies left over from the previous season, and maybe even emergency preserves.

Senya pushed on the wooden door, which stuck for a moment before giving way. She stepped into the musty cabin, blind in the relative darkness. The floor creaked loudly beneath her boots as she ventured further inside, but she stopped when her foot brushed against an overturned chair. She bent down to right it, but paused as her eyes adjusted to the dim room.

Nearly every piece of furniture in the lodge had been upended or smashed. The shelves built into the walls were completely empty, with most of their contents broken on the floor. Everything of value had been stripped away. As she took in the damage, her eyes fell across a large brown stain that marred the middle of the floor. She approached it and knelt down, scratching at the thin layer painting the floorboards and inspecting the flakes that caught beneath her fingernails. She knew trappers didn't dress their kills inside their lodges, but she also recognized the remains of dried blood.

A pit opened in her stomach as she backed out of the ransacked cottage. Wanting to banish the images from her mind, she turned back towards the remnants of the fire. She paused when she saw a gleam of ivory among the spent charcoal. It took her only a few moments to recognize the shape into a human jawbone.

Before she knew what she was doing, she plunged back into the forest, her heart racing uncontrollably. She sprinted until she couldn't breathe anymore, and then she continued another hundred yards for good measure. Her legs suddenly gave way, and she collapsed into the soft mulch, heaving unsteadily for air. No matter how much she told herself the scars of the crime that had taken place at the cabin were old, she couldn't help but glance over her shoulder every few seconds to make sure nothing had followed her out of the clearing.

As Senya moved north towards Alcazar over the next few days, she purposely avoided any trails that looked like they had been recently traveled. The animal trails were easy enough to find, and they had the added benefit of leading her past bushes and trees ripe with fruit and streams where she could drink. She knew she could have easily caught game — the rabbits she saw were so oblivious they let her get into striking distance before noticing her presence — but she let them go. After seeing what had happened at the hunting lodge, she didn't want to light a fire to alert others to her presence.

As she progressed, new smells started to mix in with the perfume of the forest. A thin layer of smoke permeated everything, and it only grew stronger the closer she got to Alcazar. Now and then, she would catch a whiff of sulfur that reminded her of the boiling pools in the slime caverns. Beneath those scents, there was something harder to define, yet even more familiar — a faint metallic smell that left a copper taste in her mouth.

Instead of following the low path of the valley that hunters and trappers frequented, Senya ranged further to the east, up onto the ridge that separated the Serrata Valley from its neighbor. From here, she could see the plume of black smoke billowing up into the sky long before she ever saw Alcazar. The closer she got, the more the trees thinned out, and she stopped on the ridge a few miles away from her home.

Below her, the valley lay naked — completely devoid of the dense forest that blanketed it two years ago. Stumps where the great trees had once grown littered the landscape, only interrupted by deep trenches that had been gouged into the earth. In the middle of the ring of devastation, an enormous stone tower rose where the temple of Alcazar should have been. Smoke billowed all around it, and the air in front of its dark façade shimmered with heat. The entire town was enclosed by a smooth stone wall that rose at least thirty feet high. Tents littered the plain surrounding the newly erected fortress, and even from her distance, Senya could see the steady flow of traffic traveling along the road that connected Alcazar to Serrata to the north.

Numb, Senya sat down on the rocky outcrop. She didn't know what she had expected to find upon her homecoming, but it wasn't this. This wasn't the Alcazar she had grown up in, where the congregation and merchants and trappers had thrived among the dense forest. She wondered if there was anything left of the temple where she had played and learned and slept, or the healing ward where she'd spent so many of her afternoons.

Before she'd left the tomb, she'd promised Father Silas she would find the Hearthlord and re-enter his service, but she didn't know where she stood with the rest of the Hearthborn. The image of the bones in the fire flashed before her eyes again, and she hugged her knees. She needed to find the Hearthlord on her own if she wanted to plead her case.

The sun sank in the sky as she watched the steady buzz of activity around the fortress. A small line of flickering lights moving across the valley towards her perch caught her attention. As they got closer, she was able to make out a line of people marching eastwards towards the ridge. The men in the front and the back were clad in the shiny black armor of the Hearthborn, but everyone else wore drab gray tunics.

Senya collected her things and dropped down from her outcrop, moving through the wiry brush that remained of the forest towards the torchlight. They were following a well-worn path of switchbacks that climbed steadily up the mountain. Senya made sure to keep well out of sight as she tailed them, which was easy enough under the cover of darkness. The slow-moving group was quiet except for the clanking of armor. The trees grew thicker as they gained elevation and distance from Alcazar. Senya could smell their destination a mile before they reached it — the stink of sulfur and smoke hurt her eyes and made it difficult for her to breathe.

She stayed back as the group spilled out into a clearing that was well-lit by a raging bonfire. As they dispersed, she skirted around the edge of the trees to get a better look.

The clearing formed a semi-circle around an opening in the mountain, where the smell was strongest. Senya recognized the handiwork of the Rothschilds from the smooth edges of the opening, but there were also piles of rock littered around the mine's entrance. A couple of haggard Castellanos emerged from the cave, carrying iron pickaxes with them. They were both covered in a thin film of black dust. They approached a shed near the mine, where a Hearthborn was waiting to receive them. He relieved them of their pickaxes and gave them waterskins, and then they retired to the bonfire, where another group of dirty workers was resting.

The new batch of workers shuffled towards the shed, where the Hearthborn supervisor passed out pickaxes and sacks. Now Senya was close enough to see clearly, she could confirm all of the workers were Castellanos — the only Hearthborn in the camp were the supervisor and the soldiers who had escorted them up the mountain. As the new group disappeared into the mine, she turned her attention to the laborers resting by the fire. Her gaze fell upon a woman patiently ladling porridge out to the miners, and her breath caught in her throat when she realized she knew her.

It took all of Senya's strength to stop herself from bursting out of the forest and running to Auron's mother. Memories of evenings spent playing in the creek near her house rushed through Senya's mind, and she could almost taste her stew again. She searched wildly for any sign of her friend, but she didn't see him. After studying the soot-covered faces, she recognized a few more townsfolk from Alcazar, although she was sure she'd never seen some of the others before.

Senya waited for what must have been hours. The newcomers from Alcazar eventually re-emerged from the mine, now just as filthy as those who had gone in before them. They surrendered their tools and drank the water the Hearthborn gave them. Once the second shift of miners had been given a few minutes to rest and breathe the relatively fresh night air, the Hearthborn rounded everyone up and led them to a shoddily constructed wooden barracks at the edge of the clearing. One by one, they ushered the Castellanos inside, and then the supervisor shut the door. Two of the Hearthborn lifted a heavy wooden bar, which they rested in place in front of the door.

The Hearthborn put out the dwindling fire, then retired to tents that had been erected at the opposite end of the clearing. Even after darkness engulfed the camp, Senya waited another thirty minutes for good measure before leaving her hiding place. She stole up to the side of the wooden barracks, where the bars of a window were just out of her reach. She set her backpack on the ground and climbed on top of it, gaining enough height to peer through into the cramped room beyond.

Most of the Castellanos were sleeping, obviously exhausted from their labor, but a few looked up at her as she rasped, "Auntie Mariana!"

She felt tears of joy well up in her eyes when the familiar face appeared on the other side of the window. A pair of fleshy arms constricted around her, hugging her and pulling her tight against the bars of the window. "Senya?" Mariana cried in a whisper. "Have you returned from the Hearth?"

Senya was confused for a moment, but then she understood. The Hearthborn wouldn't have told the villagers of Alcazar that they had left her and Father Silas for dead. They must have instead said that they had ascended to the paradise beyond the altar. She felt somewhat relieved she didn't need to explain — she didn't know what Mariana would think of her if she revealed that she had let Father Silas die.

A thousand questions bubbled up to the front of her mind, all fighting to be asked first. What had happened to the valley? Why had all the trees been cut, why had Alcazar been demolished to build the imposing fortress, and why were the faithful villagers locked in a cramped hut? What had happened to everyone else?

She found herself paralyzed by the sudden onslaught, but Mariana saved her by clasping her callused hands over her cheeks. The initial shock had left her face, and what remained now were deep lines of concern. "You have to find Auron and the girls," she said, her voice much more serious now. "After the Hearthlord came back, they took all the children north. They said it was to train them for the Hearth and that they would come back as angels, but that was two years ago. Now, with the war with Aesterland…"

Senya flushed. Auron would be fifteen now — technically old enough to be initiated into King Ferdinand's legions, but his sisters, Julia and Valeria, were only eight and ten. What use would they be in a war with the powerful nation to the north of Castilla? She had seen the injuries soldiers sustained while in the ward, and she didn't want to imagine any of them suffering the same fate.

"Hold on," she whispered. "I'll let you out of there." She extricated herself from Mariana's grasp, and despite the woman's protests, slinked around to the front of the barracks. She tugged at the heavy wooden beam that bolted the barracks shut, but it didn't budge. She crouched down and set her shoulder beneath it, then pushed up with all of her might, but she couldn't move it more than a few centimeters. After trying unsuccessfully for a few minutes, she returned to the window. More of the workers were crowded around it now.

"I can't open the door," she said helplessly.

"It doesn't matter, angel," one of the workers rasped. Senya recognized him as one of the trappers who had sometimes wintered in Alcazar. He looked much older than the last time she'd seen him, and the creases on his face were dark with soot he hadn't been able to wash away. "I escaped once before, but the Hearthborn found me." He held up his left hand, revealing two missing fingers. "This was the price I paid."

Senya looked over at the darkened tents where the Hearthborn slept. These were the people who had prayed at their temple for decades, who had given their lives to serve them. Why were their trials so harsh? Her eyes burned as the image of Father Silas's emaciated corpse flashed before her once more.

"Senya," Mariana said, her voice weak, "is this the paradise the Hearthlord promised?"

Senya looked at the faces of the prisoners — dirty and exhausted, some hopeful, others twisted with disdain. For a solitary moment, she allowed an ugly ball of doubt to grow inside her, but just as quickly, it collapsed into shame. Had she learned nothing from her trial? If her faith could be so easily shaken, what was the point of all the suffering she'd endured? "We have to trust the Hearthlord," she said.

An expression Senya couldn't quite read passed Mariana's face, but then it was gone, and Mariana pulled her into another hug. "Find Auron and the girls," she said. "Tell them to come home." Senya nodded, and Mariana clutched her tighter. "Be careful."

Senya pulled away abruptly when she heard one of the Hearthborn stir in his tent, and she ducked into the trees when torchlight sparked on the other side of the camp. She watched as one of the Hearthborn approached the window, and after talking with the miners for a few seconds, he looked towards the dark forest she had retreated to. Before he could take a step towards her, Senya fled deeper into the safety of the forest.

XIX

Nell felt a dizzying wave of vertigo grip her as she peered out over the wall. Highcastle's fortifications rose fifty feet into the air, giving the garrison a commanding view of the fertile plains surrounding the city. From here, the invaders below looked like a swarm of black ants crawling across the countryside.

She took a step back from the parapet and rejoined her mother, who was conferring with Richard Piaget, the captain of the guard, and Angela de Lucerne, one of her ministers. "Ten thousand soldiers made it back inside the city, Your Grace," Piaget reported. "We can draft more from the populace, but it will take time to train them. We haven't received word from any of the forces at the southern border. I think it would be safe to consider them lost."

Nell blanched at the report, but Queen Helene only nodded. "What of the troops at the northern border?"

"Five thousand are stationed there," Piaget replied. "We can recall them, but then the Nords may press the advantage."

"That won't matter if the invaders take Highcastle," Nell interrupted, ignoring the look of disapproval from her mother.

Piaget frowned and said, "With all due respect, Princess, there were seventy thousand at the southern border. Even if we were to recall the northern divisions, we cannot meet the enemy in open combat."

"What about the tunnels?" Nell asked, lowering her voice a bit in case any ordinary guards were in earshot. "We could use them to pincer the enemy, couldn't we?"

"They were not designed to transport armies," Piaget said. "Any sizable force would be discovered before they were able to organize on the other side."

Queen Helene glanced at de Lucerne and asked, "And our food reserves?"

"We had enough for five years, but didn't account for the number of refugees," de Lucerne replied promptly. "With careful rationing, we could withstand three years without resupply."

The queen was quiet as she thought. She paced to the other side of the battlement and looked out over the majestic city. Despite the invaders setting up camps just outside, the outer markets of Highcastle were still bustling, although there were markedly more people crammed into its streets than usual. After a few minutes, Queen Helene returned and said, "Captain, organize a delegation. Tell the enemy commander that I will entertain peace negotiations."

The color rose in Nell's cheeks as the captain nodded. Once he left to carry out the order, she turned angrily to her mother and asked, "Why would you negotiate with them? If we have enough to withstand them for three years, it gives us time to organize a resistance."

"Aesterland is more than just Highcastle, Eleanor," Queen Helene said calmly. "There are millions of people beyond these walls who are also my responsibility. Are you willing to sacrifice them to prolong the inevitable?"

"You should at least try before you kneel to these barbarians!" Nell exclaimed heatedly.

Queen Helene pursed her lips, and Nell knew she had gone too far. Slowly, she forced herself to unclench her fists. How many times had her mother told her hysteria was unbefitting of a queen? Still, she could not tolerate the idea of the invaders violating her pristine city, and she couldn't understand how her mother could be so quick to surrender.

"We have already been defeated, Eleanor," Queen Helene said gently. "Our army is all but gone. Now we must do what we can for our people."

Not trusting herself to say anything more, Nell stalked away, leaving her mother and de Lucerne on the battlement.

S iegfried gingerly climbed down from the back of the cart, leaning heavily on his crutch when his feet touched the ground. After five long weeks, his leg had healed enough to put a little weight on it, although it was still too sore for him to walk far on it. He shuffled out of the way as the other prisoners unloaded supplies from the cart, wandering up the road towards the empty houses of Wiltshire.

Confined to the cart trailing behind the Jenseiter host, Siegfried had been forced to witness the destruction left in their wake. He supposed he was glad Wiltshire was abandoned — he had also seen towns that had been completely ransacked, as well as others that had been subjugated. Without the army to protect them, the villagers could do little more than flee or kneel to their conquerors.

Wiltshire bore only a passing resemblance to the small town he'd left four months ago. Back then, the road had been a narrow path used by farmers and the occasional merchant, but now it had been expanded to make way for the constant stream of soldiers that flowed through it in both directions. Siegfried had initially been surprised when their cart had turned off the main route that connected the southeastern border to Centralia. Centralia was a major trading hub and boasted a highway that connected directly to Highcastle, where Queen Helene held her court. When they had reached the fork, Siegfried had noticed only a small fraction of soldiers split off to head towards the capital, while the rest took the smaller eastern route.

Along with the Jenseiter soldiers came thousands of Castellano workers. They were usually relegated to the sides of the road, where they cleared trees and dug ditches to expand the route. After a few weeks, the flood of soldiers passing Siegfried's cart had slowed to a trickle. About a week ago, he'd started to see more soldiers heading in the opposite direction - these with their own carts of Aesterkind prisoners.

He followed the trail of prisoners to the Wiltshire barracks, where they were unloading supplies for the night. The barracks, like many of the houses, was already occupied by Jenseiters, so the prisoners were setting up their tents in the training yard to camp for the night. Siegfried sat down on one of the logs that surrounded the cookfire, resting his crutch across his lap. He frowned as he watched two little boys dump armfuls of firewood into the hearth. Two carts of Aesterkind prisoners had joined his own as they'd moved north along the eastern road, both of which had been filled with civilian children.

The oldest Castellano boy, Auron, joined Siegfried on the log. Unsurprisingly, he was accompanied by Fabian. Although he had since learned the diminutive Aesterkind boy had grown up in Castilla, Siegfried still found the way he cozied up to the Jenseiters distasteful. The other Aesterkind prisoners kept their distance from him, but Auron had been given the task of watching Siegfried, and Fabian followed Auron everywhere, so Siegfried had no choice but to tolerate his presence.

That wasn't to say Siegfried particularly liked Auron, either. At first, he had tried to glean some information about the invaders from him, but it was all "Hearthlord this" and "angel that" with him. Castellanos had a reputation for being superstitious, but it quickly became clear to Siegfried that Auron was a zealot. After a few days, he had given up on learning anything of substance.

Once the Aesterkind prisoners brought enough firewood, the ashen-haired Lieutenant Nichts approached with Javier, another of the Castellano boys, and Auron and Fabian both rose to attention. Nichts was one of the few Jenseiter soldiers who didn't share the blonde hair and red eyes of the other invaders. The only other one traveling with the prison caravan was an orange-haired woman called Kepler.

Both Nichts and Kepler were part of the Jenseiter special forces, a division called the Reinbann. They were distinguished by the light chainmail they wore. Siegfried had spent hours upon end watching the constant stream of soldiers and workers that marched past the slow ox cart, and he had come to understand how few of them there actually were. He doubted he had seen more than one in ten thousand.

Lieutenant Nichts waved his hand, putting the boys at ease. Nichts gestured towards the hearth and asked, "Whose turn tonight?"

Auron stepped forward and responded, "Mine."

Nichts stepped aside, and Auron knelt beside the fire pit. He adjusted the logs and stuffed some kindling beneath them, then laid his palms on the pile. Siegfried had watched this ritual dozens of times, yet the hairs still raised on the back of his neck as the flames licked Auron's knuckles. Smoke rose from the fire as the kindling caught, and Auron fed his infant creation with more sticks until one of the logs was set ablaze.

"You're getting faster," Nichts said in an approving tone.

Auron shrugged as Javier seethed beside him. Since they'd left the southern border, the two Castellano boys had rotated the duty of lighting the campfire every night. A month ago, it would often take both of them well over ten minutes. Javier had gotten his average time down to five minutes, but Auron was regularly able to light the fire in thirty seconds.

Both of the Castellano boys walked behind the cart during the day. About a week in, Siegfried had noticed Auron nonchalantly drop a blackened scrap of trash onto the dirt road. He had watched him for a while longer, and to his surprise, Auron disposed of an incinerated scrap every five minutes.

The next morning, he'd watched as Auron had furtively pulled a handful of leaves off of a tree and stuffed them into his pocket. The Reinbann recruits weren't supposed to practice without the supervision of their mentors, but there was a reason why Auron was improving more quickly than Javier.

Nichts sat down on the log next to Siegfried's. He glanced over his shoulder at Captain Sprenger, who was observing the prisoners from near the entrance to the barracks. Sprenger nodded, and Nichts turned to the boys with a smile. "We are going to start combat training today," he said. Auron beamed at the news, but Javier and Fabian seemed less excited. "Come with me, you three. There's supposed to be a nice practice field behind the barracks."

Siegfried frowned as he watched them leave, disappointed he wouldn't see how the Reinbann learned to fight. He considered trying to follow them for a moment, but abandoned the idea when he noticed Sprenger glaring at him. Instead, he turned his attention to Sergeant Kepler and the cluster of Aesterkind children gathered around her.

Kepler dug into the hard dirt that surrounded the cookfire, scraping up a handful of dust. She paused for a moment as she explained something slowly to the children, and then flipped her palm upside down, demonstrating how the small pile of dirt remained suspended in her hand. After a few seconds, she relaxed, allowing the dirt to rain back onto the ground.

The children spread out and began accumulating their own piles of dirt. Siegfried watched the training silently, long since used to the nightly routine. After an hour or so, Sprenger would signal for the Reinbann soldiers to conclude the training, and then the prisoners would be fed and herded into their tents. For the first few weeks, Siegfried and the other captured soldiers had worn shackles at all times. After the first cart of civilians joined them, the soldiers relaxed a bit and only restrained them at night. Now, they were only shackled when they stayed in subjugated towns. Siegfried didn't think they would bother tonight as Wiltshire was the only town for thirty miles, and he hadn't seen anyone but Jenseiter soldiers since they'd arrived.

As he watched the Aesterkind try to make dirt stick to their hands, Siegfried was struck with the familiar feeling of isolation. He didn't quite understand why he was traveling with this group. During Kepler's first lesson, weeks ago, she had rested her palm on the ground, and Siegfried and the other prisoners had watched in amazement as a gauntlet of earthen armor crawled up over her forearm. Chills had run down Siegfried's spine as he'd been reminded of the armored golem that decimated his unit.

After letting the prisoners touch her armor, Kepler released it, allowing it to dissipate in a mist of fine dust. She'd instructed the prisoners to hold out their hands, and she'd deposited a small lump of clay into each of their palms, except for Siegfried's. When she reached him, she had looked at his outstretched hand with confusion for a few moments, then she'd gently closed his fingers and shook her head. Ever since then, Siegfried had been excluded from the training.

In the beginning, he'd watched Kepler as closely as he could. He would scrape up clumps of grass and dirt and attempt to perform the same simple exercises as the others, but the dirt always fell to the ground. After a few days, four of the five other prisoners had managed to suspend a fist-sized clump of dirt from their fingertips, while all Siegfried had to show for his efforts was a dirty hand. He'd finally resigned himself to the reality that he didn't possess whatever capacity they had to form the armor.

Since then, Siegfried had seen a dozen other Reinbann officers, and he had noticed they all had distinct characteristics from the horde of blonde invaders. Kepler's hair was a lighter shade of orange than the typical Aesterkind red, but her husky build and green eyes were strikingly similar to many of the prisoners. Likewise, Nichts looked more like the Castellano boys than he did Sprenger or the other soldiers. In fact, Siegfried hadn't seen a single blonde Jenseiter wearing Reinbann armor.

Siegfried had spent plenty of time contemplating the meaning of Berthold's message since the battle at the southern border. The banners the Jenseiters carried were emblazoned with the eagle of the Feracht family. Before he'd faced them, Siegfried had never met anyone outside of his family with his red eyes. While they clearly shared some ancestry, the blonde soldiers avoided him in the camps, leaving him in the custody of the Reinbann.

While on the cart, he'd noticed the passing soldiers had a habit of gawking at him. They usually quickly averted their gaze when he looked their way, but some of them didn't. They would either smile or sneer at him as they passed. On several occasions, Siegfried had caught Captain Sprenger staring at him intently from afar, and he was one of the few who didn't pretend he hadn't been. Even now, Siegfried could feel the captain's gaze boring into his back.

He resisted the urge to look over his shoulder, instead focusing on the Reinbann training. Only a couple of the Aesterkind managed to replicate Kepler's trick by the end of their practice. Kepler gathered the lot of them around the fire and said, "Good work, everyone! We should reach the Duchess within the week. Keep practicing, and do your best to impress her."

Siegfried stirred at this new information. He had learned the Duchess, Diana Feracht, was the commander of the army that had broken the eastern front of the border, and she also handpicked the members of the Reinbann. He had always known he and the other prisoners were being taken to see her, but never had there been any indication of when they would finally reach her.

An Aesterkind woman accompanied by a soldier approached the fire, and Siegfried immediately recognized her as one of the servants who used to cook for the outpost. She looked at him for a moment, then quickly dropped her gaze to the iron pot in her hands. She knelt beside the fire and set the pot on the grill over the flame, allowing its contents to heat up before adding the vegetables she'd been carrying in her apron.

The prisoners set up the tents while the soup came to a boil. There were only two mid-sized tents for the twenty of them, but most of the civilians were smaller children who slept together in a tight huddle. Siegfried was exempt from the work of setting up the tents because of his injured leg, leaving him alone with the servant girl.

After a few minutes, he noticed she kept glancing up at him. He frowned; although he had been stationed in Wiltshire for six months, he had never before talked to her and didn't know her name. She managed to catch his gaze, and he leaned forward in resignation. She quickly looked around to gauge the distance of the nearby guards, then, satisfied they were out of earshot, she whispered, "Did you come through Brexton?"

Siegfried nodded; the prison cart had passed through the small town on the way up from the border. It hosted the nearest outpost south of Wiltshire, and it was clear there had been a skirmish there. The houses had been reduced to ashes by the time he passed through, and the workers had been busy digging graves alongside the road.

The girl seemed to read Siegfried's expression, and she looked down, tears in her eyes. Siegfried grimaced and, eager to turn the conversation, asked, "How long ago did they take Wiltshire?"

"Two weeks," the girl replied. "Lieutenant Barrow ordered everyone to evacuate. They were going to fall back to Riverdale, but my mother isn't well, so we stayed. My brother was in Brexton — when I saw prisoners, I thought maybe—"

"They didn't take any prisoners in Brexton," Siegfried said. The girl immediately turned away from him, and he could hear her begin to sob softly. He tensed up, unsure of what to do, but then the soup began to bubble, and the other prisoners trickled back into the camp. The next time the servant looked up, the tears were gone, although she avoided Siegfried's gaze when she gave him his bowl.

Nichts and his recruits returned a little while later. Auron happily grabbed a bowl of stew and sat down next to Siegfried, bringing with him the musty scent of smoke. Fabian looked less chipper, and when he neared the fire, Siegfried noticed his clothes were still covered in dirt. Javier reluctantly joined them, moving much more slowly than he had been before. As he spooned the contents out of his bowl, Siegfried saw the hole that had been burned through his sleeve, revealing a large welt on the skin underneath.

By the time they were done eating, the only light left came from the dim embers of the dying fire. Siegfried was quiet as he listened to the others chat, preoccupied with the memory of the mass graves along the side of the road. He looked up at Nichts' charges, wondering how long it would be before they wore the uniforms of the Reinbann. The invaders weren't training their prisoners for nothing, and he knew they would eventually be given the order to ransack a village or put down a rebel.

"What's wrong?" Auron asked through a mouthful of stew.

Siegfried frowned and asked, "Why did you join them?"

Javier laughed dryly. He glanced over his shoulder, making sure none of the soldiers were watching, and rasped, "Do you think we were given a choice? What do you think happens to the ones the Duchess doesn't select?"

"It is a high honor to serve the Hearthlord," Auron said defensively.

Javier rolled his eyes, clearly tired of Auron's rhetoric. Siegfried had heard several Castellanos call the Imperator of the Jenseiters "the Hearthlord". While the Duchess had overseen the campaign through the eastern half of Aesterland, the Imperator had broken through the western pass and presumably led the way up towards Highcastle. News of the western campaign was scant, as the eastern and western roads quickly grew further apart past the southern mountains, but after Siegfried had heard the western pass had fallen, he had accepted the likelihood Berthold had died in the battle. The elite Feracht Corps would not allow the line to break without giving their lives to defend it.

"What happens to them?" Siegfried asked.

"They're executed," Fabian said softly.

Javier nodded grimly, but Auron let his spoon drop into his stew and glared at his fellow recruit. "Why would you say that?" he demanded.

"I saw it happen," Fabian replied. "In Alcazar. After you left, they took the acolytes who couldn't do the fire trick away. They would have taken me too if I didn't manifest this..." He traced the ground, raising up a small wall of dirt where his finger had been.

"They took them to the Hearth," Auron argued. "They ascended."

"Like Senya?" Fabian asked quietly.

Auron stared at him, anger flashing in his dark eyes. "What are you saying?" he asked, a dangerous edge to his voice.

For a moment, Siegfried thought the two boys would come to blows, but Fabian dropped his gaze to the ground. "I'm sorry," he said quietly. "Sometimes, my faith..."

Auron grasped Fabian's shoulder comfortingly, and Siegfried scowled. He set his empty bowl on the ground and braced on his crutch, slowly pulling himself back to his feet. He'd had enough of the cultists' nonsense for one night. He shambled towards the tent, crawling inside and claiming a corner at the back edge. The others gradually filtered in behind him, until the soldiers extinguished the fire and ordered the rest of the prisoners into the tents.

Siegfried's insomnia had only grown worse since he'd become a prisoner. For a long time after everyone else drifted to sleep, he stared at the dark canvas at the corner of the tent, listening to the hum of crickets outside. The soldiers always posted guards outside of the prison tents, and the sound of their metal armor shifting rang like bells against the still countryside. The past couple of nights, he was lucky if he could find two or three hours of sleep.

In the small hours of the morning, he heard the sound of clattering hooves in the distance. The cadence was odd — there were two or three animals, and they were clearly galloping — nothing like the steady rhythm of ox hooves. As the sound grew closer, he wondered if it could be royal horses. The monarchy of Aesterland bred a small herd imported from the southern reaches of Reese, thousands of miles away. The only one he had ever seen had been ridden by General Bridges, the flank commander at the southern border and an archduke in his own right. Oddly, the sound came from the east, from the road that led into the Black Forest.

The rapid staccato of the hooves ceased as the small party reached the barracks. Siegfried could hear the guards rush to greet them, but the voice that responded was too soft for him to make out. One of the guards left for the interior of the barracks while the riders waited, but when they returned, Siegfried heard the familiar intonation of Lieutenant Nichts.

The rider spoke to Nichts quietly for a few minutes, and he responded only with short affirmatives. Then the riders were off again, this time heading south. He could hear the sounds of hurried commotion for another fifteen minutes after they left, but then the quiet of the night took hold once more.

The next thing Siegfried knew, it was morning and another one of the Aesterkind prisoners, Jenkins, was impatiently shaking him awake. He obligingly crawled out of the tent so the others could begin the process of packing it back up. He leaned on his crutch as he watched them, hazily wondering if the events of the previous night had been part of some dream.

After loading the tent into their ox cart, the prisoners sat down to eat a hurried breakfast. Siegfried was somewhat surprised when he didn't see Auron, who usually began his watch just before the prisoners were loaded back into the cart. After he finished the scrap of bread he'd been given, he hoisted himself up into the back of the prison cart. Once Sergeant Kepler corralled all of the children into the other cart, they departed, and Siegfried was able to confirm Lieutenant Nichts and the Reinbann recruits were no longer traveling with them.

Siegfried scarcely had enough time to wonder where they had gone before another oddity caught his attention. Rather than continuing north, where the road would meander along the edge of the Black Forest to the border with Norogard, they took a right turn just outside of Wiltshire, heading east into the forest itself. This road, once little more than a trail, had been expanded since the last time Siegfried had seen it. A chill ran down his spine as they entered the shadows of the dark forest. The small hunting village of Eberswalde was two day's journey into the forest, but beyond that, there was nothing until the road passed the ruins of the Feracht family estate.

The stream of soldiers that accompanied their caravan dwindled, but the flow of troops coming from the opposite direction increased in compensation. They were left to struggle alongside the ditch that lined the way as the troops marched past them.

When they'd been traveling through the fields that dominated the countryside, it had been easy for the soldiers to pull their cart off to the side of the road during the busiest parts of the day to let the troops pass by, but it was impossible with the murky undergrowth of the Black Forest. The trees here were different from the towering oaks at the southern border — they were short and stout, with gnarled branches and spines instead of leaves. The trees that had been cleared to widen the road had been dumped just beyond the ditches, forming makeshift walls of timber that separated them from the swamp.

Their carts pulled into a small recess along the side of the road that night, but there wasn't enough room to make a proper camp. Instead, Captain Sprenger ordered that they remain shackled inside the carts with nothing more than thin blankets to weather the chill of the night. Sergeant Kepler came to give them a ration of dried meat and bread, but there was no Reinbann training. Some of the younger civilians started to cry, but the others managed to quiet them before the noise drew the soldiers.

The foliage overhead was so thick that the forest fell completely dark after the Jenseiters put out their campfires. This was the night Siegfried had grown up with, and after nearly a year away from his home, he had forgotten its comforting embrace. He rested his head against the sideboard of the cart and tried to sleep.

Despite the blankets, all of the prisoners in Siegfried's cart were shivering by the next morning. The soldiers unchained them long enough so they could relieve themselves, but as soon as they returned to the cart, they were put in shackles again. They departed unceremoniously from the small recess, slowly moving against the tide of soldiers coming from Eberswalde. The forest only grew darker as they pressed on, and it started to rain late in the day. There was an audible sigh of relief among both the soldiers and prisoners when they reached the perimeter of Eberswalde as twilight crept upon them.

As a child, Siegfried had sometimes accompanied his older sister Bridget to the market in Eberswalde. Although she was only four years older than him, Bridget had taken most of the responsibility of running the household after their mother had fallen ill. While their mother had been content to allow Litchfield, the family butler, to manage the servants, Bridget preferred more control, and she'd made it her habit to directly oversee even mundane tasks. Siegfried knew Litchfield had privately rejoiced the day Bridget married and left to live with her new husband in Highcastle.

As they entered the village, Siegfried saw that it, too, had been drastically expanded since the last time he'd seen it. The central town hall and hunting lodges still stood, but a significant swath of the encroaching forest had been cleared to make way for rows upon rows of Jenseiter tents. The place was swarming with blonde soldiers, but there were nearly as many Castellano and Aesterkind laborers. A wall had been partially constructed around the town, and their carts passed beneath the skeleton of a massive gate. None of the towns they had passed through thus far had seen so much development.

Their carts pulled to a stop just after the gate, and Captain Sprenger left with one of the other soldiers for a few minutes. Siegfried glanced behind him towards the lodges, squinting when he saw a familiar woman's face looking at him through a window. After a few moments, he recognized her as Mary Heller, Eberswalde's elderly grocer. Her face flushed white when their eyes met, but then she abruptly closed her shutters.

Before Siegfried could be sure if he'd really seen her, Captain Sprenger returned to the carts with an older officer. The two stopped a few feet behind Siegfried, and although his back was to them, he could hear them clearly as they spoke.

"Major, the Duchess gave specific orders," Captain Sprenger said. "She wanted to see any Reinbann recruits or special assets personally."

"The Imperator summoned Lady Diana to Highcastle. I do not expect her to return for several months." The elderly officer paused, pacing along the back of the cart. Finally, he continued, "There is a Reinbann encampment here. They can hold the recruits for the time being."

Both men paused once more for a few moments, and Siegfried felt their attention rest on him. The major finally broke the silence, offering, "The prison is still under construction, but there's a holding pen. It's late — take him there for now."

Captain Sprenger ventured, "Sir, I have orders to return to Castilla after I transfer custody."

"You will leave tomorrow morning," the major promised.

With that, the major left, leaving Sprenger to mutter something beneath his breath. He barked at one of the guards, who climbed up into the cart and stepped over the cramped prisoners to unlock Siegfried's shackles.

Siegfried grasped his crutch and silently stood up. He carefully negotiated his way off of the cart and stood next to the guard and Sprenger while the other soldiers led the carts through the mud, deeper into the camp. Once the Aesterkind were out of sight, Sprenger took off towards the center of town at a brisk pace, and the guard nudged Siegfried after him.

Night was well upon them now, and with the heavy mist of the late autumn rain, Siegfried couldn't see much outside of the glow of the torches lining the streets. He kept his eyes on the ground, carefully picking his footing in the mud. Sprenger led him through a row of houses, all of which were now tightly shuttered, and down the main street that used to host the market. As soon as they turned the corner, Siegfried caught the stench of death in the air, but it was too dark to make out its source.

Sprenger finally stopped at a stable. The structure was presently empty, although the smell of stale manure was enough to mask the corpse-stink he had detected earlier. The three of them took shelter from the rain beneath the high roof, and after a few seconds, Sprenger lit the lantern hanging from the center post, illuminating the entire stable.

Of the eight empty stalls, half had been converted into makeshift cells. Iron grates had been installed at the entrance of each cell, which were secured by a heavy wooden beam across two brackets on either side of the supporting walls. Sprenger and the guard shifted the beam of the center stall with a grunt of effort. Once the door was open, they looked at Siegfried expectantly, and after a few moments of silence, he hobbled into the cell. They closed the door behind him, and he sat down on the soft hay that lined the floor as Sprenger spoke quietly to the guard near the lantern. Siegfried couldn't hear them over the sound of the rain, but once they were done talking, Sprenger took his leave and the guard sat on a bale of hay across from Siegfried's stall.

Although the front of the stable was open, the structure was protected from the wind, and it was surprisingly warm. After a month of sleeping on the cold ground, the hay beneath Siegfried felt almost like a bed. He wondered idly if these were to be his quarters until the Duchess returned from the capital. Thirty minutes after Sprenger left, a Castellano servant brought two bowls of hot stew on a tray. The soldier slid Siegfried's portion beneath the grate, then returned to his seat to eat his own.

Siegfried savored his stew as he listened to the rain. Once he was done, he pushed his empty bowl back under the door and leaned against the hay. He stared up at the dimly lit planks of the ceiling, remaining still despite the feeling of restlessness that crept upon him. The rain continued as the night wore on, and after a few hours, Siegfried could hear the exhausted guard's snores. The lantern quietly died, throwing the stable into shades of darkness.

Unable to sleep, Siegfried sat up and moved closer to the crossed iron bars at the front of his cell. His eyes quickly adjusted to the new darkness, allowing him to see into the street beyond the front of the stable. The last time he'd been here, the Eberswalde market had consisted of a few permanent stalls with space for the odd merchant cart that passed through. In the darkness, Siegfried could still make out the shapes of low stalls, but there was another structure across the street he didn't recognize.

At first, Siegfried thought it was a stage of some kind. However, when he squinted against the darkness, he noticed there were two stout posts on either end and a solid beam connecting them overhead, ten feet in the air. In the middle of the open air framed by the structure, he could vaguely make out two suspended forms, and he realized he was looking at a hangman's gallows.

As soon as he made the connection, the smell of manure was no longer able to mask the stench of death that lurked beneath, and he raised a hand to his throat. Now he knew what the structure was, Siegfried found he could no longer tear his eyes away from it. He remained still at the grate, and as the night faded into morning by degrees, he could make out more detail.

The two bodies swayed gently in the autumn wind, causing the ropes they were suspended by to creak idly. They were both adult men, and judging from the sorry state of their clothes and the partial decomposition of their bodies, they had been hanging there for at least a few days. When the blue shade of the predawn light filtered onto the street, Siegfried noticed the silver clasp on the ragged cloak of one of the men. His fingers went numb when he saw it was molded in the shape of a bird. His eyes darted down, to the black vest with silver buckles and the worn leather boots. These weren't the clothes of a soldier or a peasant, but they were all too familiar to him.

Slowly, he raised his gaze to the hanging man's face, and although the corpse's weathered countenance was hidden by his long gray hair, Siegfried knew he was looking at the remains of his father, Dieter Feracht. With a great effort, Siegfried turned his attention to the man hanging beside him, and he found the same eagle sigil on his clothing. Now that the seal of Siegfried's blissful oblivion was broken, he immediately recognized Heinrich, his eldest brother. Siegfried's blood turned to ice as he thought about the two of them standing next to each other on the pedestal before the order was given.

Blood dripped from his palms as he clenched the bars of the iron grate. This was the reason he had been ferried from the southern line, following in the path of devastation paved by the bloodthirsty Duchess and her armies. This was why all of the Jenseiters had gawked at him — they must have known what awaited him at the end of the road. Each man wore a wooden plaque on his chest, suspended there by a cord draped around his neck. Both plaques had a single word inscribed upon them: *Pretender.*

Siegfried looked at the empty space to the right of his father, and he knew he would soon join them if he didn't do something. With a final look at the gallows, he broke away from the grate and explored his makeshift cell with renewed purpose. Although the Jenseiters had modified it, the stable was an existing fixture of Eberswalde, and some of the old planks in the corner were soft with rot.

He glanced at the guard, who was still sleeping peacefully, and then knelt at the back of the cell and began to dig beneath the wall. Once he'd cleared enough room for his fingers, he grasped the soft wood and tugged, breaking off a small section. He continued this process until he managed to hollow out the rotten section, but then he was met with healthier planks and only had enough room to stick his arm through. The other planks were secured firmly against the support beams with nails, and no matter how hard Siegfried pulled, they would not give.

Siegfried looked back around the cell for a tool he could use to help him. After a few moments, he picked up his crutch. He jammed it through the opening and jimmied it back, applying as much force as he could on the plank. The nails gradually gave way, and one by one, he was able to loosen the planks enough to pull off. After a few more minutes of panicked work, Siegfried had made a hole big enough to shove his shoulders through.

He crawled out onto the muddy grass behind the stable, then reached back for his crutch. The pink rays of dawn were just beginning to warm the sky, and only a few of the Jenseiters were stirring. As stealthily as he could, he limped to a cluster of shacks, then waited for two patrolling soldiers to pass before making a run for the edge of the dark forest. He allowed himself a moment of relief when he ducked under the support beams of the half-finished wall and into the cover of the trees, but he knew he had to keep going. It wasn't long before he heard distant shouts from the town as his absence was discovered and the alarm was raised.

Siegfried gritted his teeth as he pressed further into the wilderness. In the difficult terrain, his crutch was all but useless, and the pain in his leg was steadily growing worse as he was forced to put his weight on it. He could feel himself slowing down the further he went, and when he looked back, he could plainly see the trail he was leaving behind. He stopped abruptly, drawing in a deep breath to calm himself. After a few moments, he began thinking more clearly again.

He knew that in his state, the Jenseiters would quickly catch up with him and drag him back to Eberswalde. He would never be able to outrun them with a crippled leg. His best chance for now was to disappear. He continued forward more deliberately, searching for a place to hide. He stopped when he spotted a pond blanketed with a thick coat of algae.

He turned and took a moment to kick leaves over his tracks, then, ever so slowly, he lowered himself into the water, taking care not to disrupt the algae. He allowed himself to sink down into the icy depths, then slowly swam to the other side of the pond, where there was a cluster of floating branches laden with a net of moss. He poked his head up beneath the canopy just enough to draw breath, then waited.

Scarcely five minutes passed before a small troop of soldiers reached the end of his trail. They stopped at the edge of the pond, looking around in confusion and conferring quietly among themselves. Their eyes darted past his hiding spot a few times, but between the moss and the dim light, Siegfried remained camouflaged. Finally, after a few minutes of deliberation, they split up, all six of them stalking away in different directions.

Siegfried listened as their crunching footsteps faded into the distance. After a few minutes he cautiously surfaced, shivering violently from the cold. Now behind the soldiers, he could see the paths they had taken through the thick undergrowth, and he traced the one who had gone directly west. Siegfried took care to move quietly, pausing every few seconds to listen for movement. In the stillness of the forest, it was easy to hear the clanking of the heavy plate armor.

After half an hour, Siegfried could hear the telltale metallic sound of the soldier returning from his unsuccessful search. Siegfried ducked behind a tree, waiting patiently until the soldier passed him. Without a moment's hesitation, Siegfried lunged from behind the unsuspecting soldier, knocking him to the soft forest floor. He drew the soldier's dagger from his belt, and in a swift motion, planted it in his neck. The soldier gurgled helplessly as Siegfried removed the knife, but his struggles ceased a few moments later.

Numbly, Siegfried rolled the dead soldier over, frowning when he saw the man was probably even younger than him. There was a look of terror in the red eyes that stared blankly up ahead, but Siegfried brushed his hand over the boy's face, closing his eyelids. He fiddled with the chin strap on the soldier's helmet, but he stood up when he heard the crunch of a twig breaking behind him.

Before Siegfried could turn around, he felt a hot streak of pain shoot up through his chest, and he looked down at the red stalk of metal blossoming from his torso. He grunted deliriously and staggered forward, clutching the wound in his breast as the sword disappeared. He whirled around, leaning heavily on his crutch as his vision spun wildly out of his control.

Captain Sprenger, looking much thinner without his plate armor, held up his bloodied sword, murderous intent lurking in his gaze. The captain looked down at the soldier Siegfried had killed, a flash of regret crossing his face, but then returned his attention to Siegfried. Siegfried wondered how long Sprenger had been following him, but his questions evaporated when Sprenger took a step towards him. He could tell the captain did not intend to bring him back alive.

As Siegfried watched the officer approach, he heard the dull roar of blood rushing through his head. His vision grew dim as he struggled to focus on the encroaching blade, and his knees buckled beneath him. He gritted his teeth and forced his weight onto his legs, ignoring the shooting pain in his shin. If he was going to die, he would at least die standing.

Time seemed to slow as Sprenger brought his sword down on Siegfried, and although his vision was almost completely black, he swayed to the side, swinging in turn with the wooden crutch in his hand. He was surprised when he felt the tension of impact beneath his grip, and Sprenger grunted in pain when he hit the ground. No longer able to see anything, Siegfried moved instinctively towards the sound of Sprenger's labored breathing, easily finding the captain's throat beneath his grip. With blood hemorrhaging from the wound in his chest, he didn't know how long his strength would last. If he was going to die, he would at least take his killer along with him.

A fog settled over Siegfried's mind for a time, and the sensation of Sprenger's throat faded beneath his fingers. The cold despair that had engulfed Siegfried upon seeing the gallows melted away, leaving him calm and serene. Dully, he wondered if this peaceful nothingness was death.

Siegfried blinked in surprise when he felt something icy drip onto his forehead. He looked up, his vision snapping sharply back into focus as he watched the rain filter through the thick foliage overhead. He was sitting with his back against the trunk of one of the forest's stout willows. His entire body was sore, but the sharp pain in his chest was gone. He raised a hand to his wound, looking down in surprise when he didn't feel the open gash beneath his palm. He pulled the neck of his shirt open, and although his chest was still slick with blood, all signs of the wound were gone.

Disoriented, Siegfried stood up, staggering towards the unmoving bodies before him. The young soldier was where he had left him, but he was now joined by Sprenger, whose bloodshot eyes were glazed over. The veins in his neck and face were bulging, and they looked almost black against his unusually pale skin. Worse still, his mouth was open in a permanent fixture of horror. Unable to look at him any longer, Siegfried rolled him over onto his stomach.

He turned his attention to the other soldier, and after looking around to make sure no one else had followed him, he stripped the young man of his armor. He cleaned the blood from the armor with rainwater and rubbed it dry with Sprenger's tunic, then, with some effort, outfitted himself with the Jenseiter disguise.

As he removed his boots, he noticed his broken crutch lying unwanted on the forest floor near Sprenger's body. He paused, surprised to find the persistent ache in his shin that had plagued him since the battle at the southern border was gone. He clawed at the splint that supported it, removing the bandages to reveal an unblemished patch of skin where the cauterized scar had been.

Siegfried stared at his leg for several minutes, wondering if this was all some fever dream that accompanied the final throes of death. The cold rain only continued to patter down on top of him, filling his new helmet with tiny echoes of contact, and after a while, he pulled on the soldier's greaves. The young soldier had carried a mace, which Siegfried tossed aside. Instead, he cleaned the blood from Sprenger's sword and sheathed it at his side.

Now fully equipped, he turned west once and made his way deeper into the forest. His family's estate was only a day's travel east of Eberswalde, but there was nothing left for him there. It would take him weeks to reach Highcastle, but that was okay. His despair had returned, but now it was accompanied by something else — the warm promise of vengeance. The Duchess had ordered the deaths of his father and Heinrich. It didn't matter that she was protected by an entire army of Jenseiters. As far as Siegfried was concerned, he had already died under Sprenger's blade. The least he could do was take the woman who had ordered his death with him.

XXI

S enya could smell the battlefield long before she ever reached it. As soon as she cleared the mountain ridge that separated Castilla from Aesterland, the stink of death was everywhere. She waited at the edge of the forest for nightfall, watching the living sea of crows that blanketed the meadow beyond.

After reaching Alcazar, she'd headed toward Fortizia in the west, hoping to find the Hearthlord there. Though she kept off the road to avoid the Hearthborn, it was easy to get close enough to the odd camp to eavesdrop. Within a few days, she'd learned the Hearthlord was somewhere in Aesterland, in a place called Highcastle.

After that, she'd turned north. It had been easy to avoid contact in Castilla, where each pocket of civilization was insulated by sprawling forests. She knew Aesterland would be different, though. The merchants who visited Alcazar described hundreds of miles of tamed farmland. Without the cover of trees, she would have to rely on darkness.

Honestly, she was more worried about patrolling Aesterkind archers than Hearthborn. At the clinic in Alcazar, she'd heard plenty of stories about them — that they moved like lightning with their leather armor, and how they could put out an eye at a hundred yards. For every soldier who made it down to Alcazar to be healed, there were a dozen more who died along the way. The thought of running into one of them terrified her.

It began to rain, and for some reason, her mind turned to Fabian. She frowned as she pulled her hood up and watched the mist that slowly gathered on the meadow. His family had lived in Alcazar for such a long time that she didn't think of him as Aesterkind, but he had been born there. She closed her eyes, and she could see his gentle smile once more.

The moisture tamped down the smell, and after an hour or so, Senya's stomach settled enough to eat. By dusk, the fog was so thick that she couldn't see more than fifteen feet in any direction, so she climbed to her feet and cautiously ventured forward.

She listened intently for any movement as she wandered into the mist. Although she could no longer see the birds, she could still hear them — their feathers rustling, their soft murmurs, and the clacking of their beaks as they tore off some new morsel. She tried to keep her distance from them, not wanting to think about what they were feeding on, but the further she went, the harder that became.

A few minutes after she left the safety of the forest, she saw the first body. It was lying face down, and the flesh that remained was bloated and purple. A crow sat atop its leather cuirass, and it flicked its gaze up to her as she tried to skirt around it. It cawed rudely at her, and when she stepped back, she felt a hand upon her shoulder.

Panic shot through her spine as she spun around. A scream bubbled up in her throat as she took in the monstrous face that stared back at her, and there was a flurry of wings as the crows around her took flight. She tripped as she scrambled back — the thing in the mist wasn't Hearthborn or Aesterkind — it wasn't even human. Its eyes were hollow sockets, and its mouth was stretched into a silent scream as it reached for her with a skeletal arm.

Without thinking, she ran, oblivious to the horrible cries of the crows all around her. The corpses littered the ground now, and it was all that she could do to avoid stepping on them. The smell was like a miasma, as thick as the fog itself. Her eyes watered from it, but she kept going, desperate to outrun the thing behind her. As she fled, she saw more of them at the edges of her periphery, each one as twisted and mangled as the first.

She didn't know how long she ran, but by the time she charged up a gentle hill, she could no longer catch her breath. Her body was completely drenched with sweat beneath her heavy coat, and her vision was blurry. Her legs gave out at the top of the hill, and she collapsed, gasping for air as she waited for one of the monsters to claim her. At least she wouldn't die drowning in mist — it was clearer up here, and she could even see the faint outline of the moon through the clouds overhead. A little further ahead, there were the charred remains of what had once been an outpost. It didn't look like it would offer much protection, and she could no longer move to reach it, anyway.

A few seconds passed, and then a minute. It was hard to tell with the sound of blood pounding in her temples, but everything seemed quiet. Senya unbuttoned her coat, letting the cool air flood in around her. It took another few minutes for her to recover enough to get back on her feet.

From her vantage point on top of the hill, she could see the sea of fog all around her, but the night was calm and there was no trace of movement. She wondered if there was some reason the creatures couldn't reach her here—maybe they couldn't leave the mist? She heard the idle sounds of the crows again, and to her dismay, they were all around her. She must have run for miles, but she hadn't escaped the battlefield.

Not wanting to go back into the fog, she turned to the ruins of the outpost. She ducked beneath a blackened length of timber and ventured inside. The smell of charcoal was a welcome relief, and the walls seemed sturdy enough to hold what remained of the roof overhead. Senya moved to a dry corner of the room and took off her backpack. She pulled out Father Silas's coat and, even though she was still too warm, draped it over her shoulders.

Little by little, her racing heart slowed as she listened for sounds in the night. She must have slept, because the next thing she knew, beams of sunlight were shining in through the holes in the roof. She squirmed when she saw the outline of a charred hand beneath a pile of rubble, and quickly packed her things.

Judging from the dew on the grass, it was early morning. All that remained of the heavy fog of the previous night were a few stray wisps. She climbed atop the ruin to get a better view, but her heart dropped as she took in the landscape. It had been wrong to call what happened here a battle. The meadow to her south was blanketed with a patchwork of bodies, but to her north, it was even worse. She saw some flecks of shining plate where a Hearthborn had fallen, but overwhelmingly, it was Aesterkind who died here. It had been an absolute massacre.

What had the Aesterkind done to deserve this? As soon as the thought crossed her mind, Senya felt guilty. In the Frostlands, everything had been so simple, but since she'd crossed the ridge, she found herself questioning the Hearthlord's will more and more often. She'd thought her time in isolation had strengthened her faith. She dug her nails into her palms as she scolded herself. The Hearthlord's will wasn't for her to understand. If she returned to him like this, having learned nothing from her trial, what reason would he have to give her a second chance?

She squinted as she searched the carnage for the monsters she'd encountered the previous night, and sure enough, she saw them - upright, twisted forms planted among the bodies. A shiver ran up her spine when she realized how many of them there were — hundreds, at least. One of them was stationed just north of her hill, although it wasn't facing her. She watched it for a long time, waiting for it to turn and notice her, but it never moved. In the daylight, she could make out the ripped leather cuirass around its form. Whatever it was, it had once been an Aesterkind soldier.

It took her a while to work up her courage, but she couldn't stay up here forever. She climbed down and descended the hill, keeping her eyes on the creature. It remained still, and her curiosity got the better of her as she circled around it. She got as close as she dared, inspecting it with a mix of wonder and horror.

Like the first one she'd encountered, this husk's face was frozen in a wail of pain. She could see exposed bone in its face, arms, and legs, but there was also a hard crust of ash where its flesh should have been. Its twisted form was tilted forward, as if it had been running. Senya turned to the others and saw they were all facing the same way—north. They'd been trying to retreat.

The terror that had gripped her the previous night deteriorated into sorrow as she imagined the last moments of this Aesterkind's life. So much fear and suffering, and for what—

She stopped herself. She didn't want to think about it anymore. She pulled her hood up over her head and lowered her gaze. If she just focused on the ground directly ahead of her, she could carve a path around the corpses. She could move forward, and trust this massacre had been in service of the Hearthlord's goal to bring peace to mankind.

XXII

Nell sighed as she looked out of the tower window. The streets of Highcastle were flooded with black-armored soldiers, and they had closed all of the city gates but one. She could see a long line of travelers crowding the southern road that remained open, trickling in through the checkpoint the Jenseiters had established. Even from the palace, she was normally able to hear the vibrant sounds of the city, but ever since her mother surrendered to the Imperator and opened the gates, everything had become muted.

She lingered by the window, reluctant to turn away from the beauty of the city. Highcastle was ancient, built by the enlightened queens of the past. Though their construction methods had been lost to history, the smooth stone edifices of their mastery continued to stand a thousand years after they disappeared. The palace was built upon the central hill, and it was surrounded by concentric circles of neatly organized stone residences and market squares. Geothermal springs from beneath the earth flowed through aqueducts, which provided most of the citizens with a ready supply of hot water. The entire city was a marvel of engineering.

She forced herself to turn away and made her way to one of the many bookshelves that lined the stone walls of the palace library. Even before the occupation, she'd spent most of her time here, but now it was one of the few places left where she could get away from the Jenseiters. She pulled out a dusty tome from one of the lower shelves and heaved it onto her reading table.

She shifted some of the other books that littered the table to make room for her new find. Her tutors were among the courtiers who'd been driven out of the castle since the occupation, so she'd been reading what she pleased for the first time in ages. She'd taken to the histories of Athelstan, a courtier of Queen Oriane the Great four hundred years ago. His writings concerned the mundane accounts of the ancient court, but they were notable for being the oldest surviving documents in the grand library.

Even the exhaustive list of new taxes the queen had levied could be interesting, though. Professor Durand, her history tutor, had taught her to read between the lines of such accounts. Athelstan's writings of his time at court contained a classic example; fifteen years of Athelstan's accounts showed that taxes were stable, but then, they suddenly increased threefold. The subtext was clear — there had been some kind of cataclysm that had left the country nearly bankrupt.

Today, Nell was more interested in one of Athelstan's lesser writings that documented his travels after his retirement. Athelstan had first ventured south to Castilla, then back through Aesterland and the ravaged Black Forest, before turning east into the Neseveen Desert. He wrote of the ancient city-state of Talashan, then the richest city on the continent, and finally made his way to Reese in the south. His journey ended there, as Norogard had been closed to foreigners at the time.

Four hundred years later, Castilla and Aesterland remained, and Norogard had become a sprawling empire in the east, ceding the territory that had once belonged to Talashan and Reese. Nell had been sure that if she saw a full-fledged war in her lifetime, it would be Aesterland defending itself against Nord expansion. She frowned as she flipped through the account, not really reading it but comforted by the crisp texture of the pages.

Aesterland had survived the cataclysm that had occurred in Athelstan's lifetime, and centuries later, all that remained of it was an account of its effect on taxes. Nell drew some solace from the thought that Aesterland would make it through this new disaster, and maybe when people who lived hundreds of years after her read her memoirs, they would see it as only an interesting side note of Aesterland's illustrious history.

She froze when the library door creaked open behind her. "Princess," a familiar voice called, and she looked up to see Matilda, one of her mother's ladies-in-waiting, waiting at the end of an aisle of bookshelves. "The Queen has summoned you to the council chamber."

With a last look at the book, Nell stood up and followed Matilda out the library door. She did not look up to acknowledge the two soldiers who fell in behind her as she descended the spiral staircase that led down the tower, used to their constant shadow by now. Once she reached the bottom of the stairs, she continued through the grand corridors of the castle, keeping her gaze on the floor to avoid the unnerving red eyes of the Jenseiter courtiers. After a few minutes, she reached the hallway that housed the council chamber, where her father waited beside the soldiers posted at the door.

Nell met his gaze for a moment, but he looked away, shame lingering in his eyes. The once steady King Consort had become more and more withdrawn over the last couple of weeks, but this was not a good sign. Nell set her jaw as she turned to the door, which was flanked by two soldiers wearing the full regalia of Jenseiter plate armor. When they'd first entered the city, she couldn't help but be impressed by their technology. It was no wonder her mother's armies had fallen so easily to these invaders — their steel was stronger and lighter than Castellano iron. The arrows of Aesterland's famed bowmen could do no more damage to them than a child throwing rocks.

They opened the door, but Nell paused before she went through, distracted by a third guard. The soldier looked much thinner than the others, although part of it was the lighter chainmail. It took Nell a few moments to realize the soldier was a woman, but the strangest thing about her was the blue gaze that peered from behind her helmet. She was the first Reinbann Nell had seen in person.

Nell gathered herself and walked through the door into the council chamber. She squinted against the dim light of the chamber, waiting for a moment for her vision to return before stepping forward into the room. She heard the door shut behind her, but she kept her eyes forward.

Queen Helene was seated at the head of the table, looking somehow older and frailer without her crown. A map was laid out across the table, although Nell wasn't able to see much of it from her angle. A woman Nell hadn't seen before sat halfway down the long table. She'd looked up when Nell entered, and now her single piercing eye was focused intently on her. She was wearing a black dress uniform inlaid with gold threads, and the white Feracht eagle was stitched onto the breast of her stiff jacket. An ornate eyepatch covered her right eye, and a pale scar adorned the temple of her otherwise unblemished face.

"Eleanor, I don't believe you have met Her Illustrious Highness, Duchess Diana Feracht," Queen Helene said, gesturing to the woman. "She just arrived this morning."

Nell frowned as she turned her gaze back to the Duchess, but she managed a small curtsy all the same. A thin smile rose to the woman's lips. Nell noticed a shadow move in the darkness behind the queen, and she took an uncertain step back when the Imperator emerged from the back of the chamber. She had only been in the same room with the imposing man a few times, but whenever she was, she was always overcome with an oppressive feeling of suffocation.

Even in the castle surrounded by his soldiers, he was equipped with a full set of Jenseiter armor and carried a long sword at his side. Instead of a helmet, a golden crown rested on his brow, which was inlaid with a large diamond at its center. He was older than Diana, and his face bore deep scars around his eyes. As he approached the table, Nell noticed for the first time that his crimson eyes didn't exactly match each other. One was bright and piercing like Diana's, but the other was a deeper shade of red. All of the other red-eyed Jenseiters she had encountered were blonde like Diana, but the Imperator's hair was mostly black, although it was peppered with prominent streaks of gray.

Nell forced her attention back to her mother, and she was surprised to find that her voice sounded weak as she asked, "Why have you summoned me, Mother?"

Queen Helene reached for a goblet of wine and took a deep draught of it. She took a breath and began, "The Imperator and I have finalized the terms of our alliance." Nell felt a nerve twitch as she heard the euphemism, but she knew what it really meant. "To mark the occasion, we have agreed that a wedding is appropriate."

Nell's mouth suddenly went very dry as she asked, "Whose wedding?"

"Your wedding, Eleanor," Queen Helene continued. "You are to marry an esteemed noble from Jenseits, Duke Bastian von Weyler. The Imperator and I believe this union will cement the peace between Jenseits and Aesterland."

"Indeed," the Imperator said, approaching the table. "You will thank my granddaughter for finding such a suitable match for you, Princess."

A faint look of confusion passed Nell's face as she glanced between the Imperator and the Duchess. The former looked to be in his fifties, while the Duchess was probably in her early thirties. She looked like she could have been his daughter, not his granddaughter.

Nell's attention was drawn back to the Imperator when he continued, "You will not go to the altar alone, Princess. It is only natural to celebrate our alliance with a match of our own. Diana will join you to wed one of the proud sons of this land."

For a solitary moment, Nell could see a look of distress pass over the Duchess, and when she noticed her mother's surprised face, it was clear that it was the first time she was hearing this information, as well. The queen smiled nervously as she responded, "That is wonderful to hear. I'm sure this will serve to bring our countries ever closer. Eleanor, why don't you go find your father and tell him the happy news?"

"Yes, Mother," Nell responded automatically. She glanced back at Diana, who was now staring blankly ahead, the emotion drained from her pale face. With another curtsy, Nell turned, trying to retain control of her breathing as she exited the room.

She clawed at her throat as soon as the doors closed behind her, gasping for breath. Blood rushed to her cheeks as she processed the news, and she felt her father's bony hands fall over her shoulders. Nell allowed herself to be led away, and the march through the corridors to her bedroom was a muddled haze.

Nell broke away from her father and sank onto her bed. He sat down next to her and placed a comforting hand on her knee. "Have you met him?" Nell asked numbly.

"No," he replied. "From what I understand, he is the governor of some territory in Jenseits. He will need to make arrangements for his replacement before he joins us here."

"We will live here, then?"

"Your mother sacrificed much so that a Pendergast could remain on the throne."

Nell felt a streak of fury course through her at the hypocrisy, and she muttered, "If Mother hadn't surrendered, she would still be on the throne."

Nell looked up when he gently clasped her hands in his own. "It was not easy for your mother to do what she did. Try to understand, Nell."

"We could have escaped," Nell protested. She couldn't remember the last time she had argued with her father, and she was surprised to find how weak the convictions she'd harbored since the surrender sounded now that she gave them a voice. Desperately, she said, "We could have taken the tunnels—"

"We could have," he allowed. "You, me, your mother, and even some of the servants — we could have fled into the wilderness. We could have abandoned Aesterland and left it at the mercy of these brutes." Nell looked away, but her father touched her cheek, regaining her attention. "We — you — must be an example for our people to look up to. When they see you accept our new arrangement, they will accept it as well. This is how Aesterland will survive."

XXIII

Siegfried looked up at the massive stone archway as he walked beneath it, raising his hand to his helmet to keep it securely in place. The towering stone walls that surrounded Highcastle had become visible two days ago, and now that Siegfried was up close, they seemed impossibly high. He frowned as he returned his attention to the back of the soldier marching in front of him—the walls had done little good after the queen had decided to open the gates to the invaders.

It had been surprisingly easy for him to infiltrate the Jenseiter platoons he'd traveled with to the capital. After he'd found the crowded road that cut through the Black Forest, he had joined the nearest group of soldiers heading west. As long as he kept his helmet on, he was able to blend in.

Posing as a messenger, he'd moved between platoons for the last three weeks, never staying with one long enough to raise suspicion. Unfettered by his injuries, he easily covered fifteen miles a day, nearly twice the distance most units could manage with their slow supply carts. He usually ate his meals with separate squads, and he always broke away into the countryside to sleep. He had only been with the squad he passed into the city with for a few hours, and as soon as they cleared the checkpoint at the gates and entered the crowded streets of the capital, he slipped out of the formation.

The highway passed through a few prominent interior cities, but Siegfried hadn't ever seen anything like the capital. The square adjacent to the gates was dominated by a sprawling grid of merchant stalls, and as Siegfried walked between the crowded rows, he estimated there must have been hundreds of them. Jenseiter units patrolled the stalls, but there were far more Aesterkind going about their business as usual. Siegfried scowled as he passed two civilians haggling over the price of a bushel of wheat, wondering what the army at the southern border had even fought for.

The first thing he noticed about the city was its stench. The sides of the square and the crevices between the stalls were filled with garbage. The low drone of thousands of flies was ever present beneath the chatter of conversation. Although it was a cool winter day, the market was warm with the heat of so many bodies. It didn't take long for Siegfried to grow nauseous, so he pushed his way to the edge of the crowd.

He stopped when he reached the end of the market, looking up at the terraces of stone that sprawled out before him. He made his way up a sloping road, surveying the tidy residences to either side of him. The structures were obviously ancient—every edge had been eroded into a smooth surface. Although the street was still filthy, the smell wasn't so bad without the suffocating heat. Ahead of him, he could see the palace spires in the distance rising from behind another massive wall.

The road was less crowded than the square had been, allowing him to wander freely. Although it had been more than a year since he had written to his sister, he knew that she and her husband lived just up the hill from a particular tavern, the Rosethorn Inn. According to her, her lush of a husband spent as many nights there as he did at court. Back then, the Feracht name hadn't meant much outside of military circles, and he had been one of the few nobles willing to accept her without a dowry.

It didn't take Siegfried long to locate the tavern — the merchants seemed more than eager to give him directions. Once he reached it, he asked the bartender inside after David Fontaine, Bridget's husband. At first, the bartender denied knowing him, but after Siegfried placed a hand on his sword, his memories resurfaced.

Siegfried left in high spirits and turned into the small market square outside the tavern. He found the narrow staircase hewn into an alleyway that led up toward Bridget's townhouse and began trekking up the steep incline.

The staircase ended at a flat avenue, which was markedly cleaner than the street below. There were a few more broad terraces carved into the hills that separated Bridget's street from the palace district, each one packed with structures even grander than the last. Siegfried wandered up the cobblestone road until he found the residence the bartender had described. The townhouses in this section of Highcastle were fairly uniform, but the red door and dwarf willows growing in its garden set Bridget's house apart from the others.

Siegfried opened the gate and approached the door. He had to knock twice before an elderly butler opened the door a crack. The man squinted suspiciously at Siegfried and asked, "How can I help you?"

"I'm here to see Bridget," Siegfried said.

"The mistress is not in at the moment," the butler replied stuffily. "May I take a message?"

Siegfried frowned, but then he saw movement behind the butler. "Tell her it's Siegfried," he said impatiently.

The butler closed the door, leaving Siegfried to wait awkwardly at the threshold for a few seconds. He felt a chill run up his spine, and he suddenly got the distinct impression he was being watched. He glanced nervously over his shoulder, but the street behind him was totally empty. Before he had time to fret, the door swung open and his older sister threw her arms around him.

He tensed slightly as he looked down at her — the last time he'd seen her, she had been taller than him. She swept him inside, leaving the butler to close the door behind them. "I can't believe it's really you, Ziggy!" she exclaimed, tears of joy in her eyes. An involuntary scowl rose to Siegfried's lips at the pet name. "I haven't heard from you in ages! What happened to you? Why are you wearing Jenseiter armor?"

Siegfried put his hand on his sister's shoulder, stopping her mania for a moment. He looked at her seriously and said, "Father and Heinrich are dead."

Her ecstatic grin fell by degrees as her face grew pale. "You're joking, right?" she asked. Siegfried shook his head, and Bridget began to tremble. "What do you mean? How could that be?"

"Let's sit down," Siegfried suggested, and Bridget silently led him into the drawing room. Siegfried helped her sink into a sofa, then sat across from her in a stiff chair. He took off his helmet and rested it in his lap, fidgeting uncomfortably when he saw the tears streaking down Bridget's cheeks. He glanced at the butler, who was staring daggers at him from the doorway, and he ordered, "Bring us some tea."

Once the servant left, Siegfried turned back to Bridget and explained, "I was captured after the battle at the southeastern border. The Jenseiters took me up to Eberswalde. They were there, up on the gallows. I would have been executed, too, if I hadn't escaped."

"Why?" Bridget whimpered as she wiped the tears from her eyes.

Siegfried frowned at the question. "The Jenseiters carry the Feracht sigil. It was like the Duchess was making an example out of Father and Heinrich. They had plaques hung around their necks that said 'pretender'."

"Pretender to what?" Bridget asked. "Feracht is a dead house. No one around here has ever heard of it before."

"I'm not sure," he said honestly. "Has there been any word from Berthold?" When Bridget shook her head, he grimaced and said, "I heard the battle at the southwestern pass was even more of a massacre than the one in the east. He probably didn't make it, either."

"David was at the southwestern border, too," Bridget said, her voice hollow from grief. "It's been weeks since his last letter. I heard the Jenseiters were taking prisoners, so I was waiting for a ransom letter, but now…" Her voice trailed off, and Siegfried looked down at his helmet. He'd seen plenty of prisoners of war in the east, but the further west he'd gone, the fewer he'd encountered. It seemed the Imperator's campaign had been much more lethal than the Duchess's.

The butler returned, balancing a ceramic teapot and two ornate cups on a silver tray. He put the tray down on the low table and poured tea for Bridget. Her hands shook slightly when she accepted the cup, but the drink helped settle her nerves a bit. Once the butler had served Siegfried, Bridget waved him away, and he left them alone.

Siegfried watched his sister over the steaming cup in silence, letting her process the news. By the time she had finished, her tears had dried, and her hands were steady when she replaced her cup on the silver tray. "We have to kill the Duchess," she said, her voice now firm and sure.

A smile crossed Siegfried's lips. Bridget was dressed in the finery of an Aesterkind noblewoman, but she was still a Feracht at heart. In her eyes, he could see the same burning desire for vengeance that had fueled him in his odyssey across the country.

He patted the sword sheathed at his side and said, "Help me get close to her. She's in the castle, right? Do you know anyone who could smuggle me in?"

"Maybe," Bridget said, her eyes wandering up to the ceiling as she thought. "I don't know if you heard about the wedding next week." Siegfried nodded — the Jenseiter camps had been abuzz with the news that their Duchess was going to be wed to an Aesterkind. Bridget smiled in excitement and continued, "The palace will be packed with nobles. I may be able to get an invitation. You could sneak in then, and hide until—"

"I'm not going to hide," Siegfried interrupted. "I want the whole world to see what happens when you cross our family."

Bridget bit her lip. "You'll die, Ziggy," she said softly.

Siegfried leveled his gaze on her seriously and said, "If you help me, you will probably be executed, too. Even if you don't help me, Highcastle won't be safe for you anymore. You can still run if you want."

Bridget frowned, but the resolute expression on her face did not change. "I'm not letting you do this alone, little brother," she said with a reassuring smile. Siegfried was surprised at the sense of relief that fluttered through him. He had been on his own for so long that he'd forgotten what it was like to have someone he could trust. He knew that he was consigning both of them to death, but the Jenseiters had already taken everything from them. The Ferachts of Aesterland had faded into an obscure, desolate house over the centuries, but together, they could end their line with a flourish the Aesterkind would never forget.

XXIV

Despite the brisk chill of the winter morning, Siegfried felt uncomfortably hot beneath his heavy armor once he finished climbing the hill to the Promenade District. He paused near a public fountain to catch his breath and take in the lavish architecture around him. This district made Bridget's neighborhood look like a shantytown. The mansions here were more like sculptures than houses, and everywhere Siegfried looked, there were depictions of the ancient monarchs and heroes of Aesterland.

Likewise, the citizens on the streets were a class above those below. The women wore silk dresses and expensive white fox furs on their shoulders. Their hair was styled fashionably high, and most of them were weighed down by pounds of jewelry. The noblemen were a bit more understated in their dress, but Siegfried still caught the odd diamond pendant among them.

Siegfried cupped his hand in the water and took a sip, not surprised when he found that it, too, was crisper than the water from the fountains below. He glanced back at the high castle walls and tried to imagine what it must be like in the palace. He smiled — he knew he wouldn't have to wait much longer to find out.

After he'd had his first hot bath in months, he and Bridget had conspired over an excellent dinner. They'd agreed Bridget would try to make contact with her friend in the palace, one of Queen Helene's ladies-in-waiting, while Siegfried scoped the exterior. He took another sip of water and looked at the heavily guarded gatehouse on the other side of the square, where a neat line of nobles was waiting to be inspected by Jenseiter soldiers. He hadn't expected to be able to infiltrate through the Grand Entrance. There were other gatehouses along the castle walls that were used for deliveries or restricted to soldiers.

For the second time that morning, Siegfried got the creeping feeling on the back of his neck that he was being watched. He nonchalantly turned from the fountain, surveying the square around him, but no one paid him any mind. He flicked his eyes up when he caught a glimpse of movement from above, but he only saw a flash of white among the statues lining the roof of the building behind him. He frowned as he scanned the skyline, but there was no longer anything there.

After a few more seconds, Siegfried turned away and made his way east. His plan for today was to circumnavigate the miles of walls and identify all of the entrances. Tomorrow, he could come back to observe the ones that were promising. It would be ideal if he could find a way into the castle without involving Bridget. Then, she could still escape Highcastle before the assassination and maybe make a new life for herself somewhere. With her black hair, she could pass as a Castellano refugee in a remote village.

As he walked, he found himself inspecting the network of narrow alleys that separated the houses. Within them, there were chutes the servants could use to dispose of their refuse, where jets from the aqueduct washed the garbage down to the lower districts. He found himself pondering whether they could prove useful afterwards, but he quickly shut down this line of conjecture. It was stupid to think there would be an afterwards. There was no way the Jenseiters would just let him leave after he killed their Duchess. He knew he needed to harden his resolve, both for himself and Bridget. If he spent too much time worrying about her, he could waste the one opportunity he was going to get.

"Halt!" Siegfried looked up in surprise as the order cut through his thoughts, cursing under his breath when he saw a unit of three patrolling Jenseiters making their way toward him. He quickly stood at attention and saluted the approaching officer, surreptitiously ensuring his helmet was still in place and covering his dark hair. He relaxed slightly when he confirmed it was, but the officer's look of disdain did not change.

The officer stopped a few feet in front of Siegfried, and the other members of the patrol fell into a neat line behind him. They wore the same black plate armor as Siegfried, but he noticed theirs was decorated with a golden trim, and the style of their helmets was more ornate than his own. He frowned — on the road, the Jenseiter armor had all seemed the same, but he should have realized there would be differences among the top echelon of their army.

"You need clearance to be up here," the officer said matter-of-factly. "Let me see your papers."

Siegfried pretended to look through the small satchel latched at his belt as his mind raced. After a few moments, he feigned surprise and said, "I seem to have misplaced them…"

The officer scowled. "What outfit are you with?"

"The Reinbacher Company," Siegfried said, giving the name of the last unit he had traveled with on the way to Highcastle.

"You don't sound like you're from Reinbach," the officer observed, his suspicion growing. "You will have to come with us." The officer turned to order one of his subordinates to apprehend him, giving Siegfried the moment he needed to dart away.

While the plate armor provided unparalleled protection, running in it was awkward. Nobles going about their business stopped to watch as he clanked away from the patrol. He turned into one of the alleyways he had spotted earlier, prepared to throw himself down one of the garbage chutes to escape, but to his horror, his frame was too bulky with the heavy armor to fit.

Siegfried cursed when he turned around to see the patrol blocking the entrance of the alleyway. He had done them the favor of cornering himself. He drew his weapon, causing the soldiers to do the same. The alleyway was fairly narrow — probably only six feet wide. The soldiers wouldn't be able to come at him all at once.

He allowed the officer to approach him and blocked his first swing, getting used to the timing of the man's movements. After two more strikes, he had a good read on him, and he parried the next attack. The officer grunted when Siegfried stuck his sword into his exposed armpit, and he threw him to the side while he waited for the next soldier to attack.

His next opponent was larger and slower, but also much more wary after seeing how easily Siegfried had dispatched the officer. He wielded a hammer, and he used his size to press Siegfried back into the end of the alley. Siegfried allowed his back to hit the wall and waited for the soldier to raise his weapon before darting forward, drawing in too close for the man to maneuver. He drew his knife with his off hand and plunged it into the man's throat, leaving him for dead as he rushed at his final opponent.

Siegfried threw himself to the right as a javelin soared past him. As the third soldier prepared another throw, he threw his knife, which connected with the soldier's palm. The soldier looked at his hand in shock, giving Siegfried plenty of time to cover the rest of the distance between them. He cut him down with a clean stroke of his blade.

He panted for breath beneath the heavy armor, trembling from the sudden surge of adrenaline. He couldn't believe how careless he'd been. It was lucky his opponents had been so weak. If it had been a Reinbann squad instead, he doubted he would be walking away from the debacle unscathed. He took off his helmet to wipe the sweat away from his forehead and drew in deep mouthfuls of the pungent air.

He grunted when a sudden sharp pain blossomed in his thigh. He looked down at the javelin running through him and turned furiously to see the officer at the end of the alley, who had somehow stood up despite the torrent of blood gushing out of his armor. Blinded with rage, Siegfried tore the javelin out of his leg and limped over to the dying man.

He grabbed the officer's throat and squeezed, trying to replicate the sensation he'd felt while fighting Sprenger near Eberswalde. He waited for a minute as the man twitched beneath his grip, but nothing happened. Eventually, he dropped the corpse in disgust and turned to leave. His vision swayed dangerously as he took a pained step forward, and when he looked down, his leg was completely drenched in blood.

Siegfried sank to the slimy floor next to the garbage chute and pressed his hands against the wound in an attempt to stop the bleeding. He looked up dully when he heard a soft thump near him. There was a girl there, but one look was enough to convince Siegfried she was a hallucination. She didn't look like anyone Siegfried had ever seen before — her long, unkempt hair was bone white, and her skin was a deep shade of bronze. She wore a ragged conglomeration of furs and hides. Siegfried hadn't known hallucinations could stink, but this one overpowered even the pungent stench of the garbage chute.

He rested his head against the grimy wall behind him as a sinking exhaustion spread over him. His arms fell to his side as his vision slid out of focus. He watched the hazy form of the girl through half-lidded eyes as she knelt beside him and placed her hands on his wound. He grimaced as he turned his gaze upwards to the cold winter sky, ignoring his hallucination as he ruminated on his stupidity. What had the point of surviving Eberswalde even been? He had trekked across the entire country, for what? Just to die in some filthy alley? He clenched his fists, furious with himself.

As his anger broiled, some of the warmth returned to his body, creeping slowly from his core back into his limbs. He was surprised when his vision sharpened once more, and a few minutes later, he felt strong enough to sit up properly. To his surprise, the girl was still there, and she looked up at him uncertainly when he grasped her wrist. He moved her hand away from his thigh, looking down in amazement at the pale scar that remained where his wound had been. Now that his mind had cleared some, he could feel a glowing sense of power emanating from her — similar to what he felt when Nichts and Kepler had used their abilities. She hadn't cauterized his wound though; she had repaired it.

He looked down at the girl's hand, surprised to see the familiar shape of the Feracht eagle etched onto the back of it. He released his grip on her wrist when she pulled away. She scrambled to her feet and backed away a few paces, looking from her wrist back to him, her expression a complex mix of terror and hope. Finally, she asked, "Are you the Hearthlord?"

Siegfried couldn't suppress the derisive scowl that crossed his lips, and the girl retreated another step. He braced himself against the wall behind him and gingerly stood up, testing to see if his leg would accept his weight. It felt as strong as ever. His expression softened when he looked back at the girl, and he said, "No. My name is Siegfried." The girl's eyes fell to the ground in disappointment. His growing curiosity got the better of him, and he asked, "Why would you ask that?"

"You look like him," she said quietly. "It's more than that, though." She struggled to put her thoughts into words for a few moments, before she finally gave up and finished lamely, "You feel like him."

Siegfried frowned, not sure what she meant by that. He was about to ask the girl her name when she jumped up to grab the cracked edifice of the building behind her. He watched dumbly as she scaled the twenty feet to the roof, making it look as easy as climbing a flight of stairs. She glanced over the edge at him, and when the sunlight met her hair, he realized she must have been the one who had been stalking him since he'd arrived in the city. Before he could stop her, she was gone, leaving him alone in the alley with the corpses.

Unnerved by the bizarre encounter, Siegfried quickly jammed his helmet back onto his head. He wiped off as much blood as he could from his greaves, then slipped out of the alleyway back onto the street. A few of the nobles who had witnessed the chase were lingering, but they dispersed quickly when he looked their way. After checking to make sure no more patrols were within view, Siegfried retreated the way he'd come. He took the first proper staircase he found, but his heart did not stop racing until he was well within the lower districts.

XXV

"It's been too long!" Matilda exclaimed as she clasped Bridget's hands. The smile that spread over her face was infectious, and Bridget felt some of the twisting anxiety in her stomach ease as she mirrored her friend. Matilda swept Bridget to the side of the spacious hallway as two Jenseiter soldiers passed by, and Bridget quickly ducked her head, hiding her face behind her cloak. Matilda had offered to take the heavy garment when she'd entered the warm castle, but Bridget had declined, and now she was sweating beneath it.

Matilda didn't do much to conceal her scowl of contempt after the soldiers had passed. She took a moment to compose herself, and her smile returned as she offered, "Let's go up to my suite. It's hard to get away from those brutes anywhere else."

Bridget nodded, and she followed Matilda through the complex web of corridors to a spiral staircase, which led up to the royal apartments. Matilda chattered away the entire time, bemoaning the occupation of the Jenseiters and how difficult it had been to memorize a new set of noble families. Bridget only laughed at the odd joke, doing her best to keep her head down and avoid meeting the red gazes of the soldiers or nobles they passed along the way. Earlier that morning, Siegfried had impressed upon her the absolute necessity that she not be discovered. While none of the Jenseiters had given her so much as a second glance so far, she'd underestimated the stress of being so close to them.

She'd been barely paying attention to Matilda's prattle when her friend looked back at her expectedly, apparently waiting for some kind of an answer. Bridget smiled nervously and admitted, "Sorry, I got distracted. What did you say?"

Matilda rolled her eyes and said, "I hope you don't mind that I invited Berthold to tea, as well. When you didn't mention him in your letter, I wasn't sure if something had happened between the two of you."

Bridget stared at her blankly, sure she had misheard. Finally, she asked, "Berthold, my brother?"

"Yes, your brother, soon-to-be Duke," Matilda said impatiently. Bridget swayed unsteadily backward, causing Matilda to catch her arm in concern. "Are you all right?"

"Sorry," Bridget said, trying to regain her composure. "I just haven't eaten anything today. Of course, it's fine. Let's keep going."

Matilda looked uncertain, but after Bridget forced a smile onto her lips, she shrugged and they continued along the hall, past a set of grand mahogany doors guarded by two burly soldiers. Bridget was glad when they kept going past them and turned a corner down a smaller hallway. She paused when she saw the tall man waiting outside of Matilda's apartment, trembling with relief when Berthold looked her way.

She broke away from Matilda and rushed towards him, throwing her arms around his waist. Unlike Ziggy, he actually reciprocated her hug, and she couldn't hold back the tears that ran down her cheeks as he pressed her head into his chest. Matilda hung back awkwardly, taken off guard by the emotional family reunion.

Berthold shifted slightly as he looked down the hall, and he suggested, "Let's go inside."

Matilda unlocked the door and let them in. Bridget disengaged for long enough to remove her heavy cloak, but then she threw herself back into her older brother's arms. "I thought you were dead," she cried. "Why didn't you send word?"

Berthold stiffened at the question. Bridget took a step back from him, seeing him properly for the first time now the initial shock of emotion had passed. It had been four years since he'd last been in Highcastle, when he'd been promoted to the commander of the Feracht Corps. His face was more gaunt now, and a simple eyepatch covered his left eye. He wore an unusual black military uniform, and her eyes lingered on the white Feracht insignia emblazoned on his chest. How could he show their family crest so openly, while Siegfried had warned her to hide it?

"I'm sorry, Matilda," Berthold said, turning his gentle gaze to her, "but could you give my sister and me some privacy?"

"What?" Matilda asked, taken aback.

"You can't tell anyone she was here," Berthold continued. "Please. This won't take long."

Incensed, Matilda performed an exaggerated curtsy. "Yes, Your Excellency," she said ruefully, then stormed out of her apartment and back into the hallway.

Once she'd left, Bridget asked, "She said you were soon to be a duke?"

"Duke Consort," Berthold corrected, rubbing his temple idly. "I'm going to marry Diana Feracht in a few days."

"The Jenseiter Duchess?" Bridget asked in disbelief. "What do you mean? Don't you know what she did to Father and Heinrich?"

"I know," Berthold said, his shoulders slumping. "I haven't heard anything from Siegfried, either. She may have killed him, too." He paused to collect himself, then said, "There wasn't a safe way to contact you, but you need to go into hiding. If she finds out about you, I may not be able to protect you."

"How could you marry her?" Bridget asked, the pitch of her voice rising uncontrollably as she shook with rage. Berthold placed his hand on Bridget's shoulder to calm her, but she slapped it away immediately. "You're betraying your own country, Berthold! Your own family!"

"This is the only way for our family to survive," Berthold said, his voice calm despite her accusations. "The Jenseiters are too strong. The Imperator wiped out my entire division by himself, and their armies cut through ours like we were nothing. We can't fight them. Unless we fall in line, we'll be annihilated."

"I don't understand," Bridget said, unable to believe her brother's cowardice. "Why you? Why would they kill everyone else and leave you?"

"The Imperator is our ancestor, too," Berthold explained. Bridget scoffed, but he held up his hands and said, "He's from another time, from before the cataclysms. He was asleep for centuries, but Diana reawakened him. He said he wants to restore our house to its former glory." He frowned and continued, "I think Diana was trying to eliminate us to prevent any other claims to the throne, but she couldn't get to me. Trust me, marrying me is the last thing she wants to do."

"You're a coward," Bridget seethed.

Berthold's calm demeanor finally cracked under the accusation, and he asked, "Why should we sacrifice ourselves for the Aesterkind? Do you know the Ferachts used to rule this nation before the Pendergasts?"

"You're disgusting!" Bridget screamed, no longer even wanting to look at him.

Berthold clenched his fists, but he withheld any further comment. For a tense minute, they were both silent. Finally, when Berthold spoke again, he had regained his calm timbre. "You don't have to agree with me, Bridget, but you do need to get out of the city. Go as far into the countryside as you can. Once this whole situation has stabilized, I will find you. Just be patient."

Bridget didn't say anything, but she drew away when Berthold stepped forward to give her one last hug. He dropped his gaze and, without another word, left the apartment. She collapsed onto a chair, and before she knew it, she was sobbing with a strange mixture of fury and despair. The emotion poured out of her until she couldn't breathe, and as she gasped for air, her resolve slowly reformed, harder and sharper than it had been before.

She'd been taken off guard by Berthold's re-emergence, but at the end of the day, what did it really change? He had chosen his path, just as she and Siegfried had chosen their own.

XXVI

Senya lingered in front of the bakery, swallowing when her mouth began to water. The smell of fresh bread was intoxicating. Since she'd first discovered the establishment, she'd made a point to come this way every day just to stare at the loaves beyond the threshold. It wasn't that she lacked for food in the city—rats and pigeons were easy enough to catch—but the only thing she dreamed about anymore was biting into a fresh roll.

She took a step back when a burly Aesterkind man in an apron emerged in the doorway, blocking her view. "Got any coin today, girl?" he asked impatiently. When she shook her head, he gestured to a group of Hearthborn patrolling a little ways up the street, and warned, "Better get lost, then."

Senya scurried away into the throng of people crowding the lower market. She pressed through the steady flow of Aesterkind towards the sewer, where she dropped down into the muck. Rats scurried out of her path as she made her way through the passages that ran beneath the streets of Highcastle. Every now and then, there was a burst of neon green mold to light the way, but otherwise, the tunnels were completely dark.

The sewer steadily tilted downward, until finally, it opened into a massive cavern beneath the heart of the city. In its center, there was a great pit, so deep and dark that Senya didn't dare get close enough to look inside. A few times a day, it erupted with steam, scalding anyone who happened to be passing nearby. This was where all of the refuse of the city ended up, including the refugees who'd been driven north by the Hearthborn invasion. Every inch of ground that wasn't slick with sewage had been staked for a ramshackle hovel.

Most of the refugees would be out now, trying to scavenge food from the districts above, but still, the cavern echoed with the moans of the sick and dying. Disease was rampant in the shantytown. Some of the ill burned with fever, others developed weeping boils all over their bodies, and still others were slowly consumed by the same glowing green mold that lit the passageways.

There had been fights, too — refugees accusing each other of encroaching on their territories or stealing what little belongings they hoarded. Once, a ragged man had pushed another into the pit, and the cavern had gone completely quiet for a few moments as his screams echoed from the abyss.

The cistern was dismal, but it was also the only place these people could go. The public houses in the city above were filled to bursting, and most of the refugees didn't have enough money to afford them, anyway. The Hearthborn patrolled the streets, and anyone caught sleeping in the street was arrested and taken away, somewhere outside the city. The only mold-infested refugee Senya had seen above had been executed on the spot.

In Alcazar, when pilgrims came to pray at the altar, the congregation hosted them in their own houses — hospitality was a core pillar of the Hearthlord's teachings, after all. It made Senya sick to think about how many people the nobles in the upper districts could shelter in their mansions. Instead, they let these people suffer in the filth. That wasn't even mentioning the palace, if the Hearthlord just opened the gates—

Senya shook her head, dismissing the thought. It had been a few weeks now since she'd entered the city, clinging to the underside of a supply wagon. At first, she'd been elated that her long journey to Highcastle was complete. The Hearthlord's divine presence radiated from beyond the high, smooth walls that protected the palace. He was so close, and yet those walls had proven to be nigh impenetrable.

They soared stories above any of the nearby buildings, and she hadn't been able to find a single section with crevices she could climb. The gatehouses were well-guarded, too — all of the carts that went in were thoroughly inspected, rendering her previous tactic useless. When she first discovered the sewers, she'd hoped they might provide an entrance, but every time she thought she was getting close, she was met with a locked grate. It was frustrating, but she reminded herself to be patient. Even if she couldn't find a way in, the Hearthlord would eventually come out, and then she would finally be able to present herself to him.

She carefully made her way through the maze of shacks to the far end of the cavern, where she'd managed to find a shelf in the natural cave wall fifteen feet above the cistern. She climbed up into her pocket and took off her coat. It had deteriorated more in the three months she'd been in Aesterland than the entire time she'd spent south of the Icetooth Ridge. Between the cold rains, her treks through the sewers, and the humidity of the cistern, the once lush fur was now a matted tangle, and that was where it wasn't completely threadbare. Her boots and tunic had fared little better — everything was falling apart from the damp conditions. Still, she was always hot in the city, even after she'd ripped out the fox furs she'd lined her coat with.

She paused as her gaze fell upon the white pelts stacked beside her pack. How had she not thought of this before? Trappers in Alcazar could live an entire season off just one rare arctic fox pelt, and she had four. Unlike her coat, they had remained fairly dry through her travels, and with a little cleaning, they would look as new as the day she'd skinned them.

Her mind raced with what she could do with a few shillings. She could feast on bread for a week, maybe even afford a new pair of boots. With a happy heart, she shrugged her coat back on and shoved the furs into her pack. She paused to choke down a few strips of the charred pigeon she'd saved from the previous night, then pulled up her hood and scrambled down into the shantytown.

It didn't take her long to navigate the sewers to a far-flung section of the lower district, where she emerged in a seedy street filled with brothels and cheap taverns. At this time of day, it was quiet, giving her a bit of privacy at the public fountain.

The water she splashed onto her face was bracing, but by the time she'd scrubbed most of the grime from her skin, her hands were numb from the cold.

Once she was reasonably clean, she took out one of the pelts and gently brushed through it with her fingers, taking care not to pull out the soft fur. It was slow work, and she had to take frequent breaks to wash her hand again in the fountain. By the time she finished, the sun was already sagging in the sky, and some of the district's patrons were returning to their favorite haunts.

She took a steep staircase up to the next tier of the city, then followed the street until she reached the tradesmen's district. There were a couple of tailor's shops here, but she picked the closest one and stepped inside.

A tall man with thinning hair looked up at her from behind a counter as she entered, an immediate frown darkening his face when he assessed her. It was the same expression she saw whenever she bumped into anyone in the upper districts, so before he could tell her to leave, she unclasped her pack and pulled out one of the pelts.

"I want to sell this," she blurted out.

The tailor gaped for a moment and he took the pelt from her, but he stiffened again as he moved his lamp closer. He inspected it before asking, "Who did you steal this from?"

Senya bristled. "The hand that conceals will wither and rot," she muttered as her anger passed. This Aesterkind was a heathen, after all — how could he know how deeply insulting such an accusation was?

The tailor snickered, then flicked his gaze up as another customer entered the shop. "I'll be right with you, sir," he said before returning his attention to the pelt. He lowered his voice and said, "I suppose it doesn't matter, anyway. What's your price?"

Senya looked at him blankly. She had a vague idea a fox pelt would have sold for a few reales in Alcazar, but she wasn't sure what that would be in Aesterland's currency. The bread roll she'd been craving for the past week was five copper farthings, and the fox had given her about four good meals. She consulted her fingers, then offered, "Twenty farthings."

Without hesitation, the tailor pulled out a coin purse from beneath the counter, and Senya watched in amazement as he stacked a small pile of copper in front of her. She was about to reach for the coins when she heard a bark of laughter from behind her.

Before she could turn around, another man joined her at the counter. He was huge — well over a foot taller than her, with broad muscles that could have belonged to a miner. His nose was crooked as if it had been broken several times, but his grin was friendly when he looked down at her.

"I'll give you ten libertines for it, and call that a bargain," he said, pulling a coin purse from his vest. He set a golden coin down on the counter, and Senya looked uncertainly from him to the tailor. In the lower market, she'd seen people trade with copper farthings, and now and then, a silver shilling would change hands. This gold coin was new to her, and she had no idea how much it was worth.

The tailor grimaced and immediately dumped his entire coin purse onto the counter. "Fourteen libertines, seven shillings, and thirty farthings," he offered, a thread of desperation in his voice.

The other man laughed and shrugged. "I can't beat that," he admitted. He nudged Senya and said, "That's a fair price, girl."

Senya smiled and gathered the coins from the table. Even without knowing how many reales the hoard converted to, she knew it was more money than she'd ever seen in her life. With this, she could rent a room in one of the boarding houses in the mid-district, eat at a tavern, maybe even pay for a hot bath. She opened her bag to deposit the coins, pausing for a moment when she saw the white fur inside. She'd originally intended to sell all of them, but this was already plenty.

She looked back up at the tailor as she shrugged her pack over her shoulder, but he was glaring furiously at the other man. "Thank you," she said meekly, then turned and hurried out of the shop.

With her fortune in hand, she raced through the streets, heading back to the cistern. All that was left to do was pack up the supplies she'd stashed there, then she could leave that wretched place behind forever.

She slowed her pace as that thought festered. The hoard in her pack would certainly be enough to lift her out of the sewer, but what about the masses of refugees who remained there? She looked up at the darkening sky thoughtfully. It had only been that morning she'd scorned the nobles of upper Highcastle for shutting their doors to the refugees, but hadn't she just been contemplating the same thing? Even if she sold all of her furs, it may not be enough to house all of them, but even a few shillings each would surely offer them some comfort.

Her mind was made up when she turned around, but she immediately bumped into the huge man from the shop again. He was so solid that she bounced back to the ground, but he offered her his hand and easily pulled her to her feet.

"Sorry about that," he said jovially.

"It was my fault," Senya replied, lowering her head shyly. After a moment, she continued, "Thanks for your help earlier."

The man waved his hand. "That old man was trying to cheat you. How could I just stand aside?" Senya looked away uncomfortably, but the man squatted down to her level and said, "I noticed you had a few more furs."

"Oh, right," Senya said, glancing back at her bag. "I was going to go back and sell them, too."

"I only had ten libertines to offer you back there, but I have an associate who would pay much more," the man said helpfully. "You could get thirty each, easily."

"How many shillings is a libertine worth?" Senya asked.

"A hundred," the man replied. Senya's heart skipped a beat at the revelation. It was more money than she could comprehend. The man grinned when he saw he'd won her over, and he clapped his hand on her shoulder. "Come with me. I'll make sure you get a good deal."

Senya allowed him to lead her down the street, back to the staircase she'd taken up from the lower district. The streets were dark now, and starting to grow livelier with the clientele of the local taverns. Senya's escort ignored them and steered her through the crowd until he diverted her down an alleyway.

The alley reeked of garbage and urine, but it wasn't any worse than the cistern. They reached a gate of sorts, though it was little more than two stacks of derelict crates. A few rough-looking men were stationed in front of the entrance, but they nodded in recognition when they saw Senya's companion. One of them pushed aside a crate with a grunt, creating an opening for them to pass through.

A couple of cracked lanterns had been set up beyond the threshold, revealing a small courtyard piled high with an assortment of merchandise. It seemed like the back alley shop had everything—from chipped battle axes to intricately decorated vases to quietly twittering birds in wooden cages. In the center of it all was a copper throne, upon which sat an obese man with an emerald set into his right eye.

With some effort, the man leaned forward and smiled, revealing a full set of golden teeth. "What have you brought me today, Carver?" he asked sweetly.

Senya looked up at her escort when he nudged her forward. "Show him," he encouraged.

She placed her bag on the sticky ground and reached inside, jostling past the coins she'd gotten from the tailor to pull out one of the remaining pelts. The man squealed in delight when he saw the fur, and he motioned for her to approach. She obliged, and he raised the fur to his cheek. "So soft!" he exclaimed. "Is this real?"

Senya nodded. She looked back when she heard the jostle of the coins, surprised to find Carver had picked up her bag. "There's two more of them in here," he said, looking past her to the merchant. "And another at old Farrow's shop."

"How splendid," the merchant crooned. Senya flinched when she felt his hand against her cheek. "It's bold of you to try to fence stolen goods on the Eel King's turf, young lady."

Senya opened her mouth to protest the accusation, but before any sound came out, a thick arm wrapped around her neck. She began to struggle, but then she felt pressure against the back of her head, and everything started to go dark. Distantly, she heard Carver's voice as he asked, "What do you want me to do with her?"

The emerald in the merchant's eye glinted as he pawed through the contents of her bag. "I'll let you go with a warning this time. Next time you have something valuable, bring it to me first." He flicked his gaze up to her captor and said, "Put her back where you found her."

Senya felt her feet leave the ground, but everything else was a blur until she could hear the sounds of revelers on the street once more. No one gave them a second glance as Carver carried her out of the alleyway and through the crowded street, back to the public fountain. Her impaired consciousness slowly returned as he released his grip on her and sat her down next to a sleeping woman whose clothes were stained with dried vomit.

She tried to rise, but Carver kept a firm hand on her shoulder and chided, "Not just yet, girl. He said to let you off with a warning."

"What—" Senya began, but then what was left of her vision exploded into stars. She gasped in pain as she raised her hands to her face. Blood was pouring freely from her nose, and when she tried to stem the flow, the lightest touch sent her awareness spiraling away once more. It took a few seconds for her vision to return to her, and by the time it did, Carver was gone.

She tried to stand, but her knees refused to support her weight, so she slid back down against the fountain. She just wanted to go back to the cistern, to wrap herself up in the safety of Father Silas's coat, but then it occurred to her that it, too, had been in the backpack they'd taken from her. A sob escaped her, and suddenly the unfairness of everything overwhelmed her.

She shook quietly next to the fountain as tears streamed down her cheeks. Even though the streets around her were humming with the drunken crowd, she felt as alone as she ever had in the Frostlands. Absorbed by her misery, she hardly noticed when the drunks loitering around the fountain scattered, until there was a pair of black greaves directly in front of her.

A bolt of panic shot through her, but her head spun violently when she tried to get up again. The soldier knelt down, and she was surprised to find she recognized the face beneath the helmet.

"Siegfried?" she asked dully.

"You look like shit," he said, offering her his hand.

She reached for it but then hesitated. "What are you doing here?"

"Looking for you," he explained shortly. "Come on."

Senya took his hand, and with a grunt of effort, he pulled her to her feet. She swayed unsteadily for a moment, but he wrapped his arm around her waist, and with his support, she was able to keep up with him.

"You didn't tell me your name last time," Siegfried said as they made it to the quiet streets beyond the tavern district.

"It's Senya."

XXVII

S iegfried tapped his foot impatiently, counting the seconds as they dragged by. The moment he'd entered the townhouse with Senya, his sister had whisked the girl away. He'd followed them as far as Bridget's room, but then she'd slammed the door in his face, leaving him nothing to do but wait for what felt like hours.

That wasn't to mention all the time he'd spent that day tracking the girl down. After she'd healed him, he hadn't been able to get her out of his head. He was sure the strange power she'd used was the same as his. The Castellanos and Aesterkind who'd unlocked their abilities all had Jenseiter teachers. If he could just find her again, she could become his.

Of course, that task was much easier said than done. His only lead was the stench he remembered from their first encounter — a clear sign she probably resided somewhere in the lowest district of Highcastle. Unfortunately, the ring of stone hovels was far larger than all of the upper districts combined. He'd started the morning in the largest market at the entrance of the city in his Jenseiter armor.

The merchants had been of little use, but a beggar who overheard him offered information in exchange for coin, and Siegfried learned she lived among the vagrants in the sewers. Siegfried had gone through a string of beggars then, each one leading him closer to the eastern slums where he'd finally found her. At some point, he'd exhausted the small purse of coins he'd taken with him that morning, but intimidation had proven just as effective.

He stood up when he heard the door open, and a few moments later, Bridget triumphantly steered a freshly bathed Senya into the room. Bridget had dressed her in one of her own gowns, and without the heavy fur coat she'd worn before, Siegfried realized how small she was. Bridget had cleaned all the blood from her face, but her nose was still swollen and dark bruises had formed beneath her eyes. Senya met his gaze for a moment, then, looking embarrassed, averted her eyes to the ground.

"Sit," Bridget commanded, and Senya obligingly sank into an overstuffed chair. Bridget let out a soft sigh before turning on Siegfried, and he froze when he saw the dangerous look in her eyes.

"I didn't mean to wake you up—" he began.

"That isn't the issue here," Bridget hissed. She pointed to Senya, who was gently probing her broken nose, and demanded, "What did you do to her?"

Siegfried balked. "I didn't do that," he said. "She was like that when I found her."

"Why did you bring her back here?" Bridget asked.

"I think she may be able to help us," he explained. He looked back at Senya when he felt a familiar glow of warmth coming from her. She had closed her eyes, and she didn't react when he took a step towards her. Siegfried glanced back at Bridget and said, "Watch."

Bridget crossed her arms, but she remained still as Siegfried squatted down next to Senya and observed as the bruising beneath her eyes faded away. There was a small crack as the bridge of her nose realigned, and when she opened her eyes again, all signs of the damage had disappeared.

"Amazing," Bridget said flatly. "Ziggy, the wedding is in two days. I don't see how—"

Siegfried quickly raised his hands, stopping Bridget before she could finish. He gently took her shoulder and led her back into the hallway. "I think she is one of the cultists from Castilla," he said quietly. "She called the Imperator 'Hearthlord' earlier. I don't want her to find out what we're planning."

Bridget huffed in exasperation. "Still, I don't see how you think she can help us."

"I healed myself like that in Eberswalde," Siegfried explained. Bridget gave him a dubious look, but he reaffirmed, "It's true, but I haven't been able to do it again since then. I'm going to get her to teach me how."

"In two days?" Bridget asked. "I thought you were scouting new entrances to the castle all day. We're running out of time."

Siegfried grimaced — Berthold's presence in the castle had effectively stymied their original plan. Although he hadn't reported Bridget to the Jenseiters, he'd warned Matilda not to bring her back into the castle. Siegfried's encounter with the elite soldiers patrolling the upper districts had also revealed his current disguise was unlikely to work inside, either. As it stood, he still wasn't sure how he was going to sneak in for the wedding.

"I'll figure something out tomorrow," Siegfried promised, trying to sound more confident than he felt. "Why don't you go back to bed? I didn't mean to bother you with any of this."

Bridget paused for a second, then said, "Ziggy, she's just a kid. You should leave her out of this. Highcastle won't be safe for her anymore if you get her involved."

"I don't think Highcastle was very safe for her, as it is," Siegfried said, brushing off Bridget's concerns. She glanced back into the lounge, where Senya was watching the two of them, then sighed and relented. Siegfried watched as she retreated to her bedroom, then slipped back into the lounge and closed the door behind him.

Senya nervously lowered her head, but Siegfried noticed the way her eyes lingered on the tray of stale biscuits on the table. He slid the tray closer to her, and after a moment of hesitation, she snatched one up and crammed it into her mouth.

Siegfried sat down on the couch next to her chair and watched as she ate two more before she looked back up at him self-consciously.

"Thank you," she murmured, crumbs flying from her mouth.

Siegfried smiled disarmingly and said, "Have as many as you want." He poured her a cup of water, and she eagerly gulped that down, as well. He considered for a moment how to present his request to her, until finally, he decided it was best just to be direct. When she slowed down a bit, he leaned forward and said, "I want you to teach me how to heal myself."

She paused halfway through a biscuit as she looked up at him in surprise. With some effort, she choked it down and replied simply, "I can't."

Siegfried bristled, taken aback by the abject refusal. He slid the plate away from her and demanded, "Why not?"

Senya gazed mournfully at the remaining pile of biscuits just beyond her reach. Siegfried cleared his throat, and she finally turned her attention back to him. "Your power is the same as the Hearthlord's," she said. "Mine is different. I can't teach you."

"I healed myself once before," Siegfried argued.

Senya took another sip of water. "The Hearthlord is all-powerful," she said reverently. She considered for a moment, then her expression brightened. "He could teach you. You could come with me when I meet him."

Siegfried frowned and reluctantly pushed the silver platter towards her again, allowing her to continue her feast. "When are you going to meet him?" he asked.

Senya shrugged. "He's in the castle. The sewers go beneath it, but all the exits I've found so far have been locked."

Siegfried straightened up at this information. Matilda wouldn't be able to smuggle him in through the gatehouses, but perhaps she could still send something out to them. "And if I could get a key? You would take me with you?"

Senya beamed and nodded. "Of course! Your sister should come with us, too. The two of you are the first people I've met who felt so much like the Hearthlord. Not even Lady Diana—"

She broke off when she saw the scowl that rose to Siegfried's lips. He quickly suppressed it, twisting it into a smile to set her at ease. "You've met the Duchess?" he probed.

Senya nodded uncomfortably, moving her hand up to cover the long scar carved into the side of her neck. It took Siegfried a moment to put two and two together, and then he asked, "Did she do that to you?"

"It was part of my trial," Senya said softly. "That's why I have to find the Hearthlord, so he will accept me back into his service."

"If they treated you like that before, why would you want to go back?"

Senya gave him a blank look, as if she'd never even considered the question. After a few seconds, she said, "I was born to serve the Hearthlord."

"Says who?" Siegfried asked.

"Father Silas," Senya replied as if that settled the matter.

Siegfried scowled. He'd had enough of cultist nonsense from the Castellanos, and his patience for it from this girl was quickly wearing thin. Still, even if she couldn't help him unlock his abilities, she'd proven useful in other ways. In the morning, he would have Bridget send word to her friend, and convince her to steal a key for them. Senya could have her audience with the Hearthlord, and meanwhile, Siegfried would plant a dagger into the Duchess's heart.

XXVIII

Nell drew in a deep breath of fresh air when she emerged on the walkway atop the battlement. A moment later, her aging fiancé appeared behind her, and as he captured her arm beneath his elbow, she was once again submerged in the miasma of cologne that lingered around him. She put on her best smile as he led her to the edge of the wall, all the while imagining if he tripped and plunged thirty feet down to the courtyards below.

"What a magnificent city you have here, my dear," Bastian von Weyler drawled as he looked out over Highcastle. "A tad overcrowded, I daresay." He smiled as he patted her captive hand. "After tomorrow, I will sort that out."

"We took in a number of refugees recently," Nell said tactfully. "Perhaps if we returned them to their lands—"

Von Weyler laughed. "I didn't mean to worry you with such matters, dear," he said dismissively. "We will find you something more deserving of your attention, I'm sure. My late wife quite enjoyed horticulture. She would have absolutely adored the gardens here."

Before Nell could respond, he abruptly turned, jerking her along with him as he toured the walls. He paused for a moment when he saw a small cluster of figures standing atop the next balcony. Nell immediately recognized Diana and her own fiancé among them, and von Weyler ran a nervous hand over his balding head, slicking back what remained of his graying hair.

As they approached, she caught a whiff of smoke in the air. The soldiers in the Duchess's entourage stepped forward, blocking their way. Von Weyler bowed deeply when Diana looked back at them, and with a flick of her hand, the soldiers parted, allowing them to step up onto the balcony.

"I'm glad you arrived safely, Bastian," Diana said, turning her gaze back to the courtyard below. She was flanked as always by her blue-eyed Reinbann body-guard, but she made no show of familiarity with her future consort. Berthold had been relegated to the far corner of the balcony, where he stood alone.

"The escort you sent was much appreciated, Your Grace," von Weyler said.

Diana merely nodded. Von Weyler hesitated for a moment, then pulled Nell forward, and she could finally see what was holding the Duchess's attention. There was a great bonfire in the center of the courtyard.

A chill ran up her spine when she saw one of the soldiers heave a massive tome into the blaze with a grunt. Even from this distance, she didn't have to ask to know what it was — Athelstan's memoirs. She frantically looked at the piles of books scattering the courtyard. The entire royal library must have been down there. She wanted to scream at them to stop, but between the thickening smoke and von Weyler's cologne, she knew if she opened her mouth, she was going to vomit.

She extricated her hand from her fiancé and staggered away from the balcony. Everything was spinning, and her knees felt weak. She was sure she was going to fall, but then a callused hand caught hold of her. She looked up in surprise at Berthold, who had stepped forward to support her.

Von Weyler's mouth gaped open, but Diana had not moved from her spot. "Not feeling well, Princess?" she asked placidly.

Nell's cheeks reddened as she regained her footing. "I'm afraid not."

"Why don't you get some rest then? It would be a shame if you were sick on your wedding day." Von Weyler made a move toward her, but Diana continued, "There are a few matters I would like to discuss with you, Bastian. Perhaps Berthold could escort the princess back to her chambers."

"Of course," Berthold said. He offered Nell his arm, and she gratefully clung to it as he led her back the way she had come.

When she'd first been introduced to Berthold the previous week, Nell had been surprised to find she recognized him as the commander of Aesterland's elite Feracht Corps. During his promotion ceremony, she had even shared a dance with him. That must have been years ago, though. Since then, he'd lost an eye in some battle or another, but he was still tall, young, and well-built. Diana hadn't seemed to warm up to him, but Nell would have switched him with von Weyler in an instant.

She supposed he was a strange match for the Duchess, though. As far as Nell could tell, Diana Feracht held the highest authority among the Jenseiters except for the Imperator himself. Berthold was an accomplished soldier, but he was no duke. The fact they shared the same surname had also struck her as odd — so much so that she'd looked up his lineage. The Aesterkind Ferachts had been granted a Dukedom in the Black Forest by Queen Oriane the Great herself, four hundred years ago. While they were no longer a great house, they were unassailably Aesterkind. How Berthold's family was connected to the rulers of the Jenseiters remained a mystery to her.

Nell's head cleared a bit as they gained some distance from the smoke, and once they rounded a corner, she asked Berthold if they could stop for a moment. He obliged, and she sat down heavily on a delicately carved stone bench. She looked up at the gray winter sky overhead, trying to control the burning surge of emotions rising in her throat. She could feel the tears welling up behind her eyes, but she knew if she started to cry now, she wouldn't be able to stop.

She could scarcely count the number of times she'd reassured herself her life wouldn't change so much after she was wed, but she knew the books were just the beginning. There were no records from before Queen Oriane's time — they had been all lost to the tumultuous period the historians called the cataclysms. Now, she stood at the precipice of her own cataclysm.

She looked at Berthold as he sat down next to her, although she could no longer bring the false smile back to her face. He frowned as he studied her, before finally he said, "I fought the Jenseiters on the western front, Princess. It may seem bleak now, but please believe me, this is the only way."

"We will lose everything that we are," Nell said softly.

"We already have," Berthold replied, lowering his head. He drew in a deep breath, and then he stood up. He offered her his hand, and when she looked up at him, his gentle smile had returned.

XXIX

Senya paused as she reached the sprawling mold formation that grew over the nexus of tunnels, waiting in its eerie neon glow for Siegfried and Bridget to catch up. The previous two days had been utter bliss — so much so that it had been a little hard to climb back down into the sewers that morning. Hot baths, lavish meals, and a feather bed at night — Bridget had provided every luxury she could imagine. A part of her felt guilty about enjoying such splendor while she knew there was an entire community suffering beneath their feet, but when she'd mentioned it to Siegfried, he'd only laughed.

Now that she was here, though, her heart hammered with nervous excitement as she looked into the dark tunnel ahead. It wouldn't be long until they reached the castle, and then she would finally be able to see the Hearthlord again. Her mind raced when she thought about what she would say to him, and how he would respond. It had been more than two years now since he left her and Father Silas in the tomb.

She felt the phantom edge of the dagger against her neck once more, and she raised her hand to the scar. Why was she thinking of that now? Her trial had been an instruction in faith — if the Hearthlord sensed any doubt in her heart, she knew he would reject her. Now, when she was so close to finally redeeming herself, why was she dwelling on the past?

She jumped when something bumped into her, but when she looked up, it was just Siegfried. Bridget stepped into the glow behind him, keeping a hand on the red wig that covered her dark hair. It had been immaculately styled that morning, but after an hour trudging through the sewers, it was starting to look more like a rat's nest. Neither of them had dressed appropriately for the journey; Siegfried was wearing his Hearthborn armor, and Bridget's multi-layered dress was probably almost as heavy.

"Which way?" Siegfried asked, looking ahead at the maze of channels.

"There," Senya said, pointing at a tunnel across the rushing current of murky water. She led the way to the stream, taking care as the floor became slippery with algae. The causeway ahead was one of the biggest she'd encountered in the sewer system, spanning almost seven feet. It wasn't deep — probably only three feet or so, but Senya had been careful so far to avoid getting any of the dripping muck on the clothes Bridget bought for her.

Senya took a running start, then leapt across the river of filth to the narrow ledge on the other side. She dipped her knees slightly to set her balance, then let out a soft breath of relief and looked back at the siblings.

Siegfried grimaced as he took his position, and she moved out of the way to give him room. He overshot his jump a bit, and his breastplate slammed hard into the slick wall. Senya grasped his shoulder as he kiltered back towards the sewage, but after a tense moment, he was stable on his feet.

Bridget remained where she was, looking helplessly at the causeway. After a few seconds, she clumsily took a few steps back, her high heels clicking loudly against the cobblestone, but she hesitated as she turned her gaze back to the span. "There must be another way around," she said.

Senya frowned and peered towards the source of the sewage, beyond the neon glow. This was always where she had crossed before, and she hadn't ventured any further along the channel. "Maybe," she said with a shrug. "We can go look to see if there is a crossing."

She made to move past Siegfried but paused when he shook his head. "There's no time." His expression softened a little as he asked, "Do you remember the way back?"

Bridget's face blanched. "You don't have to do this alone," she said.

Siegfried smiled, though his eyes remained cold behind his helmet. "It's not too late for you to leave the city."

Senya could sense the tension between the two, but she didn't understand. Although it was fainter, the Hearthlord's presence lingered in Bridget the same as Siegfried. Now that they were so close to meeting him, why would she suddenly leave the city?

Before she could ask, Siegfried prodded her forward and ordered, "Let's go."

Senya automatically did as she was told, but when she glanced over her shoulder back at Bridget, she could see there were tears in her eyes.

Siegfried was quiet as they continued along the tunnel, leaving them with only the sound of rushing water and the echoing clank of his armor. The passage steadily climbed upwards, until it ended in a ladder hewn into the stone that led up to a locked grate. A clear stream of water was pouring down from the aqueduct above it. Senya winced when she felt the heat coming off of it — it was much hotter than the water that coursed through the rest of the city.

"I'll go first," Senya volunteered, and Siegfried reached into his pouch for the key that had been delivered to the house the previous day.

Senya held it tightly as she ascended the ladder, keeping her body as close to the wall as possible to avoid the spray from the boiling waterfall beside her. Once she reached the top, she snaked an arm through the narrow bars. It took some maneuvering, but a couple of seconds later, the iron lock on the other side clicked, and she pushed the grate open and scrambled up onto the landing above.

She had to crouch to avoid hitting her head on the low ceiling. As she tried to get her bearings, she realized the small passageway she'd emerged into may not be a sewer after all. It was immaculately clean; its white marble glistened with moisture, and the hot water running in the channel beside her was completely clear. It was also uncomfortably warm. The water threw off rivulets of steam, creating a sweltering fog in the cramped duct. The sound of footsteps echoed from overhead, and when she looked up, she could see glimpses of the courtiers passing by through thin slits carved into the floor.

She couldn't stay here long; she was already faint from the heat. She waited for Siegfried to appear at the grate, then quickly moved through the shaft until she found another hatch.

Before she could push on it to escape the steam, Siegfried hissed at her to wait. She obligingly moved out of his way, allowing him to cautiously raise the hatch and poke his head above. He looked around for a few moments, then muttered, "It's safe."

She followed him up into what must have been a storage room. Siegfried moved a cluster of brooms out of his way as Senya replaced the cover behind her. She raised the hood of her cloak over her head, hoping this would be the last time she would have to disguise herself like this.

Siegfried cracked open the door and peered out into the hallway beyond. A steady stream of people rustled through the corridor, all in the same direction. Siegfried cursed softly as he closed the door and turned back to her. "The wedding must be starting soon," he whispered.

"The wedding is today?" Senya asked in surprise. Even in the cistern, Princess Eleanor's betrothal had been a popular topic of discussion, but she'd never bothered herself with the details. "Should we wait until it's over?"

"No," Siegfried said. "Everyone will be distracted with the ceremony. This is probably the best chance you'll get."

"You're coming too, aren't you?" Senya asked.

Siegfried nodded. "There's someone else I need to see first, though. Go ahead without me."

Senya frowned, put off by the deviation in their plans. She'd gotten accustomed to the idea of approaching the Hearthlord with Siegfried over the last couple of days, and suddenly the prospect of meeting him alone seemed daunting. She shook her head, reminding herself that whether or not Siegfried was there, this was what she'd been striving towards for two long years.

She moved past him to the door, but before she could open it, Siegfried put a light hand on her arm and said, "Be careful."

Before she knew what she was doing, Senya hugged him, causing him to tense up beneath her arms. She immediately felt silly for doing it, so she released her grip and took a shy step back. Stammering, she said, "I'm sorry. I just — thank you."

Siegfried looked awkwardly at the floor, and Senya couldn't help but smile. "I'll see you after the wedding, I guess," she said.

"Yeah," Siegfried muttered.

Senya took another moment to re-adjust her hood, then opened the door and slipped out into the crowded hallway. There were more Hearthborn here than she'd ever seen before — and not just soldiers. More than half of the courtiers were blonde, and the rest had the bright red hair of the Aesterkind. Even though she felt out of place, it was easy to blend in with so many people, and she followed the momentum of the crowd into another, much grander corridor.

Everyone was surging towards a set of doors at the end of this hallway, where the squeeze was causing a bit of gridlock. As Senya approached the doors, she felt a sudden pulse course through her as she entered the Hearthlord's divine presence. She didn't know how she could have initially mistaken Siegfried for him. At this distance, it was like she'd been submerged in a vicious current — even the air she breathed in felt heavier.

She looked up, and the pounding sensation in her sinuses grew stronger. He was there, just above her. She searched the hallway until she found a door guarded by two Hearthborn soldiers, beyond which a staircase led to the next floor. She stood rooted at the spot, letting the crowd shuffle past her as she stared at the door. As hard as she tried, though, she could not work out how to get past the guards.

Desperation began to creep in. Her plans for how to go about making contact with the Hearthlord had always been vague, and she hadn't really considered that he would be well-guarded at all times. Maybe if she went outside, she could try to climb in through the window, but what if the exterior of the castle was as smooth as those of the walls that protected it?

The pounding sensation in her head steadily intensified, making it harder to think. Just as she had resolved to try to rush past the guards, a dark figure appeared at the doorway, and the crowd parted in reverence as the Hearthlord emerged into the hall. Senya suddenly found herself alone, shaking, and unable to move in his presence.

She looked up as he stood before her, and he lifted his hand to her hood, lowering it without a word. A murmur rippled through the crowd, and the Hearthlord reached down to take her hand. His eyes flicked down to the black eagle imprinted on her. Terror rippled through her as she met his gaze, and all the things she'd wanted to say were impossibly far out of reach.

He rested his hand on her shoulder and said, "Welcome back."

Although it was snowing outside, it was hot in the massive banquet hall. Nell could feel beads of sweat forming around her brow, where her hair had been teased up into an elaborate style. The threads of gold and diamonds woven into her red curls were heavy on her neck. It didn't help that her wedding dress was composed of seven different layers of fabric. Although it was the traditional garb of Aesterkind royal brides, it was also sweltering, and her knees felt weak as she gasped for breath.

The wedding party stood atop a dais raised a few feet above the crowd. A ring of Jenseiter soldiers stood guard at the edge of the stage, separating them from the courtiers. The Imperator had chosen to watch from one of the boxes on the second floor of the hall. She glanced up at his booth but was surprised to find there was someone in there with him. She quickly looked away when he met her gaze. In all honesty, she was glad that he wasn't on the stage. He still made her uncomfortable, and his suffocating presence along with everything else may have been too much for her to bear.

Von Weyler stifled a cough beside her. The old man had somehow squeezed into a dress suit, although its buttons looked like they may burst at any moment. He was wearing his heavy cologne again today, but after standing next to him for so long, she'd detected another smell beneath it — like sour milk. She supposed she should be grateful he was pleasant enough, but her stomach turned when she thought about the consummation that would come after the wedding.

She glanced at her fellow bride, who stood at the other side of the dais. The Duchess was doing even less than Nell to hide her contempt for the whole affair. A snarl had been plastered on her lips all morning, and she kept looking impatiently at Queen Helene, who'd been giving a speech for the better part of an hour. Diana had chosen a military uniform over a dress, and with the sword at her side, she looked as if she was more prepared for a battle than her wedding.

Berthold caught her eye, and he gave her a reassuring smile. Nell forced herself to return it, then quickly turned her attention to the floor. In a way, she knew Berthold was right. Aesterland had already been defeated, and this charade would be only one of many humiliations as they became a client state of the Jenseiters. Still, Nell could not quiet the voice in the back of her mind that told her this was all wrong.

Nell felt someone touch her clammy hand, and she looked up to her mother, who was pulling her forward to the center of the dais. Queen Helene had finally finished her speech, initiating the moment Nell had been dreading for the last month. She stood to the queen's left while von Weyler took a position on her right, and the queen said gravely, "My daughter, my sole heir and the Crown Princess of Aesterland, is the future of our people. With this union, we cement our alliance with Jenseits, for the prosperity of both our realms."

Von Weyler fumbled with his pocket for a moment, then pulled out a golden ring. Nell weakly raised her hand, and he took it and negotiated the ring onto her finger. Once it was in place, he stepped forward and raised the veil that had partially obscured her embarrassment so far. He pawed at the back of her neck, and Nell closed her eyes as he kissed her. Again, he was gentle, but his rubbery lips only exacerbated her nausea. She felt an immense rush of relief when he finally released her, and she quickly returned to the side of the stage where she'd been waiting before. A sterile applause rippled through the room.

Diana and Berthold replaced them in the center of the dais. Queen Helene opened her mouth to speak, but she paused when one of the soldiers at the edge of the dais moved out of formation. Diana turned to question the soldier, and Nell saw a flash of steel as the soldier lunged towards the Duchess. Diana's hand moved like lightning, redirecting the soldier's gauntlet to shift his dagger a few inches to the left. She grunted softly when the blade emerged from the back of her uniform near her shoulder.

The rogue soldier took a step back and drew his sword, as did Berthold. Queen Helene retreated behind the line of Jenseiter soldiers who were closing in on the assassin. Everyone stopped for a moment when Diana's cutting laugh broke out across the stage. She shoved past Berthold, who had stepped forward to defend her, and drew the saber at her belt. Despite the blood blossoming around her shoulder, Nell had never seen the Duchess look so happy.

Diana gestured to her soldiers, who fell back to the edges of the dais. Nell had no idea why the Duchess was entertaining the efforts of an assassin — with one word he could be apprehended and executed on the spot. She looked up at the Imperator, who hadn't moved from his box. He also seemed content to let the situation unfold.

Her attention was drawn back to the dais when she heard the sharp cry of colliding steel. The assassin's attacks were relentless, but Diana was able to intercept his blade each time he struck. The assassin's strikes grew more desperate with each lunge, until finally he committed to a powerful overhead slash. Diana used the butt of her saber to knock his sword out of his hands and countered with a swift stab, which found its way between the joint in his shoulder plate. Blood splashed across the ground as the assassin took an unsteady step back, and Diana's grin fell into a snarl of contempt.

She took another step towards him, and he circled her to avoid being pushed back into the wall of soldiers. Diana rushed forward, and although he managed to block her sword with his bracer, she kicked him back. Nell had been so entranced by the duel that she hadn't noticed how close it had gotten to her and von Weyler, and she looked to the side in alarm as the assassin tumbled into her new husband, knocking him down.

She met the assassin's eyes beneath his heavy helmet, surprised to find they were red like the other Jenseiters. She hadn't ever considered there would be political strife within the Jenseiter forces. She looked down at the dagger in the assassin's hand and screamed when he raised it to her own throat. He roughly grabbed her hair and pulled her head back, using her as a shield as he backed towards the edge of the dais.

Diana spat and sheathed her saber. Nell could hear her mother screaming at the soldiers to move aside, but they didn't budge until Diana waved her hand. With that, the ring around the dais opened so the assassin could drag Nell off of the stage.

Nell let herself be pushed through the crowd of onlookers, which parted nervously around them. His blood seeped into the back of her dress, and she knew that even with this desperate tactic, the rogue soldier wouldn't be able to get far. As long as she stayed calm and didn't upset him, she would eventually be rescued.

Once they had cleared the doors of the banquet hall, Nell's kidnapper moved more quickly, although a retinue of soldiers stalked after him. His breath was hot on her neck as he rasped, "Tell me how to get out of here."

She obligingly pointed to a side corridor, which he took. After navigating a few more of the palace's grand passages, they emerged out of the front gate near the stables. The assassin shouted at a stable boy to bring him a horse, but the child stood rooted, trembling with fear. Nell screamed when she felt the assassin press the dagger harder against her throat, drawing a thin line of blood. Upon seeing his princess in distress, the stable boy jolted into action and retrieved a horse. He hastily threw on a saddle and bridle and led the animal out to Nell and her kidnapper.

Nell recognized Tulip, her mother's stallion. Tulip could sense the tension in the air, and he whinnied softly when the assassin climbed up into the saddle, never releasing his grip on Nell's hair. He grasped the back of her dress and heaved her up in front of him, and then awkwardly thrust forward with his hips. Nell glanced back at him, unsure of what he was doing, but then she realized he had no idea how to ride. She gently kicked Tulip's sides, causing the animal to trot forward towards the outer palace gates.

"Give me the reins," she said once they had gotten some distance from the palace. "And get that dagger away from my throat. If we hit a bump, you're going to cut me."

The assassin grumbled for a moment, but he relinquished the reins to her anyway and lowered the dagger a few inches, although not enough to relieve Nell's discomfort. She kicked Tulip's sides with a bit more force, and he broke out into a gallop across the cobblestone streets surrounding the palace.

The nobles in the Promenade District threw themselves out of the way of Tulip's massive hooves, but it wasn't long before they hit a square surrounded by stairs and narrow alleyways. While Nell had spent an eternity surveying the city's labyrinthine roads from the castle towers, she'd never considered the route a horse would need to take. Tulip circled nervously at the grand staircase that led down into the lower districts, refusing to go any further.

Nell yelped in surprise when her kidnapper pulled her off of the back of the horse. He dragged her into one of the alleyways, and she felt her stomach turn when the distinct smell of garbage invaded her nostrils. The assassin released her as he fumbled with the straps securing his bulky breastplate. By the time she realized that she should have fled, he managed to release the clasps, and the two halves of the armor fell to the ground with a heavy clank. Nell winced when she saw his tunic was drenched in blood from the wound in his shoulder.

She barely had time to feel sorry for him before he grasped the back of her hair again. He steered her to the sewer at the end of the alley, and before she could protest, he shoved her into the chute. She sputtered incomprehensibly as she rocketed down the filthy slide, until she met an abrupt stop atop a pile of refuse at the bottom. Before she had time to recuperate, her kidnapper barreled into her, knocking the breath out of her.

He swayed unsteadily as he yanked her to her feet. Nell retched in disgust as he limped along the edge of the sewer. His pace was already slowing considerably, and she knew it was only a matter of time before he succumbed to his injuries.

Once again, she found herself pitying this pathetic figure. If he'd been trying to assassinate the Duchess, he had failed spectacularly, and he'd most certainly endangered her life in this clumsy attempt at escape, but he was doing more than any Aesterkind she'd seen thus far to resist the invaders. She'd spent so much time brooding about her fate — and the fate of her country — over the last month, but she'd never even considered sneaking a knife onto the dais to eliminate one head of the Jenseiter state herself.

Against her better judgment, she planted her feet, causing the assassin to stop in his tracks. He raised his dagger as he looked back at her, but she put up her hand and said, "You won't be able to escape the city like this. Let me help you."

The assassin eyed her suspiciously, but after a few tense moments, he returned the dagger to its sheath at his belt. With hands trembling from exhaustion, he removed the rest of his heavy plate armor. When he took off his helmet, Nell was surprised that he had black hair instead of the typical Jenseiter blonde. He was also much younger than she'd expected. Without his armor, he looked less like an experienced revolutionary and more like a scared boy.

"My name is Nell," she offered. "What's yours?" The assassin looked away in disdain for a moment, but he turned back in surprise when she ripped a strip off the outer layer of her dress and handed it to him. "For your wound," she said.

He accepted the fabric begrudgingly and awkwardly tied it around his shoulder, putting some nominal pressure on his injury. Once he was done, he muttered, "It's Siegfried."

Nell pressed past him and led the way up a narrow passage that connected the sewer to the streets of the market district above. The alley spilled out into a major thoroughfare she recognized. She let down her hair and threw her expensive jewelry into the sewer, then ripped off two more bulky layers of her dress. Satisfied with her disheveled appearance, she grasped Siegfried's hand and led him out into the street.

Her disguise was enough to bear them across the crowded avenue, and she quickly turned into another alley that led to a series of back streets. Before long, they reached her destination — a small cemetery hidden away behind the forgotten arterials of the city. It had reached its capacity centuries ago, and its headstones had long since faded away into smooth rocks. The only structure that remained intact was a large marble monument depicting Queen Oriane the Great.

Nell headed towards the monument, but she paused when she saw the hidden passage beneath it had already been revealed. The series of tunnels that ran beneath Highcastle were a state secret, known only to the royal family and their inner circle. She took a step back when a dark figure emerged from behind the monument, and the familiar feeling of suffocation blossomed in her throat.

"I'm glad to see that you are unharmed, Princess," the Imperator said as he drew his sword.

S iegfried scowled as he sized up his new opponent. He wore a full set of the
Jenseiter plate armor, although instead of the helmet he donned an ornate
crown. To complete the ensemble, he had a billowing white cape fastened with a
huge topaz brooch. There was no mistaking it — this was the Jenseiter Imperator.

He had been stupid to trust the princess, and she had somehow led him directly
into this trap. With his armor discarded and nothing besides the dagger as a
weapon, he knew he was at a severe disadvantage. His rage had slowly been
building since the Duchess had humiliated him on the dais, though, and now it
exploded beneath his palms. It was the same throbbing sensation he'd been trying
to replicate since he'd escaped Eberswalde.

"What is your name, boy?" Siegfried looked back up at the Imperator, who had
passed Nell and was now approaching him.

With his helmet gone, there was no point in trying to hide his identity any longer.
"Siegfried Feracht," he responded proudly, raising his dagger in front of him.

The Imperator smiled. His weapon remained lowered, and Siegfried tried to
gauge how long it would take him to cover the distance between them. If he could
take him by surprise, he may be able to overcome the difference in range. "Why
did you attack my granddaughter?" the Imperator asked.

Siegfried spat. Everything had spiraled so quickly out of his control. He still couldn't understand how the Duchess had been able to defeat him. When he'd realized that he couldn't kill her, that he was going to die without accomplishing anything at all, he'd panicked. The pulsing in his hands intensified, and he darted forward. The Duchess was out of reach now, but the Imperator was an acceptable substitute for his rage.

He had to throw himself to the side to avoid the flash of steel that cut through his intended path. A cold sweat broke out across his forehead — the Imperator's sword was even faster than Diana's had been. He ducked when the blade came at him again and barreled forward. His only hope was to close the distance — now was not the time for retreat.

The Imperator caught Siegfried's wrist as he stabbed, and Siegfried's vision burst into stars when the Imperator slammed the butt of his hilt into his head. Blood ran freely down his temple as he staggered back, but the Imperator was in front of him again instantly.

Pain exploded in Siegfried's chest, and his vision turned red. He stumbled blindly backward until his back collided with a gravestone, and he sank down against it, shivering at the cold sensation creeping up his limbs. More blood filled his mouth with each wheezing breath he took. He looked up weakly as the Imperator advanced towards him, but then a muffled shout broke out across the graveyard, and the Imperator abruptly stopped and turned toward the source of the noise.

Siegfried pressed his back against the gravestone as hard as he could, slowly raising himself back to his feet.

"Please, stop!" Senya cried as she climbed out of the tunnel. She rushed past the princess towards the Hearthlord, but she paused when he turned his heavy gaze upon her. Desperate, she fell to her knees before him. She didn't know why this was happening, but the quiet serenity that had blossomed within her an hour ago withered away when she looked past the Hearthlord at Siegfried's broken body. She didn't know why he had attacked Lady Diana, but she didn't want to see him executed. "I — I can heal him, and Lady Diana, too. It will be like this never happened."

The Hearthlord lowered his sword and approached her, and she averted her eyes to the ground. Being in his suffocating presence for so long had already exhausted her, and it felt even stronger now, making it difficult to breathe.

"Get up," he commanded.

Trembling, Senya climbed to her feet, flinching when she felt the Hearthlord's rough hands against her cheeks. He tilted her face towards him, and she shivered as she stared into his cold eyes.

"You helped him infiltrate the palace."

Senya nodded weakly. She opened her mouth to explain, but then she felt the Hearthlord's grip tighten.

Pain. For a moment, it consumed all of her thoughts. Distantly, she heard someone screaming, and it took her a few seconds to realize the sound was coming from her. The Hearthlord's fingers felt like red embers pressing into her skin, setting the rest of her body ablaze.

When she'd reunited with the Hearthlord, she was sure that she would finally find the meaning of all of her suffering, that everything she had seen on the long journey to Highcastle would finally make sense. As her vision blurred with tears, she felt the steady faith that had borne her through those freezing nights alone in the tundra begin to crumble. For a moment, she was back in the tomb, watching as the statue transformed into a man while she bled out beneath his grip. Was this what it meant to serve the Hearthlord? Was this what Father Silas had died for?

Her vision blurred as she raised her hands to the Hearthlord's vambraces. She could barely feel the polished metal beneath her fingers, and her thoughts felt further and further away. She vaguely heard the Hearthlord grunt in pain, and then she was falling for what seemed like an eternity. A dull thud reverberated through her body as she hit the ground. She gasped for air as she planted her palm on the ground, trying to get back up, but her muscles felt like jelly.

She sensed movement beside her, and she felt her back leave the ground as someone dragged her across the overgrown grass. She blinked as she looked up, but her fading consciousness could barely process the hazy red outline above her. The heaving form overhead paused for a moment, and then rolled Senya's limp body to the side. Once more, Senya was falling, and then there was only darkness.

Nell looked over the edge of the ditch into the dark tunnel, wincing when the Neseveen girl smashed into the dirt below. She relaxed slightly when the girl groaned, glad the fall hadn't killed her outright. She turned her attention past the monument to Siegfried, who was darting from one gravestone to the next while avoiding the frenzied Imperator's blade.

Everything had begun to feel like a nightmare. Nell had only been able to watch while the Imperator stabbed Siegfried, but she didn't know what more she could do for the poor boy. The chances he would escape his botched assassination attempt had always been incredibly slim.

However, something had stirred within her as she'd watched what the Imperator had done to the girl. Her terrible screams still echoed in Nell's ears. The crumpled form lying at the bottom of the tunnel — that was the price of anything but unconditional fealty to the Imperator.

She bit her lip as Siegfried ducked behind another monument. He was covered in blood, but he seemed to have regained his strength. Still, it was all he could do to avoid the Imperator's devastating attacks. Nell blinked when the top half of the monument slid off of its base, separated by a single stroke of the Imperator's sword. She didn't know how such a thing was possible, but it made about as much sense as whatever the Imperator had done to the girl, or how Siegfried could still be running despite his grievous injuries.

Although the Imperator had supposedly come here to rescue her from her kidnapper, she found herself hoping Siegfried would be able to defeat him. Every time Siegfried narrowly dodged his blade, her heart jumped in her chest. After a few more blows, though, it became clear to her that he didn't have any hope of winning against the monster — he couldn't even get close enough to strike.

She managed to catch Siegfried's gaze for a moment, and a silent understanding passed between them. Nell dropped down into the tunnel as Siegfried bolted across the graveyard toward her. He jumped down beside her, and together, they threw their weight against the rusted lever set into the wall. Ancient machinery creaked as the monument slowly shifted over them. Nell heard the Imperator's heavy footsteps overhead, and her heart raced as she pushed with all of her might.

With a loud clang, the mechanism snapped close, throwing them into complete darkness. There was a deafening sound from up above and dirt cascaded down on them. Nell blindly threw herself out of the way as the tunnel collapsed around them, scampering forward as far as she could until the rumbling overhead stopped. She was still as she listened to the raspy sound of her own breathing, blinking against the total darkness as the dust settled around her.

She crawled to her feet and fumbled against the side of the wall until she felt a metal sconce beneath her fingers. She unhinged the lantern hanging from it and turned a dial until a warm glow burst from behind the yellowed glass. She drew in a deep breath as she scanned the pile of rocks where she'd come from, sure she would find the remains of Siegfried and the girl buried beneath. To her surprise, Siegfried was just behind her, unscathed from the cave-in, and the girl was at his feet.

Nell looked up at the rocks that had collapsed around the tunnel, breathing a small sigh of relief when she saw the entrance remained sealed. The adrenaline pulsing through her veins gradually subsided as she approached Siegfried and the girl. The Neseveen's skin was pallid, and the veins in her neck and face were dark and swollen.

"Is she alive?" Nell asked weakly.

Siegfried bent down and felt her pulse. "She's just unconscious," he said after a few moments.

"What about you?" Nell asked, inspecting him more closely. His tunic was in tatters and covered in blood, but when she pulled the fabric aside, she saw that his wounds were gone.

He batted her hand aside uncomfortably and said, "I'm fine." He frowned as he surveyed their new surroundings and asked, "What now?"

"The Imperator knows about the tunnels somehow," Nell said, glancing up at the entrance above them. "We need to keep moving."

Siegfried lifted the girl onto his shoulder with a grunt, then looked down the tunnel. "Where does this lead? Back to the palace?"

"Luckily for us, this side leads outside the city." Siegfried shot her a doubtful look, but she brushed it off. "I'm not going back," she announced. She gestured at the girl and said, "What the Imperator did to her — it's the same thing the Jenseiters are going to do to Aesterland. My mother is too afraid to fight, but I'm not just going to sit around and watch anymore."

Siegfried shook his head, but he started down the tunnel anyway. Nell stood rooted to the spot for a moment, a little startled by her sudden declaration. After a few seconds, she composed herself and hurried after her kidnapper. Even if she had wanted to go back to the palace, she wasn't sure if she could after helping Siegfried escape. She didn't think she would be executed — she was the Crown Princess, after all — but what she had done would not go without punishment of some sort.

Now that she'd made her decision, she put those thoughts out of her mind. The tunnel had collapsed behind her, and there was no looking back anymore.

XXXII

"Please drink this, Your Grace."

Diana took the cup of milky liquid from the surgeon. She forced it down in one long draught, then coughed as the bitter substance burned her throat. A few moments later, a warm sensation spread through her body, and she felt herself fading into the ether.

The surgeon helped her lie down, then cut away her blood-soaked shirt. The assassin's dagger hadn't hit anything vital, but it still needed to be purified and sewn up. On the battlefield, the most efficient way to stop the bleeding was to have a Castellano cauterize the flesh, but here she had the luxury of surgeons to neatly suture it. The only thing that would have been better was a Neseveen healer, but her grandfather had left the last one for dead in his prison.

The surgeon waited a few minutes for the anesthesia to do its work, then poked her with his needle to confirm she could no longer feel anything. Satisfied, he lowered his head to begin his sutures. Diana hazily turned away as the needle pierced her flesh, smiling when she saw Natalia sitting at the other side of the bed.

"I should have been there," Natalia said quietly.

Diana's smile faded when she saw her bodyguard's cheeks were stained with tears. "My grandfather didn't want the Reinbann there," Diana reminded her gently. "Anyway, what would you have done?"

"I would have killed him before he could touch you."

Of that, Diana had little doubt. She looked past Natalia, and her lip twitched in disdain when she noticed Berthold watching from the shadows. Under the Imperator's watchful gaze, she hadn't been able to arrange some accidental death for him before their charade of a wedding. Still, she didn't intend to stay married for long. As soon as the Imperator set his sights elsewhere, she would finish what she'd started in Eberswalde. She had no need for a consort, especially not a pretender born of a long line of blood-traitors.

The surgeon finished his sutures and carefully bandaged her chest. "You must rest now, Your Grace," he said. "The sedative will take a few hours to wear off, and then there may be some discomfort."

Diana waved him off, and with a bow, he left the room. She drowsily sat up, then threw her legs over the side of the bed. She didn't have time to lie around all day. Natalia retrieved a fresh uniform for her, and Diana pulled on the tailored shirt, ignoring the dull pinch in her shoulder whenever she moved her left arm.

With a surge of effort, Diana tried to stand up, but her legs refused to support her weight, and she sank back down into the bed. Annoyingly, Berthold rushed to her side, but she was not fooled by the concerned expression he'd conjured.

"Don't touch me," she snarled as he offered her his hand.

There was a knock on the door, and then an Aesterkind maid entered with a tray of food. Diana ignored her and looked at Natalia. "Escort him outside," she ordered.

Natalia nodded and grasped Berthold's arm, then roughly pushed him towards the door. Diana sighed, glad to be rid of him for a few moments, then looked up as the maid approached her, still holding the tray. Irritated, she gestured to the table across the room and began, "Put the food there—"

She broke off when she saw the dagger in the maid's hand. With her limbs heavy from the sedative, she could only watch as the tray crashed to the floor and the maid rushed towards her. She felt a dull pressure when the maid plunged the dagger into her stomach. The maid drew it back, preparing to stab her again, but then Berthold tackled her, slamming her roughly against the wall.

Diana looked numbly down at her wound as Natalia frantically pressed her hands over it. Although there was no pain, she knew it was bad. The blood spilling out over Natalia's hands was black.

"The doctor," Diana muttered.

Natalia nodded and promised, "I'll be right back."

Diana turned her gaze to the maid as Natalia's footsteps echoed down the corridor outside her bedroom. She looked dully at the woman's black hair, confused, but then she noticed the red wig lying at her feet. The defiant eyes that met her own were a familiar shade of crimson. She had seen the same eyes somewhere before.

"Let go of me, Berthold!" the woman hissed. "This is our chance!"

Diana slowly shifted her attention to the horrified expression on her new husband's face. It took her addled mind a moment to make the connection, but then she knew. The resemblance between the siblings was striking — the last vestiges of the rotting Aesterkind Feracht tree.

Her hand shook as she reached for the saber at her bedside, but she couldn't even feel the hilt beneath her grip. She cursed as an unfamiliar panic danced in her chest. Berthold may have fooled her grandfather, but she'd seen through him the entire time. The assassin at the ceremony, and now this — this must have been his aim all along. And still, she'd been stupid enough to send Natalia away while she was so incapacitated.

The assassin winced in pain when Berthold twisted her wrist, and her dagger clattered to the floor. "What are you doing?" she demanded.

"You don't know what you've done," Berthold said quietly.

His sister screamed in fury as she struggled to free herself, but he maintained his grip on her. Diana heard heavy footsteps approaching down the hall, but the form that appeared in the doorway wasn't Natalia or the doctor. Even through the haze of anesthesia, her skin still crawled as the Imperator entered the room.

As he assessed the situation, Diana noticed that something seemed different about him. His usually pristine armor was stained with blood, and his hair was disheveled beneath his crown. There was something more than that, too, though. The scars around his eyes had faded, and the deep wrinkles in his face had softened. She was sure he normally had streaks of white in his graying hair, but she could no longer find them.

The Imperator turned towards her and asked, "What happened here?"

Diana moved her hand from her side, allowing him to see her wound. She raised a trembling finger to Berthold and said, "He orchestrated all of this, Grandfather."

The Imperator approached Berthold. "Is that true?" he asked.

Berthold blanched. "I had nothing to do with this, I swear," he said, panic creeping up into his voice.

Berthold grunted in pain when his sister suddenly threw her head back against his face. She jerked out of his grip and swiped for the dagger on the ground, but the Imperator was too fast. He caught her throat and smashed her back into the wall.

"Another of your siblings?" the Imperator asked.

"Another?" Berthold asked, raising his hand to his bloody nose. "Do you mean— Was Siegfried—?"

The Imperator nodded as he tightened his grip on the woman's throat. "Am I to believe you knew nothing about them?"

"Don't hurt her," Berthold pleaded. "I did know she was in the city, but I didn't want to get her involved. I thought she was harmless, and I didn't even know Siegfried had survived."

The Imperator smirked, and with a swift movement, he cracked the woman's head against the wall. Her body went limp, and he passed her back to Berthold. "Take her to the dungeon," he ordered. "I will not tolerate any more deception." He glanced back at Diana as he added, "From either of you."

Berthold lifted his sister into his arms and scurried out of the room, not daring to meet Diana's furious gaze. The Imperator closed the door behind him, and Diana watched numbly as he sat in the chair beside her bed. She wondered if he intended to watch her bleed out, all the while protecting her murderers. The injustice of it made her blind with rage. She was barely able to control her tone as she demanded, "Why did you let them live?"

"Did you think I wouldn't find out what you've done?" the Imperator asked, a sinister edge forming in his voice. "Why is it that my bloodline has become so weak while I was sealed away? Why are your armies so hollow and devoid of the power I left behind?"

"How could I be responsible for that?" Diana seethed. "No one in Jenseits has shown any trace of your power for three hundred years."

The Imperator laughed dryly. "Why is it that the filth in your Reinbann retain their abilities, when my descendants do not?" Diana stared at him — the war of succession in her lifetime had only been one of many. Throughout the years, each generation of Ferachts had culled their rivals, killing anyone who showed the potential to challenge the throne, until all traces of their ancestor's power had been wiped out.

"I know what you did in Eberswalde," the Imperator said. Diana looked away, but he grasped her chin, forcing her to meet his gaze once more. "You are a Feracht in name alone, Granddaughter. Berthold may be a coward, but he still has my blood running through his veins."

She winced when she felt the pressure of his hand against her stomach, and for a moment, she was sure he was going to finish what Berthold's sister had begun. Instead, she felt a warm glow creep through her torso, and when he removed his hand, her wound was gone. She looked down in disbelief, then back at her ancestor.

"Pray that you bear an heir worthy of my legacy," he said as he stood up over her. He turned to leave, allowing the rest of the threat to hang over her, unsaid.

Once she was alone, Diana let out a haggard breath, and then she began to shake with rage. She knew that without the Imperator, the way to the Motherland would have remained closed forever. Without him, the future of every Jenseiter would have grown darker with each passing year. Because of him, they would prosper for generations to come. The campaigns to conquer Castilla and Aesterland had been laughably easy. Despite all this, she had grown to regret the day she had released him.

Her eye had seemed an acceptable sacrifice, but then he had taken her authority, and now her autonomy. Jenseits had been in a slow process of decay since he was sealed away. With his return, life had returned to her homeland — they had planted the trees that had once blanketed Castilla, and with the acquisition of the vast grainfields of Aesterland, she would be able to end the famines. Still, there was a limit to how much she was willing to suffer for her people.

XXXIII

Senya awoke to the sound of arguing. She drew in a ragged breath, wincing when it caused a dull ache to reverberate through her body. A soft groan escaped her as she opened her eyes. The voices abruptly stopped, and when she looked up, Siegfried and the princess were staring at her. Judging from the strong smell of manure and the hay littering the floor, they were in a barn. With some effort, Senya sat up.

The princess smiled in delight as she brushed past Siegfried. "You're finally awake," she said, sitting beside her in the soft hay. "I was worried."

In a flash, the events of the day came flooding back. Senya frantically turned her gaze to Siegfried, who remained on the other side of the barn. He'd discarded his blood-soaked tunic, which lay balled up on the floor beside him, but when she looked at his chest, there was no sign of the injuries he'd suffered in the graveyard.

For a moment, she was relieved, but then a sharp bolt of pain ripped through her head. She raised her hand to her temple, but she paused when she saw her palm. Her skin was unusually pale, and her veins looked almost black. She tried to summon her power, but her fingers remained cold and lifeless. A hollow pit formed in her stomach as the reality of what she'd done dawned on her. She'd finally gotten what she wanted, but now, it was all gone again.

Senya unsteadily pushed herself to her feet, ignoring the vicious throbbing in her head. "Where are you going?" the princess asked as she staggered toward the door.

"I have to go back," Senya muttered, more to herself than anyone else. Maybe it wasn't too late. If she returned and begged for mercy, maybe the Hearthlord would forgive her.

She reached for the latch on the large barn doors, but before she could pull it open, Siegfried slammed his fist into the splintered wood, barring her way. A streak of unfamiliar anger coursed through her as she glared up at him.

"Get out of my way," she demanded.

"Don't be an idiot," he said. "Not after what he did to you."

"You lied to me," Senya seethed, pulling at the door handle. It rattled, but Siegfried was too strong.

"Are you this blind?" Siegfried asked. "Can't you see he's a monster?"

Senya's patience broke, and she shoved him as hard as she could. Siegfried looked surprised, but he held his ground. "Don't call him that!" she cried.

Siegfried studied her for a few seconds, and then he smirked. "You already knew, didn't you?"

Senya furiously shook her head, but the movement caused another shock of pain to drive through her temple.

"It's not true," she murmured, raising a trembling hand to her head.

How many Aesterkind had died in the Hearthlord's brutal campaign to take Highcastle?

"The Hearthlord came here to save us."

How many Castellanos had been enslaved by his angels, forced to plunder the resources from their own lands?

"Who are we to understand his divine will?"

How many days had she spent alone in the tundra, desperately trying to ward off frostbite and hunger?

"He's not—" Senya broke off, closing her eyes as the throbbing in her head grew unbearable. She took in a deep breath, and among the scents of hay and stale manure, she detected the smoke of a spent campfire. Suddenly, she was in the tomb again, approaching Father Silas's unmoving form. She felt a tear roll down her cheek — she already knew what came next. It would be easy to just open her eyes, to bury this memory once more, but then she was kneeling beside him. He wouldn't wake up. She pulled on his shoulder, and as she gazed at Father Silas's emaciated corpse once more, the web of contradictions she'd built around herself could no longer hold.

Senya opened her eyes, and the smug look fell from Siegfried's face when he saw her despair. Her god was a monster. The bitter reality crashed into her like a tidal wave, and she fell to her knees, unable to stop the convulsing sobs that came pouring out of her.

Siegfried took an uncomfortable step back, but then Senya felt a pair of warm arms drape around her shoulders and pull her close.

"It's going to be okay," the princess said softly, stroking Senya's hair.

Senya couldn't remember the last time another person had held her like this, and to her surprise, she found herself beginning to calm down. After a few minutes, she was able to regain control of her breathing. "I'm sorry," she muttered, wiping the tears from her face with a dirty sleeve.

"You don't have to be sorry," the princess reassured her. "Siegfried is right, though. None of us can return to Highcastle."

Siegfried scowled. "You could still go back, Princess. I don't recall asking you to follow me, anyway."

"Your resistance against the Jenseiters is admirable, but lacks competent leadership," Princess Eleanor said, as if he hadn't spoken. "How many of you are there?"

Siegfried gave her a blank look. "What are you talking about?"

"In your organization."

"There is no organization," Siegfried said.

The princess frowned. "What did you expect to do alone?"

"Kill the Duchess," Siegfried replied, crossing his arms.

"Well, it's a start, but I don't see how that would free Aesterland."

"I don't care about freeing Aesterland," Siegfried said darkly. "The Duchess killed my father and brother."

Senya looked at Siegfried in surprise. He hadn't told her that before. The anger on his face was plain to see, but beneath it there was a reflection of the same grief she felt at losing Father Silas. He met her sympathetic gaze for a moment, then quickly looked away.

Princess Eleanor smoothed out her tattered bridal gown and stood up. "I'm after something greater than petty revenge," she declared. "First, though, we need to get further away from Highcastle. I'm sure the Jenseiters will be searching for us. We'll need to stay out of sight."

"Inspired," Siegfried said sarcastically, drawing an annoyed look from the princess. "I was going to suggest we turn ourselves in to be executed."

"We should seek refuge in Norogard," she continued. "We share a common enemy in the Jenseiters. With their help, I will return to take back Highcastle."

Siegfried scowled. "Norogard and Aesterland have been at war for generations," he said. "What makes you think they would help you?"

Princess Eleanor waved her hand as if centuries of conflict were nothing. "If it means putting a Nord prince on the throne of Aesterland, I think they will be open to negotiate," she said. "The high road will take us to the Augur crossing. There are five thousand Aesterkind troops stationed there. I'm sure they will join us, as well."

"If the Jenseiters haven't already pushed up to the border," Siegfried said. "There are Reinbann in the east, too. I don't think the Nords would fare any better against them than we did, and the Jenseiters are making even more of them."

"What do you mean?" the princess asked.

"They've been teaching some of the prisoners how to manifest their abilities," Siegfried explained. "I've seen Aesterkind who can create armor out of dirt, and Castellanos who can summon fire—"

"What were their names?" Senya interrupted, abruptly climbing to her feet. She winced as the painful throbbing in her head resumed, but she didn't let it distract her. The entire time she'd been in Aesterland, she hadn't seen any trace of the Reinbann or the acolytes they'd taken with them.

Siegfried frowned as he tried to remember. After a few moments, he said, "One of them was called Auron. There was another cultist with him, but he was Aesterkind."

"Fabian!" Senya said, her excitement briefly overshadowing the pain. "Where did you meet them? Where are they now?"

"They were traveling up the eastern high road the last time I saw them, but that was months ago. I don't know where they are now."

Senya's shoulders slumped. The spark that had ignited at the mention of the other acolytes died as quickly as it had come. To be honest, she didn't know what she would do if she found them, anyway. If they had joined the Reinbann, it meant they were still part of the Hearthlord's divine plan. She'd made herself an enemy of their god, and she didn't want to risk corrupting them, as well.

Siegfried reached down to retrieve his stained tunic and pulled it back on. "We should get moving," he said. "It's a long way to the Augur."

Senya's blood turned to ice as she watched Princess Eleanor and Siegfried head towards the door. Soon, she would be alone once more, and this time, without any clear goal in sight. She knew Siegfried was right about the Hearthlord, but she had been born into his service. If she wasn't one of his angels, what else was left for her? Once they were gone, it was only a matter of time before she returned to Highcastle to surrender herself to him.

If she didn't, wouldn't it mean Father Silas had died for nothing?

"What's wrong?" the princess asked from the doorway, drawing her attention.

Senya sniffed back a sob. "I don't want to go back to the Hearthlord," she admitted.

Senya looked up as the princess approached her, surprised when she offered her a hand. Senya accepted it, and Princess Eleanor pulled her to her feet. "Don't be silly," she said. "You're coming with us to Norogard."

Senya felt a wave of relief at the invitation, but a deep-rooted sense of guilt tugged at her heart. "What about the acolytes?" she asked.

"They were heading north the last I saw them," Siegfried said. "Maybe we'll find them along the way."

Senya allowed the princess to lead her outside. As she drew in the crisp night air, her pounding headache began to clear. Her entire life, the only identity she'd ever known was that of the Angel of Alcazar, but the Hearthlord had killed what was left of that girl in the graveyard. She didn't know what remained, but for the first time in a while, she wasn't paralyzed by her faith. It was a long way to the Augur, and she would have plenty of time to find out who she had become.

<u>Please Leave A Review on Amazon & Goodreads!</u>

ABOUT THE AUTHOR

Beth Werbaneth is a software engineer who moonlights as a mediocre pickleballer. Sometimes when she's off the clock and it's too dark to pickle, she writes epic fantasy. She won the 2013 Amazon Breakthrough Novel Award Quarterfinalist prize for *The Carrier*. She lives in Seattle with her cats, Pancake and Sage.

Follow her on TikTok and Instagram: @bethwerbanethauthor